The Three

Kelsey O'Brien is a Paris-based writer who tells stories about intriguing figures and hidden moments from the past. Her fiction, reviews, and travel pieces have appeared in print and online.

THE THREE

Kelsey O'Brien

hera

 Penguin Random House

First published in the United Kingdom in 2026 by

Hera Books, an imprint of
Canelo Digital Publishing Limited,
20 Vauxhall Bridge Road,
London SW1V 2SA
United Kingdom

A Penguin Random House Company
The authorised representative in the EEA is Dorling Kindersley Verlag GmbH. Arnulfstr. 124, 80636 Munich, Germany

Copyright © Kelsey O'Brien 2026

The moral right of Kelsey O'Brien to be identified as the creator of this work has been asserted in accordance with the Copyright, Designs and Patents Act, 1988.
All rights reserved. No part of this publication may be reproduced or transmitted in any form or by any means, electronic or mechanical, including photocopy, recording, or any information storage and retrieval system, without permission in writing from the publisher.
No part of this book may be used or reproduced in any manner for the purpose of training artificial intelligence technologies or systems. In accordance with Article 4(3) of the DSM Directive 2019/790, Canelo expressly reserves this work from the text and data mining exception.

A CIP catalogue record for this book is available from the British Library.

Print ISBN 978 1 83598 235 8
Ebook ISBN 978 1 83598 147 4

This book is a work of fiction. Names, characters, businesses, organizations, places and events are either the product of the author's imagination or are used fictitiously. Any resemblance to actual persons, living or dead, events or locales is entirely coincidental.

Cover design by Head Design

Cover images © Arcangel; Getty Images / iStock

Printed and bound in Great Britain by Clays Ltd, Elcograf S.p.A.

Look for more great books at
www.herabooks.com | www.dk.com

For my friends

Prologue

I pace the floor of my tiny room, the walls seeming to grow tighter and closer with every step. My chest feels constricted, breathing impossible. I turn to look out of the window but am met with black, enveloping darkness. The wind howls through the trees, mournful amongst their leaves and branches. How did I come to be here, trapped between the two people I love most in the world? How can I save one without betraying the other?

The room tilts and I seek respite by sitting on the bed and placing my hand on my chest to count each fluttering heartbeat. My loyalties are pulled in equal yet opposing directions. There is nothing to be done – I am completely helpless, and yet to refrain from action is intolerable. The wind blows again and moonlight shines into the room, stretching shadows along the floor and lighting up my books, wardrobe, and other belongings in ghostly, murky colours. I pull off my wig and scratch my head in desperation. How do I untangle myself from these threads of deceit? In the corner, the ticking clock is a menacing reminder that there is no more time to waste. No matter whom I choose, someone will be condemned and – I realise with a shudder – none of us will ever be the same. Our three lives are in my hands now.

Chapter One

1791 – Now

Measuring paper, smudged notepad, a fresh pencil – these are the tools at my disposal today. 'If you could lift your arms,' I say, encircling Lady Elina's chest with the paper.

'Any difference?' she asks, detached as usual. I wish she wouldn't attempt conversation; her indifference extinguishes what little joy I get from coming to work. I need to decide how many pleats to put into this bodice, not monitor her state of mind.

'Perhaps a finger smaller… nothing we can't solve when pinning it into place.'

She sighs. 'You may as well make the entire bodice smaller. I fear this is becoming a trend.' She's maintained a healthy figure for as long as I've known her, but perhaps stress is affecting her appetite. She must feel the strain of not getting pregnant, even if it isn't her fault. She lowers her arms and steps aside. 'Have we finished?'

'I'd just like to go over the drawings,' I reply, picking up my notebook of careful sketches to show her. The evenings are still dark and I have spent the last week painstakingly completing her dress designs by candlelight. Since they will be for this summer's ball, a flattering yet ornate motif is of paramount importance to display the family fortune. 'I thought a blue silk brocade with gold and green embroidery would highlight the season. I can make a matching train and petticoat with some help from the tailors in town.'

'I'm sure that will all be fine. It matters very little to me.'

It's as if she's slapped me across the face, but with my social standing I cannot reply as I would like. She is not usually a cruel mistress so I wait, suspecting she will question her strong language shortly. Our interactions are usually carefully deferential and gracious, but something must be distracting her today.

She reads my expression and looks contrite. 'I apologise... you always create such masterpieces, I suppose I've just grown accustomed to them.'

'If I may, it's quite time-consuming work, Your Ladyship.'

As I hoped, this gets her attention but I don't think she'll demand an apology for my presumption. Her eyes glint mischievously. 'Of course it is.' She laughs a little. 'Your intermittent boldness is always refreshing, Mr Rooke.'

For years, her even temperament has surprised me – she's so different from her husband, who tends to be more impassioned. It is difficult to wound her pride, not that I've tried to do so. When I first began working here and hardly knew the first thing about dressmaking, there was a disconnect between us and it took years for me to understand that her coolness reflected her own self-restraint, not how she viewed me. While I still feel held in place by my position in the household, she has begun to exude little bursts of warmth and interest in my skills. Just last month, we discussed the reading I do to follow the latest news in gown silhouette and structure, and the clippings I add from the *Lady's Magazine* to my textile album. She was surprised to learn that I can read and write outside of business-related correspondence – the information seemed to animate her in a way she had not previously shown in front of me. How could she think that all this time I've been sending letters to London with nothing more than numbers and fabric types crudely written down? My friends are there, indeed a piece of my spirit still walks those narrow East End streets.

I finish jotting down her new waist measurement, then close my notebook with a satisfying tap. 'The dress should be completed in time, but I will need to order more boning from London before I can begin in earnest,' I tell her.

'Ah, so you will write to your business friends! I hope they reply with diverting stories from the capital.' She turns towards a large bookshelf built into the wall. An imposing presence in the room, it nearly runs the length of the panelling. I've occasionally sneaked glances at the titles and authors as I've passed by: Spinoza, Barbauld, Hume, but am oblivious to what they might mean. Her fingers pass along several spines but I'm too far away to see what they might be. 'Have we finished with the fitting?'

I cross back to her desk, where I left my effects. 'Just about... I'd hoped to have you try on the refinished stays for your red dress. I added the new outer panels and trim as we agreed.'

'Of course – thank you. I was surprised they took so long, but I don't pretend to understand the nature of your work.' She strolls back to me in her shift, lifting her arms so I can wrap the stays around her and begin lacing. She steadies her gaze to the other side of the room, cool and distant.

'It should have been a quick job, but the material was delayed coming from France, what with the riots they've had.'

The cord flies through my fingers as she spins around to look at me with bright eyes. 'It's hardly riots – they're having a full revolution, Mr Rooke.'

'Oh,' I reply carefully. How should I respond – in favour of the rebels or against? I can hardly make intelligent conversation about it anyway, knowing only what the London shopkeepers tell me. I decide to wait for her to face forward again and keep looping the lacing through eyelets on the back panels of her stays.

She continues her thought. 'I'm not surprised that imports would be affected, from what the papers are reporting. I do hope they are successful.'

I fasten the shoulder straps in front, then stand back to admire my work. The stays fit perfectly, creating a smooth silhouette with her shoulders pulled back. 'Who do you hope is successful?'

She peers down, then checks herself in a mirror across the room. 'They're lovely – worth waiting for! I mean the people. They've suffered terrible monarchs for generations, with no rights to speak of. No juries to judge whether the accused are truly guilty. Fractured political classes without a sense of shared fraternity. No food for the common people to eat while the king grows their debt without end.'

As she speaks, I walk to the armoire to find her matching jacket but first sneak a glance at her face. I've never heard her speak with such enthusiasm, and it's intriguing. 'Where did you learn these things?' I find the jacket and help her slide into it.

'I read French books and pamphlets when I can find them. Regrettably, most of my knowledge comes from our own papers, though I hardly trust what they have to say on the matter.'

The Three

This turn of the conversation is bewildering, but I try to remain focused on my work. I check how the jacket pairs with her stays, calculating. Some trim above her left shoulder is visible, but it can be pinned back. The waists are even and the colours a pleasing contrast. 'May I ask why not?'

'It sounds a bit familiar, doesn't it? No security for the working classes. No individual rights for women or, frankly, a tradesman such as yourself. The fiery revolution in France may well spark kindling on our own shores, so our government will suppress information wherever it can.'

'I must say, you seem very knowledgeable on the topic.' I suppose when one doesn't need to work for ten hours a day to keep oneself alive, there's more opportunity for reading. But this is the first time I've been captivated by Lady Elina, and it isn't due to her surprising political insight. She speaks with ferocity; her sympathy for the cause of the revolutionaries reminds me of the feeling I have as I begin to design fresh gowns with new material or needlework. She knows what it means to be awake in the world, not simply drifting through without a light on one's path. It is not a feeling I have recognised for some time.

'Really, it only takes a bit of reading of those who are at the forefront of this fight,' she says, looking off. I can see her mind weaving thoughts together, but do not know if they are about this topic, me, or something else. Her maid, Anne, returns to help her dress while I pack up my things, yet she remains quiet and pensive. I turn towards the door to leave, but she touches my arm. 'Just a moment, Mr Rooke.' She crosses to her bookcase and scans the titles, pulling down a small text from the third shelf. 'If you are interested in learning more, I would urge you to read this. It was written decades ago, but its philosophy is the very same fuelling today's French revolutionaries.'

She holds it out with a warm smile I've never experienced from her, but I hesitate to take the book. 'Your Ladyship, I hardly have the time...'

'Come now! Read it at your own pace – I won't miss it. It is worthwhile to expand our circles of thought.'

I feel my cheeks darken and look over at Anne, then down at the floor. 'It's just... I'm not sure I have the vocabulary for it, ma'am.'

Now she looks embarrassed. At least that eases my pain somewhat. 'Oh, I understand. I'm awfully... but didn't you recently say that you write regularly to your friends in London?'

'Yes, but I don't speak French, and I'm sure there would be words—'

'Oh, come now! Do try it, and I will assist you. It's translated, so you needn't worry about the French. Here…' She presses the book into my hand with an earnest look. 'We can discuss it next time. I'd be delighted to have someone I can talk about these things with. To me, they're terribly important and yet my husband hardly notices unless they directly impact his estate.'

I feel backed into a corner – is it wise to change course when relations between us have always been orderly and businesslike? Why is she sharing these ideas with me – do they point to a secret she is hiding? Or perhaps that is simply my guilty conscience getting the better of me. After all, if we grew more sociable she might learn what *I* have been hiding from *her*. I wonder whether her husband knows that she is engaged in this perilous world of revolutionary politics – I fear he would not be pleased if he found out. Still, my curiosity is piqued. 'Very well, I will attempt it. Thank you, Your Ladyship.'

She smiles as I gently place the text on top of my effects. 'Good day, Mr Rooke.'

At last I am free from her rooms and back in command of my own time. I walk down the hall, which is plastered with imposing portraits of ancestors through the years. There's a family resemblance from picture to picture, though each tries to improve on the generation before with a larger canvas or more accessories to highlight an adventurous life – if one considers a life filled with books and wigs to be adventuresome.

Nevertheless, the house and grounds remain impressive. I ignore my ageing skin in the mirrors and instead peek out the windows as I walk. I remember the first time I came here, I'd never seen such an expanse of green before. London has parks, but nothing like this. A fountain large enough to swim in, grass neatly maintained, plants intentionally placed. Nothing left to grow wild – everything in that garden is there for a reason, and it's someone's job to look after it all. Imagine!

At the top of the stairs, I pause to make a note about the whalebone order from London. I believe Davis McFarland still has his connections; he's been a reliable source of materials for decades. Even when I was just beginning my trade and had only a few clients, he was flexible with payments for my advanced orders. The city has changed much in the years since I left; every time I return it seems a layer has been removed or added. The streets are familiar yet foreign – a favoured pub has disappeared, replaced by a haberdashery, or a factory stands where I'd swear there was once a row of houses. Crowded streets are now a crush, the air is heavier and shortens the breath, and yet. It is still my city, my true home – the bustle of commerce, the organised flow of pedestrians, the variety of *life* happening every day.

1770 – Then

Leadenhall Market. At one of the stalls, a woman sells oranges. Carriages nearly crash into each other as they slosh through mud on the city streets. I pick my way through the dusty air, the smell of manure stinging my nostrils, until I reach the end of the alley. There's a grubby shop with a sooty window, but at least it's mine – not a bad outlook for my twenty-third birthday. Who could have imagined that the orphan without even a pair of shoes to his name would one day have his own workshop? I unlock the door, reminding myself to get a bell.

In no time, this place will be bustling. Not with clients, of course – I'll take their measurements in their homes. I wouldn't expect the ladies of court to trudge to this end of the city. I'll set up some tables, get a few girls in to help with the needlework. I'll turn out the finest stays this city has ever seen.

–

I have the designs to show Mrs Hatchfield of Berkeley Square. I could take a coach to get across town but decide to walk. Through the winding streets of the City I see bankers sitting in pubs, leaning close and devising schemes to topple the world in their favour. Their hands toy with their glasses like game pieces on a board only they know the rules to. The rest of us simply walk past on the peripheries. Along the Strand, stationers hawk the latest tragedy: a new string of murdered girls in some park or alley. It's of no concern to me – these monsters always favour young ladies, while I remain a target of the law and no other. Some might think it better to be on one's own in a remote village with no one to see you or know what you get up to in your spare time, but we city dwellers know how to morph into shadows when the wrong people walk past. We understand that danger lurks around every corner and that there is safety in the anonymity of a crowd, even freedom.

The air has begun to lose the warmth of summer, and soon my sunset evenings wandering through the park in my shirtsleeves and waistcoat will be a distant memory. It rained early this morning and the square is damp; mud and grass stick themselves on to my shoes unceremoniously. I walk up the front steps and ring Mrs Hatchfield's bell.

She's not pleased with the designs; wants something closer to what Lady Howard was wearing last summer. 'Why sink back into the comfort of the past,' I tell her, 'when you can create new currents and fashions for tomorrow? This new cut may be a bit more revealing than is currently conventional, but so were last year's designs. We must attempt to improve our lives, to add colour where there is none.'

'Oh, Mr Rooke. Your words are tantalising, but I have my honour to think of.'

I'm not in a position to turn away work, so I'll redesign the stays as she likes. Injured by her casual dismissal of my ideas, I try to encourage just a little originality in her. 'Perhaps with some silver embroidery along the top?'

'Yes, that would be fine.'

I've barely begun the game and must take my victories where I can find them. I'm ushered out of the Hatchfield house, rejected designs under my arm.

We Londoners often find ourselves alone, but I don't mind. I enjoy feeling solitary amongst so many others, at peace with my thoughts as I walk along the river, through the markets, and alongside the coaches and trolleys. I know my neighbourhood, and my neighbours know me – we may be stuck in the East End, but our factories and warehouses power London and there's nowhere better for fresh fish in the morning. Not that I buy a lot of fish, of course. My appetite isn't very grand owing to my upbringing, when a piece of fruit once a week was a luxury. Walking in London reminds me that my time is my own, that I'm in control of my life here – indeed I've built it myself without much help from anyone else. Mrs Hatchfield may not like my designs today, but she'll be cramming to get on my books this time next year.

Lincoln's Inn Fields. It's drier now and there are more people about, walking in pairs through the large expanse of grass. As I pass a row of boghouses, I spot him. Dark skin, clearly a fresh arrival from one of the colonies, and well dressed in a green silk velvet suit. I wonder what line of work he's in but we never exchange that kind of information. Often when you meet people this way, you barely say two words to each other – conversation is not the purpose of these interactions.

He catches my eye before walking down into the last privy in the row, which is conveniently shaded by a cluster of trees. I wait a moment, pulling out a notebook and pretending to write something down, then follow him inside.

We kiss briefly, but our hands are down each other's breeches within seconds, pulling at shirts, loosening buttons from their lodgings in an effort to grab at the firm flesh underneath. I remember his style now; we met last month under similar circumstances in Hyde Park. These sorts of encounters aren't ideal during the daytime, but sometimes it's safer to hide in plain sight. We enjoy one another briefly and completely; an intense rush of companionship that dissipates as quickly as it arrives. I know it means nothing and if we never saw each other again I wouldn't think twice of him, but inside I feel a pull for something more lasting, a connection that runs deeper.

That is not the nature of life in the city for men like us. With imprisonment or death around every corner, it is impossible to form lasting attachments. 'Until next time,' he whispers, and I stifle a smile – he's only trying to be romantic. He leaves and I linger; I picture him walking along the row of boghouses and then, my last impression that he was ever here: a cough just within earshot, signalling that it's safe for me to leave.

Outside the park, wide avenues give way to narrow streets. Fresh paint on shopfronts slowly fades until you wouldn't know the wares sold in a given place unless you'd been to the shop before. At the grocers, a boy furiously wipes the window with a brown rag, though it's unclear if he's picking any dirt up or simply smearing it around. Still, what's left of the produce looks bright and appealing – it was probably brought in from the countryside this morning. By this time of the day, there's not much left and it isn't as fresh as it was first thing, but the shopkeepers are getting worried about selling everything and will drop their prices. My preferred time to buy – I'll gladly sacrifice a little flavour for more money to spend on entertaining myself. Today, I don't need much – an apple for the rest of my walk will do.

When I return to the shop from my perambulation, a girl about sixteen years old is waiting for me on the stoop. She has her hands wrapped in cloth instead of gloves and picks flakes off an old crust of bread. When she sees me approaching, she stands and brushes herself off.

'I'm here about the job,' she says without ceremony. She's not presenting herself very well, but I've been in this business long enough to know that one doesn't judge before gauging a person's ability. Besides, she's the first applicant I've had in two weeks.

'Come in. Have you done much staymaking work?'

She scoffs, but as she peers around the shop I catch a hint of intimidation in her expression. 'Been sewing since I was seven,' she replies, unwrapping the cloth from her hands.

Dropping the designs for Mrs Hatchfield on a table, I light a fire and put the kettle on. 'Care for some coffee?'

'All right.' She looks at a pair of stays I'm currently working on, laid out on a nearby workstation.

'Those are for a lady in St James's Square – she's expecting them next week for a dance.' One of my first clients from the nobility, I can still remember the swell of pride in my chest when she decided to work with me.

The girl fingers the stays carefully, examining my stitching and construction. 'Not easy work, is it? Double stitching with the whalebones.'

She's noticed, that's good. 'My fingers are used to it.'

Upon hearing this, she holds out her hand and examines her own small fingers. 'I'm best at the fine needlework, but I know my stitching as well as anyone.'

I hand her a cup of coffee. 'Sorry, I'm out of milk,' I tell her, not that she seems to care. Sometimes, a hot drink to finish off an exhausting day is all one needs to perk back up. 'How long have you lived in London?'

' 'Bout a year now,' she replies. 'I came up from Winchester after working in a pie shop.'

'So you've only been sewing for one year?'

'Nah, I told you I been doing it since I was a girl.' I suppress a smile – she's still just a girl. 'I sewed for my mum at home, picked up odd jobs mending things, and as I got better, started doing adornments for them who had a bit more to spend.'

'Well, I know it's not much to look at, but my shop is quite high-end. I only work for ladies who can afford custom-made stays, typically requiring them for unique formal engagements.'

'Unique formal engagements,' she repeats. 'Well, I guess you must know what you're doing if you talk so fancy.'

There's something appealing about her. She's certainly confident in her abilities, yet seems capable enough and willing to learn the skills required to cater to finer tastes. I tell her as much.

'Oh, sure I am, sir. I pick things up quick too – I'm not just sayin' that. Never had lessons, I figured it out as I went along. I may not know much about the designing side, or acquiring the materials, but I can promise to work all night if need be.'

'That's very good to hear. I'm getting too busy for one person and could certainly use the extra help. I'll pay eight shillings per week with board, will that suit?'

She considers. 'Should do, sir. I get by pretty well without much. But, um, will it just be you and me living here alone together?'

I hadn't pegged her for one of those American puritans. 'Well, I have my apartment upstairs, and you would take the room at the back of the shop.'

She ponders this briefly, then nods. 'That's fine, I just wanted to check you weren't trying any funny business.'

No need to flatter yourself, my dear – I have no interest whatsoever. 'I can assure you, I would never be so familiar.'

'That's good,' she says, grinning and revealing a small gap in the right side of her smile.

'I shouldn't imagine we'll spend much time together outside of working hours,' I say carefully. 'Your business is your own, and so is mine.'

'Suits me,' she replies.

I walk around the workbench, gesturing at her to follow. 'Let me show you what I'm currently working on and how you can help. I've got quite a few linens cut out and just need to sew them together, add some detailing to the front of these stays, and line the sides of these ones – I haven't decided about whether whalebone or reed will do better.'

'As a lady, if I may be so bold,' she says cautiously, 'they're both supportive, but whalebone gives a little more, so if she's got to be movin' about in it, that's what I'd advise.'

I chuckle a little, both because I can't help myself and because I want her to know where she stands in *my* shop. 'Your advice is not necessary; I've been making stays for years and understand the difference between whalebone and reed. I've worn the stays I've created to see how they feel.'

'Have you really?' she asks, sounding surprised.

'Of course – I wouldn't be the best in London if I didn't. Not so much any more, and you are *never* to try on the stays we make – they are custom-measured and I won't have you ruining them. My difficulty with the whalebone is that the lady in question is rather large and I'm not sure it will be strong enough. It is something I will consider and decide in my own time.'

To her credit, she takes this speech well and recomposes herself. 'As you please. Shall I start on the individual pieces, then?'

'Yes, thank you.'

It would seem I've found an apprentice. And although she is a girl, it's not unheard of to have women in the shops these days – their smaller fingers handle the stitching rather well. Besides, if she doesn't please me, I can let her go anytime I like. This is how it was when I first trained as a staymaker – labour is cheap in London and it took a great deal of practice to persevere to the level I am at now.

A few days later, I'm at Mr Blankenship's shop. It's invigorating to know that I can take my time here and stays are still being sewn at my workbenches. Martha is well suited to this kind of labour and I should be able to double the shop's productivity in no time.

I ring the bell and Mr Blankenship potters out. There are signs of the younger man he used to be – firm hands, strong forearms, but as I watch him move around behind the counter, I'm always concerned he might topple over. Still, it's entertaining watching him on the ladder, reaching for yards of fabric on the higher shelves – might this be the day he finally falls off? Of course he never does, and thank goodness because he has the best connections for French material.

'I ordered two yards of the red and gold brocade on Tuesday last; has it arrived?'

He speaks in his familiar deep voice, his tone brisk. 'Of course, Mr Rooke.'

No ladder today; he's got my order ready in the back. The benefits of being a regular customer. I insist on examining the fabric every time for loose strands or stains – one can never be too careful.

'Everything seems in order. Please wrap it.'

'Right-o.'

A necessity on London's streets. You never know when a horse will gallop past, kicking up dirt, or a sudden downpour might strike. I pay Mr Blankenship and am on my way. This brocade will be used for a new client, Lady MacIntyre, to make stays she'll wear at her Christmas party. If I can impress her with the quality of my work, she'll be a valuable customer with one of the busier calendars in town. She's already approved the designs, but I'm hoping to surprise her with some of my trademark details – silk lining for comfort and levity, and fewer whalebones than she's accustomed to.

Tomorrow, I'll cut the fabric and begin lining it. But until then, some entertainment for tonight. Perhaps a trip to Mother Mack's? No, it's far too predictable – tonight I favour something a bit more diverting. Surely there will be a play on somewhere in this smoky, bustling city.

The Theatre Royal, Drury Lane. While I prefer the shows at Sadler's Wells, Mr Garrick is always entertaining. Perhaps they'll have a production of Shakespeare tonight.

It's not Shakespeare, but the show is still amusing. The actors outdo themselves as usual – bicycling onstage, dodging lamp posts. Everyone cheers and yells out to them as they go. The set pieces sway with the heavy breath in the room and two men behind me loudly castigate the story's villain, but all this flurry and commotion is why I love coming to the theatre – it beats with life. I crane my neck, looking through the swell of faces in the pit, and suddenly spot him. It's not so difficult – he stands out, dressed far better than anyone else on the floor. Are those silver spangles on the jacket he's wearing? My eyes run over him. Young, little to cause him worry, a good eye for fashion. Perhaps he is only down here to see what it's like with the lower classes, a whimsical experiment. He looks over – I've been staring too long – and smiles at me. My cheeks flush. Usually I try to be more careful, but already there's a warm feeling spreading from my chest and into my fingers.

I'm in luck – there's an extended interval and drinks flow freely. We approach each other and introduce ourselves. 'I don't think I've seen you at one of these shows before,' I say.

'Do you come to every performance?' he asks affably.

I humour him. 'Well, no, of course not.'

'Then perhaps I'm less out of place than you imagine.'

'Perhaps you are.'

A bashful smile, but no discomfort. For these few moments we are at ease together, but a shadow crosses his face. 'Excuse me.'

He must have seen someone he knows, couldn't be caught talking to a strange man for too long. If I'd been recognisable to someone here that might excuse it, but I am anonymous, simply another face amongst the many.

After reaching a satisfying point of intoxication, I wind my way home through the crowded streets. Tonight, walking alone feels hollow as the city spins around me. Along the river, little dots of light from the moored ships shimmer like gold buttons on a sailor's uniform. But they are not shining for me.

Into my shop, which now seems small and forgettable compared to the outside world. I remind myself that it's truly mine, trying to find some encouragement. Martha is nowhere to be seen, probably gone to bed for the night. I look over a new design on my desk, making a few alterations. If I move the baleen ribbons by a few centimetres I can fit an extra bone at the front, which will serve Mrs Hatchfield well.

Should I have asked for his name? No – he's clearly a visitor in my world. I've been disappointed enough by men like him, ostentatious with their money and dangling their world of ease and comfort in front of me before they grow bored of their own games and disappear. And yet there was something that hinted he wasn't like the others. There was an openness, a warmth about him that I've rarely experienced. Perhaps it was simply the confidence and security that come with having the world at one's fingertips.

Best to have avoided inevitable disappointment. I've felt the sting of rejection enough to know that I'm never served by venturing too far from my reliable liaisons in the park. Indeed, I must consider mere disinterest rather fortunate – it's far safer than being reported or beaten.

It isn't until I've blown out my candle and am undressing for the night that I find his card in my pocket.

Chapter Two

Now

Leaving the chatter of the servants in the kitchen behind me, I head upstairs for my appointment with Lady Elina. First, I stop at my room to collect the latest gown I've made for her. It should be a quick drop-off since she rarely requests any changes, and then I can plan my upcoming trip to London. Having this visit to the capital on the horizon is one of the few things breaking up the monotony of my days here. Sometimes I wonder why I stay, but my life will always require compromise in either love or ambition. Besides, I've nowhere else to go – everything I am belongs here now. And yet sometimes it feels as though I could just step back and disappear like a shadow fading into the wall. If I did, would it make any difference?

I march up the plain grey stairs of the servants' quarters, through the ornate antechamber and into the great hall with its Aubusson carpets. A large grandfather clock stands against one wall, reminding me that my time here is not entirely my own. Yet there are other instances when I look at it and feel a conflicted sense of ownership – after all the years I have spent living here, is it not partly mine as well?

On my way up the main staircase, my back moans – a consequence of decades spent bending over careful needlework. This never used to happen when I was younger. On the landing, I twist a few times, the dress swaying and rustling with the motion. I sigh, taking a final turn down the corridor to Lady Elina's door. Will she like the dress? The sleeves took three attempts to get just right, balancing the amount of fabric with the required pleats. I hope the decorative ribbons along the front skirt will drape attractively. I always try to make these outfits as flawless and sumptuous as possible – after all, they are the only things I have control over any more. I knock.

'Come in, Mr Rooke.' She's at her desk writing, a stack of books at her elbow. Before I can say anything, she slaps her hands on the surface with rigour, looks directly at me, and asks, 'How are you finding the French treatise I lent you?'

'I – I've brought your new dress, ma'am,' I stumble, caught by surprise.

'Yes, all right,' she stands and takes the bundled gown from my hands, tossing it carelessly on a nearby chair. 'There's no need to be shy! Come and have a seat, let's talk. I don't expect you to have read it all just yet, and I'm sure you have questions. There's much to discuss.'

This eager, energetic behaviour is entirely out of character. I watch the dress and my weeks of work gently crumple downwards into the chair. My hands feel empty without the weight of it in them – its power to give me excuses to make my leave is suddenly gone. Exasperated, I make an effort to unknit my eyebrows before looking back to her. She sits nearby, gazing up at me expectantly.

'I'm sorry, Your Ladyship, I don't wish to displease you but we really must look at your gown for the carnival ball at Lord Westworth's next week and see if there are any adjustments to be made.'

She pauses before replying and I worry I've angered her. But then she smiles knowingly. 'Leave it to you to focus unflinchingly on your work.' She stands and walks to the wall to ring for her maid, who enters promptly.

I lay the gown and accompanying stays on the bed so Anne can help her dress. She loosens the petticoat Lady Elina is already wearing and gently brings it down to the floor so she can step out of it. Then, Anne unties the bodice around her shoulders and carefully slips her arms out of each sleeve. After setting everything aside with the utmost care so as not to damage the valuable materials, Anne turns to the bed and lifts the shorter stays I recently completed for the carnival ball silhouette. Lady Elina taps her foot impatiently, so I step forward and offer to lace the stays at the back while she holds them in place.

Meanwhile, Anne goes to the clothes press and holds up two rumps of varying size and shape with a questioning look in my direction. I nod towards the one in her left hand, which is more round and less oblong. She returns and I move out of the way so she can wrap the rump around Lady Elina's stays, tying it at the front. Next, she helps Lady Elina into the petticoat, gently lifting it up and over her head before smoothing it down and tying it into place. Once this is done, Anne picks up the gown and turns it so Lady Elina can slide her arms through the sleeves, which end with two rows of ruffles at each elbow. Finally, Anne pins the front of the gown closed while I adjust the skirts. 'At last!' Lady Elina exclaims.

'Apologies, ma'am,' says Anne, casting her eyes towards the floor.

I circle Lady Elina, ensuring the skirts fall evenly, checking that the shoulders are in the right place in proportion to the waist. I nod, pleased with my work.

'Shall I move around for a moment?' she suggests – I often ask her to do this to see the gowns in motion and ensure her chemise does not peek through inadvertently. 'Anne, you are dismissed,' she says, pacing across the room. As the door clicks shut, she continues. 'Now, I don't agree with every point, but that discourse was decades ahead of its time. What do you make of how the author discerns between the different types of inequality?'

I try to keep my features calm, but can't help my brow furrowing in confusion. My thoughts jump from her gown to Anne's sudden absence, finally catching on her question. What kind of reply does she expect? Why does she want to speak about these obscure topics with me, of all people? It's true that I began reading the book she lent me, but I could not see anything in it that filled me with the passion and excitement Lady Elina exhibits. I suppose it must be beyond my comprehension, and that is fine – my world of clothes-making is enough and offers me ample challenges. It has taken decades to learn how to craft gowns with the same attention and skill I once applied purely to staymaking.

I straighten my posture, my back and shoulders sore from the hours spent hunched over her gown. She has yet to say a single word about it. While I've given up expecting praise from her, it is exasperating that she cannot see the efforts I have gone to. As I examine her silhouette, she turns around to look at me. Her eyes are keen, her expression genuine, and I decide to engage with her. 'I'm not sure I understand his point – surely there are genuine differences between people that make us unequal whether we wish to be or not?'

'Ah.' She nods vigorously. 'There are many who would agree with you – the male form is physically stronger than the female, which justifies the violence and brute force men use against women. It's an argument I've heard before. And yet, when you follow that to its logical conclusion, why does every man not abuse his fellows who may be physically weaker? Does our government use physical force to make decisions on how to run the country? When we engage beyond the surface, we understand that the real reason men mistreat women is because of ethical inequality, just as the discourse argues.'

'Oh... all right.' I glance over to the door, tantalisingly close yet unavailable until I have been released. A wave of bitterness towards her rushes over me in my frustration of being confined and stifled in this house, unable to dictate my own movements.

Lady Elina watches my expression – I can feel her trying to understand me – and then smiles kindly. 'You needn't be embarrassed. There are those with far more education than you who continue to believe the same thing because challenging their thoughts would threaten the control they have over society.' She sticks one leg out, admiring the way her petticoat shines in the morning light.

How can she understand so much from these books of hers, yet know so little about someone trying to work right in front of her? 'I suppose as long as those men remain in charge, our discussing it serves no great purpose.'

She watches me, nodding in sympathy. 'But you see, Mr Rooke, that power which they grip so tightly is an illusion. Look at what happened in America and what is happening in France! Once the common people understand that equality is within reach, they will stretch out their arms to take it.'

Despite myself, I begin to understand what she means and find myself once again intrigued by her enthusiasm. I remember that I need to ask if she would like any changes made to the dress, but a different question falls from my mouth. 'How do you know all of this?'

She throws a glance over to her paper-strewn desk. 'I educate myself. There isn't much else to do when one is trapped in the countryside, wouldn't you agree?'

I don't meet her eye – of course I agree but it would be rude to brush off my employment here. 'You have your social calendar, ma'am.'

She acquiesces. 'Indeed I do. You ought to see what happens when I introduce this topic of conversation at parties – lords and ladies running as if I were stricken with disease!'

I chuckle a little, then shift my stance again. My body is weary but my thoughts have begun to feel lighter. This is the first honest conversation we have had together, the first time I feel truly seen by her.

'It is not easy to make people see that our world could be different. Even those who would benefit from a more equal society cannot envision it becoming a reality, and all of us continue to suffer from this lack of imagination. May I ask...' She hesitates. 'I do not wish to be untoward, but why do you remain here instead of returning to London, when it has so much more to offer, particularly for someone as talented as yourself?'

My blood freezes in my veins. I am always guarded around her, but had begun to soften in the last few minutes and immediately brace myself again. This is not the first time I have had to face this question and, while I cannot tell her the truth, I try a variation of it. 'There are complications of life in the city that are not an issue here.'

She nods, but her expression is mixed with curiosity. She will likely ask again, as we seem to be expanding our interactions to topics outside of my work. 'In any case, I don't wish to use up your valuable time, Mr Rooke. I'm sure we both have a lot to occupy us today. Send Anne back in, please.'

She returns to her desk as I make for the door. She's right – I have many tasks ahead this afternoon. I glance at her as I leave – what could she be labouring over? Perhaps a letter to a friend.

Returning to my room, I pause over my designs and orders. I need wax for my sewing thread, but will check the kitchen before purchasing some in town. I turn to the window, watching the swans and ducks in the pond outside. Are they there because they want to be, or because the gamekeeper clips their wings?

On my windowsill is the French discourse Lady Elina lent me. I pick it up, feeling its light weight in my palm. What's the time? Not quite lunch. Perhaps I'll read until then.

Then

Dear Mr Ashby,
While I appreciate you leaving your card, I felt it may be best to write instead of calling. The jacket you were sporting the other night was most attractive – I wanted to ask who made it for you?
Yours,
Matthew Rooke
Bell Yard

Dear Mr Rooke,
The jacket is from Barnaby & Sons in Piccadilly. Yet I suspect you already knew that; perhaps you wrote with a different purpose in mind?
Yours,
Henry Ashby
38 St James's Square

Dear Mr Ashby,
You must be very bold to conjure up these hidden intentions on my behalf – after all, it was not I who sneaked my card into a stranger's pocket!
Yours,
Matthew Rooke
Bell Yard

There's no immediate response from him after that. Perhaps I offended him with my little joke, or he has grown tired of me already.

I try to put the matter out of my mind, for I have work to contend with. 'Martha!' I call as I walk downstairs. 'Have you finished lining Mrs Hatchfield's stays?'

She's like a little mouse as she scurries around the table, her shadow falling onto the splintered floor. 'Just doing the last stitches now, sir!'

I do enjoy being addressed this way – it's exceedingly rare in my life to be referred to as anything other than my name or 'the staymaker'. Mustn't let myself develop any flights of fancy, however – Martha is hardly the Duchess of Cornwall, and I'm only a step or two above her.

While she stitches the remainder of the lining, I step over to another workbench and review my designs. Heavier boning in addition to shoulder straps will support the large mantua that Mrs Hatchfield requires at the back of her dress. The superficial fabric is something new for me, painted silk from France. The flowers and vines appear to have been directly brushed on, quite painstaking work for the artist tasked with painting the entire sample. Whether this way of designing silk will become popular is anyone's guess, but I hardly consider Mrs Hatchfield a pioneer of fashion. Even her shifts are conservative, and the dressing gowns I have seen her maid set aside for her after our fittings are several years behind current styles. These insights are an advantage of my trade, as I am admitted into personal spaces where many are not and can observe what is otherwise hidden.

'Here you are. What do you think?' Martha sets the stays onto my workbench. They pick up a little extra weight as each layer of fabric is added, and especially when all ten panels are sewn together. Her needlework is even and I count twelve stitches per inch. I'm pleased with her competence thus far.

'Well done,' I say. 'You'll want to work towards fourteen or fifteen stitches per inch of fabric as you progress, but this is satisfactory. Why don't you run out and get us a snack?'

She flushes a little at the praise and looks at her shoes for a moment. 'What do you fancy, sir?'

'Perhaps some fruit from the market.'

I hand her a tuppence coin and watch her scamper out the door. I remember that age when the chance to go outside during daylight was savoured, my body swallowed whole by the city streets. Toiling in the dull light of a shop for hours on end and sewing the same pattern over and over again wore on my spirit, while even fifteen minutes of strolling amongst my fellow Londoners was enough to re-energise me. Not so any more – I enjoy my walks but these days they are a chance to centre my focus. My work, far from drudgery, is invigorating because it is *mine*; each pair of stays are my own design. It is remarkable how a sense of ownership enhances a person's outlook.

Back to Mrs Hatchfield. I begin to add the whalebones one by one, the rigorous stitching requires great strength and attention. Perhaps two more stitches, and then I can move on to the second bone—

A knock at the door, though I'm not expecting any callers. I walk past the low fire and open the door to reveal a boy, perhaps nine or ten years old. He looks well fed but still has the glimmer in his eyes one sees on the more enterprising street orphans.

He holds out a card and I already feel lighter – it must be from Henry. I check just to make sure. Yes, it's him – I recognise the handwriting. 'Already franked?'

'Yessir,' the boy calls as he twirls around to leave.

'Thank you.' But he's already hurried away to earn his next farthing. I glance to my sides foolishly, guarding a secret that does not yet exist, then tear open the note.

> *Dear Mr Rooke,*
>
> *Since you already think me bold, I would hate to spoil the image. Should you be free this afternoon, I would welcome your company at number 24 Piccadilly. I'll await your presence at four o'clock.*
>
> *Yours,*
> *Henry*

I'll have to make haste to get across town and Martha's not yet returned. No matter – I set out the pattern for the panels on Lady MacIntyre's stays along with the broadcloth and a note explaining that I've stepped out. That should be enough to get her started. Just before dashing out the door, I have the good sense to check my cravat and tie a fresh knot. I spot some dust on my shoulder and brush off my coat, admiring the embroidered geranium-and-hollyhock design on the pockets and cuffs. Stockings look fresh – perhaps just a little rouge on my cheeks and I'll be ready.

As I open the door the bell rings, giving me pause. I'm being ridiculous, abandoning work for a man I know nothing about except that he has good taste in clothing and a playful sense of humour. It's foolhardy, a selfish ambition that's sure to bring me nothing but misery.

Just before this dark cloud swoops over me, I laugh. To deny adventure is to shrink away from the sun, this city has taught me that. We must embrace life if we wish to avoid a heart full of regret. After all, this day – this moment – is the only one we've any certainty of keeping.

Number 24 Piccadilly is a simple, unassuming door. I wonder what secrets it holds – is Henry here already, or am I miraculously early? I don't spend a lot of time in Piccadilly outside of client homes and my interest is piqued by the mysterious location. From our playful notes, I'm optimistic this might be the sort of place where we can safely be open with each other. I stretch my fingers against my leg, hoping this encounter goes well and I impress him. Londoners saunter past, but no one comes or goes from the door to satisfy my curiosity. I glance over my shoulder, growing concerned. How long should I wait? What if he doesn't show up? But as I turn back around, the door opens and Henry walks through. 'Ah, there you are – I was searching for you!' he exclaims, jovial.

I smile but falter a little – was he waiting for me inside? Should I have tried the door? His welcoming expression pushes my anxieties away and I follow him over the threshold.

The light changes as the door closes. Before my eyes adjust, I catch a counter to the left and, above it, the outline of a wig. Henry reaches into his pocket and lays a shilling on the counter as we enter. As he does, a man with perfectly coiffed hair and white gloves bows to us. The floor is chequered and there's an intriguing smell wafting through the air, something earthy and spicy. We walk through the corridor, down a few steps, and come upon an expansive, elegant room. Candles light up the tables, where I see games of cards being played with gusto. To the right, a long wooden bar hugs the wall and Henry nudges me in that direction first. In the low candlelight, the sleeves of his suit shimmer with silver foil embroidery and I briefly let my eyes fall to admire his calves in their clocked silk stockings.

'Two chocolates,' he says to the man behind the bar. So he's taken me to a chocolate house! I've read about the reckless debauchery commonplace in White's, but of course you can't always trust what the papers say. I can only imagine the lies they might print about me were I ever unfortunate enough to wind up in their pages.

The man at the bar adds a series of spices to elegant silver cups, then a scoop of dark brown powder and tops the whole thing with warm wine before giving each glass a vigorous stir. He sets them on the polished bar and says, 'Five shillings, sir.'

My mouth falls open in shock but I try to recover by rubbing my jaw as if it were bothering me. Henry pays but, for such a price, my expectations are high.

We find a couple of plush chairs and take a seat. 'It's a fine establishment, is it not?' Henry asks me. 'I've been coming here for years, though I don't have terribly good luck at the games!'

I smile, trying to sit back and relax. I'm enjoying the elegance of the room, but find myself more interested in watching Henry. 'It's beautiful, though I suspect you may be among the higher-calibre clientele.' I nod towards a group of boisterous young men thumping the table as their chequer chips bounce off.

Henry laughs. 'They're harmless, really.' He drinks his chocolate and I follow suit – not exactly appealing, but it's an interesting blend of flavours. My nose fills with the scent of cinnamon and clove, while the bitter chocolate dries my mouth. I try another sip.

'You know, I'm not sure this is quite worth the price.' I don't want to be disagreeable, so I say it as if in jest.

'The taxes on it are loathsome. But you don't drink it for the taste,' he leans forward an inch, 'you drink it for the way it makes you feel.'

I run my finger up and down the side of my cup. 'I see – so although its character is not conventional, it has something deeper to offer?'

His eyebrows flit up in understanding and a sly grin crosses his face. 'Precisely.' His lips remain parted. 'Perhaps it is even an acquired taste, one that grows more enjoyable with familiarity.'

I edge my hand closer to his on the table. Already the chocolate has quickened my pulse, heightened my senses. 'Something so unique must be very difficult to give up. I'm not sure I would drink anything else.'

He's about to answer when a man dressed in a yellow velvet jacket stumbles over to our table. 'There you are, old fellow! Come on, let's have a game of whist.'

Confident, Henry keeps his eyes on me. Am I still breathing? He's asking me a question. 'Do you play?'

I have to clear my throat before I find my voice. 'Well, I... I'm not much for cards.' Of course, I've learned over the years, but I don't have the resources to waste gambling every week. And who is this intruder imposing himself on us?

'That's all right, come along!' Henry bounds up from the table with a rush of energy and seizes my arm. 'It's great fun. We can be partners.'

I like the sound of that. I follow him towards the centre of the room and we sit down at a table with two uproarious men in expensive suits.

Am I sweating? I pull out a handkerchief and dab at my face. Henry sits opposite, his friends prodding his arms in greeting.

'My good men, allow me to introduce Mr Matthew Rooke – a new friend of mine.'

I nod, trying to blend in.

'Welcome, Mr Rooke,' says a gentleman to my left with a face comprised of teeth. 'Right, lads, the game is whist – buy-in is a guinea.'

'I'll get this,' Henry says to me and carelessly tosses both of our fees into the middle of the table. I don't know whether to be enchanted or appalled – such a sum would cover a week's worth of expenses at my workshop. His friend passes our cards over, and Henry inclines his head forward as if trying to memorise them all.

'How many points shall we play to?' the man in the yellow jacket asks.

Henry looks thoughtful, but I detect a playful hint behind his expression. 'Let's just make it ten – I don't want to bore Mr Rooke for too long.' His eyes glint in my direction and I try not to blush.

'Not at all,' I reply, placing a card down, 'I am all yours this evening, Mr Ashby.' The shadow of a coy smile passes between us faster than a candle flickering.

His toothy friend on my left sweeps up the cards. 'More likely you'll lose, then wish to keep playing until you win. I know how you are, Ashers,' he chuckles, jostling Henry. I watch carefully to gauge his reaction – is there something between them?

The man puts down the knave of spades. I check my cards, but the highest I have is a six. I glance across the table at Henry, still chuckling with his friend. Perhaps they simply know each other through family connections. He tosses down a four, and I feel a slight pang of disappointment that I cannot win the trick for us.

'Come on now, gents!' says the man in the yellow jacket. 'You're starting out from behind!'

I smile good-humouredly, hopeful that our chance will come. Henry answers him, 'I'm beginning to wonder if you did something to the cards when you were shuffling them.'

'Upon my honour!' his friend scoffs. 'Only a scoundrel could suggest such a thing!'

'Indeed – the same sort who would steal his friend's notes before exams!' jeers the man on the other side.

Henry leans towards him with a smug expression. 'Parvus pendetur fur, magnus abire videtur,' he says as if this settles the issue, and the three of them dissolve into uncontrollable laughter.

I try to smile along, but it's obvious I'm removed from the three of them. I cannot reminisce about schooldays or make jokes about a mutual friend's dinner party last week. There is a divide between me and Henry, each of our backgrounds unfathomable to the other. I sigh as we all play another round – even if my shop becomes as successful as I hope it will, some chasms can never be bridged. I will never learn Latin, or choose to spend my spare time playing cards. Perhaps I should simply enjoy being part of his world this evening, but there is something about him, a hint at something deeper that compels me to want more.

At last we've come into the suits I have higher cards in. I'm about to put down a queen, but I feel Henry's eyes on me and glance up at him. He winks at me slyly and I pause, then put my queen back and play a lower card instead. When it's Henry's turn, he plays an ace and picks up the trick for us. 'Look out, boys!' he says to his friends, but saves most of his triumphant smile for me.

We don't win in the end but, true to his word, Henry stops playing after ten points. He walks me outside to the street, both of us careful not to arouse suspicion.

'Thank you for this evening,' I say, wishing for more. I want to ask if I embarrassed him in front of his friends, if he is truly interested in me as I hope he is, if we can see each other again soon. If only I could cup his face in my hands and kiss him, that would answer everything.

His smile is sweet but guarded. He casts his glance behind me and out into the street, then focuses back on me with complete attention. 'Do you need a chaise?'

'God, no.' I stifle my laugh. 'I can walk home.' It would have been nice to eat dinner together, but I suppose we would not be able to speak openly with his circle of friends prowling around anyway.

'Are you sure? It's quite far, and no trouble—'

'No, no, it's all right. Good night, Mr Ashby,' I say, nodding my head and spinning around on my heel into the city night.

It's an hour's walk back to my shop and, without Henry for company, I remember how much work remains to be done and pick up my pace. I rush past the Royal Mews and shuffle along the river. Almost immediately, I regret this decision – with ships landing and being unloaded, the wharves are filled with pigs, hay bales, casks of beer, and workers tasked with moving them away from the river and into warehouses, where carts and coaches await. I had hoped to let my mind wander, to understand what just happened at the chocolate house, but it is impossible with so much commotion. A canvas sack topples over and letters spill out, causing various men to yell at one another while the only sensible worker picks them up.

Amidst this noise and chaos, I slip into Durham Yard, an alley running parallel to the river. I am at my leisure this way, my steps on the packed earth echoing between the brick buildings. A window opens and I hop across the little street instinctively, hearing the splash of someone's toilet behind me. Why did Henry bring me somewhere his friends would be? Did he want to impress, or intimidate? Ahead, a large man carrying a sack appears. He may simply be going about his business, but the sky has grown dark – he could be a thief. I've no intention of finding out, so I hurry along and turn left, onto the main road. St Paul's looms above, a calm and steadying presence amongst the chaotic crowds. Another mile and I'll be home.

The familiar jingle as I open my shop door. Martha is hunched over a table – asleep? No, her fingers are moving. She looks over at me, sullen, but not in a position to say anything. I add a log to the fireplace, poking it until orange light pours into the room. 'Getting dark in here.'

'It don't bother me,' she replies.

'I'll be working through the night, so the light will do me good.'

She puts her needle down and looks at me. 'I know it's not my place, but you mighta considered that before you ran off for half the evening.'

She's more courageous than I imagined. 'You're right – it's not your place.'

'It's just, I came back and you'd disappeared.'

'Did you not see my note?'

She tucks her chin down, suddenly shy, 'Oh...' then casts her eyes onto the piece of paper at the end of her workbench. 'Right, well... I saved your snack.' She gestures to the end of the table, where a pear and hunk of cheese sit humbly.

I feel a twinge of guilt, but have no intention of letting her know that. 'Fear not, I'll have it for supper.' I wonder what Henry will be served at the chocolate house tonight. Or perhaps he will dine with his friends elsewhere. Will they ask him about the strange man from the card table, or will all thought of me be carried away on the night breeze?

I sit down opposite Martha and pick up Mrs Hatchfield's stays, feeling with my fingers for where I left off with the whalebone channels. I can sense her eyes on me.

'Sir, if you're going to work all night, are you expecting me to as well? Only I've been working all afternoon already.'

'And how do you know that I haven't?'

'Because you'd have brought back the fabric for Lady MacIntyre if you had.' Is there a hint of smug triumph in her tone?

'Martha, I could replace you tomorrow if I liked – mind the way you address me.' I pause, pushing the bone into its place. 'You are not expected to work all night just because I do. We each have different responsibilities – your focus is the menial labour, and I do everything else. It's only natural that my hours will be longer and more varied than yours.'

That's quieted her, but I doubt she's let the matter go. She hops down from her stool and puts the kettle on the fire.

–

The next morning, early dawn breaks through the windows and burns my eyes. There's a glimmer – the needle, inches from my face. My neck aches and I stand to stretch, looking around. The fire is out; the boning on Mrs Hatchfield's stays finished. I check the front door – yes, milk has been delivered. I make some coffee – a luxury in the morning, but it's needed today. Martha's door is still closed – I suspect she'll stay hidden for as long as she can stand it. It's nice to have the shop to myself again and I pretend she isn't back there at all.

I finish my coffee, then package a recently completed pair of stays for Mrs Thompson in some paper and twine to keep them safe from the whirling morning traffic. She is an older client I would like to move away from – her orders are infrequent, simplistic, and there is always some difficulty with payment. Still, I won't turn down any work until my books are truly too full to add anyone else. I must leave my card with some of the dressmakers in Soho again, and perhaps consider placing an advertisement in the *Gazette*.

Heading towards the door, I glance at myself in the mirror and immediately realise I must change. I dash upstairs to my quarters, searching the armoire. With a clean shift, new breeches, a fresh jacket, and my wig, I'm presentable enough for the London streets.

Grabbing the stays for Mrs Thompson, I open the front door and bump into a boy.

'Beg yer pardon, sir, are ye Mr Rooke?'

'Indeed I am.'

He hands me a letter and runs off. I check the front – it's from Henry. Holding the door ajar with my foot, I open it.

> *Dear Matthew,*
>
> *Thank you for your company yesterday. It was delightful to have some thoughtful conversation and I had a marvellous time. Would you happen to be available this evening to see Mr Garrick playing Hamlet? Perhaps you know a place where we might have a late supper after?*
>
> *Yours,*
>
> *Henry*

I falter, wanting to reply to him but knowing that I need to get this delivery to Mrs Thompson quickly so that I can collect an order of silk for Lady MacIntyre's stays, then return to the shop and cut it. It would seem my time is already running short and it's only morning. I walk to a workbench and find a piece of paper, but when I realise the ink is dry I decide to wait. Cramming his letter into my pocket, I dash out the door to pick up the silk order. I'm thrilled he wants to see me again and my steps feel lighter than usual, but I cannot lose sight of work. In addition to my hopes for the shop's success, it is my only means of survival.

I walk through St Paul's shadow, then Lincoln's Inn Fields on the way to Mr McFarland's shop. The dandelions are beginning to shrink and wilt but the trees remain verdant, not ready to abandon the summer quite yet. A man saunters next to me, meeting my eye. We give each other a cursory appraisal and he veers off towards the boghouses. I slow down, but am not inclined to join him. Something has shifted inside me – the familiar physical pull towards another man is gone, replaced by the memory of Henry smiling at me, the warmth in his eyes, the rosy colour of his lips.

I hurry through Covent Garden, with its tall stone houses and wide streets. I'll stop at Mr McFarland's shop first to collect the silk, perhaps some leather as well. I know I have at least a yard of the tawny colour I want to finish Lady MacIntyre's stays, but I suspect she will require it for future orders and would like to be well stocked. Once she sees my work on this first pair of stays, she'll want to place another order immediately. They will be the most comfortable she's ever worn, and the most stylish too.

I turn on to Panton Street and into Mr McFarland's shop. Just as I place my hand on the door, I suddenly remember I've left Mrs Thompson's stays back at the workshop. I cringe, realising I'll have to double back and lose all this time spent walking. I could catch a chaise there and back, but it's not worth it to spend any money on Mrs Thompson's order considering what I've charged her. I sigh – I will have to work late and miss spending the evening with Henry. I hope he does not mind pushing his theatre plans to another night.

After exchanging a few pleasantries with Mr McFarland and quickly collecting the silk and leather, I tuck the parcel under my arm and hurry back to my shop. The bell rings and I spin around, looking for Mrs Thompson's stays where I left them by the door. But they've disappeared. I scramble through the workbenches, carefully lifting patterns and panels of fabric to look underneath. But the stays – three days of labour, fabric, and boning – are nowhere to be found.

Chapter Three

Then

The low autumn light coming through the windows offers just enough visibility to confirm that the stays aren't in my workshop. Just then, the bell jingles and I turn around to see Martha walking through the door. I realise in an instant what has happened.

When she locks eyes with me, she pushes her lips together until they disappear. She's clearly nervous, as she should be. She has risked my reputation with a client, and more importantly, taken on responsibilities that I have not assigned her. 'What have you done?' I glower from behind the workbench.

She keeps to the edge of the room, bunching her apron in her hands nervously. Is she trying to decide what to say? I do not give her more time to contemplate an excuse.

'You delivered Mrs Thompson's stays, didn't you?'

She nods, staring at the floor. 'Sir—' she begins.

'How could you do such a thing? Client interactions are not your purview and you have risked the integrity of this business! Did you collect the second instalment of her payment, or were you even aware of that step in the process?'

She's surprised by my attack and can only stutter out a few words. 'I just... but...'

'It was not your place to deliver those stays, do you understand?' I ask her. She is still bewildered and for a moment I wonder if my rhetoric is too harsh – after all, I did forget the stays when Henry's note flustered me this morning. But she needs to understand that this is my business, not hers, and I am at risk if anything goes wrong. 'What compelled you to do such a thing?' Now I pause long enough for her to speak.

She takes a breath, steadying herself. 'I saw you'd forgotten them this morning and we're so busy right now, I figured it couldn't hurt to get one thing out of the way. I was only trying to help.' Her girlish face hardens but she looks down, as if ashamed of herself. 'I do want to prove myself as useful, sir – I want you to take me seriously.'

Her pitiful face makes me soften my tone. I can begin to understand why she did it – to gain favour rather than to usurp my position. I consider my reaction – perhaps I was stern because I am not as secure as I'd like to be in my ability to run a successful business. My ambition is great, but I must take care to manage things the right way. 'Very well,' I tell her, 'I will bear that in mind for the future.'

She nods in thanks, then sits down at a workbench and rolls her neck. She reaches for a pile of silk panels and lays them out on the table, looking over at my new pattern while she does. She smiles at them, seemingly charmed. I put the kettle on for some more coffee as she begins to stitch the panels together. I watch her while the kettle boils – such a diligent worker. My eyes catch a sheet of paper nearby with a newly drawn design; I pick it up and begin refining the pattern.

We carry on with our work until the sun has gone down. With the cooler weather and additional clouds in the sky, bright orange and pink hues filter through the windows. The bells at St Michael's chime six, but we continue apace. I'm just starting to ponder supper when there's a knock on the door.

I get up to answer it and my blood stops – it's Henry on the stoop. Glancing behind me, I usher him into the alley and close the door tight behind me.

'What are you doing here?' I whisper.

He holds himself gracefully, relaxed and easy-going. 'I wanted to see where you worked. I was hoping you'd be free for supper.'

In the chaos of the day, I forgot to return his note. He reaches out his hand for mine – I long to take it, but push him away. 'We must be careful! Wait here.' In truth, I'm exhilarated that he's come. It confirms how he must feel and, in being so open, he endears himself to me further.

Popping back into the shop for my jacket, I inform Martha I'll be dining with a friend this evening. I pause, the feeling of guilt creeping across my conscience.

'You may take the rest of the night off, if you wish,' I tell her. I can hardly lose the labour, but it seems hypocritical to make her work alone.

I return to the alley and find Henry waiting. His smile melts the day's work away — I return it.

'Come,' I say. 'I know exactly where to take you.'

We weave through the wooden houses and trading shops of the East End, walking down Fleet Street and into Leicester Fields. It's dark, but the oil lamps light our way. In an alley off the square, there is a coffee house run by Mother Mack. It's windowless and unassuming, but as we approach the door we can hear whooping and laughter coming from inside.

'What is this?' Henry asks, amused.

'It's called the Bird's Nest — the sort of establishment some might call a mollyhouse.'

'I've never heard of such a place.'

He's in for a treat, and my confidence grows now that we're in my territory. 'Follow me.'

Opening the door, we're hit with a wall that is equal parts heat and noise. It's already crowded inside, the wooden tables each crammed with several groups of men. Everyone talks over each other, gesturing wildly, glasses of beer and gin clamouring for space on the tables.

'What a pretty husband you've got!' someone calls to me.

'I beg pardon?' says Henry.

'He's just baiting. Come on,' I tell him.

We squeeze through to the bar, where Mother Mack is serving drinks. 'Mr Rooke!' she cries when she sees me. 'Where've you been?'

'Here and there. I see you're keeping well without me.'

'Well, you know — Friday nights are popular. And we got our licence back, so everyone's glad for some spirits.'

I motion over at Henry. 'Do you have any space in the back rooms for supper?'

She grabs a couple of empty glasses and wipes the counter down with a clean cloth. 'For you, love? Sure I do. Come along.'

There's a little door at the end of the bar — we walk through and down a corridor. On the right are intimate rooms with just two (or, occasionally, three) men inside. Mother Mack leads on, stopping at one of the doorways.

'Here you are,' she says. 'There's pie and mash for supper — I'll bring it through in a bit.'

'Thank you,' I say, squeezing her hand in gratitude. I've been coming here for years and used to think she had a particular affection for me, but over time saw that she treats all her customers with the same warmth and discretion. Her husband runs the place with her, but he usually stays in the kitchen until they're out of food for the night.

There's a sofa and table in the room, with a little fireplace for warmth. Henry collapses onto the cushions, looking up at me and smiling. 'Well! I can't believe I didn't know about this place. Are there others like it?'

I sit down next to him. 'Yes, plenty. But this is my favourite – the hours are good and Mother Mack is the best proprietress.'

'I've heard of places where men are sold by the hour.'

'This isn't like that. Everyone is here because they want to be.'

'Well, I certainly am.' He reaches out and takes hold of my hand. All my senses are heightened in anticipation – I feel each of his fingers between mine, the smell of his perfume. My own heart pounds in my ears as if someone is thumping against the wall (which, now I consider it, they might be). I run my eyes over Henry, admiring his jacket and vest, the way his entire outfit harmonises.

'Do you consider your fashion choices very carefully, or simply buy whatever is most expensive?'

He laughs at this. 'I confess, I don't have very refined taste and take the advice of the tailors whenever I make a purchase. But you,' he grabs my jacket, fingering its brass buttons, 'you understand how to put an outfit together.'

'Part of my trade,' I say. Then, deciding to take a risk: 'I'm rather good at removing clothing as well.'

He's not offended, just smiles. As our eyes meet, Mother Mack returns with our supper and two ales.

'Here you are, my loves,' she says, setting everything down and lighting a candle on the table.

'You're very kind,' says Henry, pressing half a crown into her hand.

'Ooo, generous!' She nods to me approvingly and I blush – I don't want Henry to think I make a regular habit of meeting men here.

The mood is festive and, once she leaves, I raise my glass to Henry's. 'Cheers! I'm pleased I could bring you here – you never know when one of these houses will be closed down. May we drink and forget the cruelties of the world.'

We tap our glasses, but he looks thoughtful. 'I've always found the reason for drinking varies with the company one keeps. Given the present moment, I find myself drinking to remember, not forget.'

Perhaps a poetic spirit rustles within him after all. The beer and food are flavoursome – even though I'm sure it's a modest meal for Henry, his exclamations are all complimentary. As we finish eating, I ask him about his family.

'What would you like to know?'

'Have you any brothers or sisters?'

'One sister, elder. She's married to a gentleman in Derbyshire.'

'And your father earns his living from colonial trade?' It's an educated guess.

He sinks back against the sofa, looking a little melancholy. 'Well, we have our estate at Stonehurst Manor, but my father has been increasing his investments across the Atlantic. I believe we're hardly involved beyond providing initial funding.'

'You don't sound very invested yourself.'

He lifts the corner of his mouth in recognition of my little joke, but still seems discouraged. 'No, to be perfectly honest I find it all quite dull. My father is not yet fifty, so he does most of the work and keeps watch over our financial affairs. I won't take over for many years, and can't bring myself to engage with any of it until then.'

I bite my lip, unsure of how to respond. I can't understand choosing not to work – for me, it has always been a necessity. And yet I take such enjoyment from my trade that I almost pity Henry for finding himself so listless.

'I'm no good at talking about it,' he says. 'And there's no point. Until I must worry about it, I simply want to enjoy London.' Ah, yes – our shared love of the capital quickly mends the pall I'd cast with my line of enquiry. Soon, we are trading thoughts on the best plays, parks, and shops. We learn that we both enjoy walking past John Flude's pawnbrokers to admire the display, and listening to the afternoon bells of St Paul's.

'You know,' he says with bright eyes, 'I've never spoken like this with anyone before – never felt so comfortable revealing my innermost thoughts about who I am. Thank you for letting me.'

Feeling a rush of closeness to him, I lean forward and kiss him. His mouth presses back on mine and I'm flush with excitement, relief, catharsis. Touching him, feeling his warmth, is unlike anything I've experienced with another man. His breath rushes past my ears and I can almost feel his heart beating under my fingertips. I catch him by the shoulders and push him backward into the sofa, running my hands over him. I reach down to his breeches, but he grabs my wrist to stop me.

'It's all right,' I say, 'we won't be disturbed.'

'I can't. Of course I want to, just not yet.'

The heat of desire is cut short by rejection's sharp sting. I sit up and lean away from him. 'There's nothing wrong with making use of your own body,' I say, feeling a little defensive.

'I'm comfortable with my body. I simply... need more time.'

I nod, hurt but trying to understand. Maybe I am his first, unless there was a cousin in the nursery when he was growing up. Perhaps I am the first he has wanted.

We sit up, a bit awkward. 'I hope you don't think—' he begins.

'It's fine,' I say, trying to recover from my embarrassment by moving the conversation along even as I wince inside. 'Another time.'

'Yes.'

Before either of us can say anything else, there's a commotion outside. It sounds like it's coming from the bar, but must be terribly loud if we can hear it in these back rooms. Gathering our jackets, we check to see if everyone is all right.

A tall, handsome man is standing up from a table as Mother Mack yells at him. 'You may not go by Thom Newton tonight, but I'd recognise such scum as yours any day of the week!'

'Madam, I assure you I am here for pleasure like everybody else.'

'Pah! You think I don't know you're the one who turned over our poor Gabriel Lawrence last month? You're nothing but a two-faced scrub.' She spits at his feet.

The man slowly makes for the door. 'Very well, I see I'm not welcome here.' He looks around the room. 'But I'll remind you that I'm friendly with the local officials – you might consider treating me more kindly.'

At this, Mother Mack begins whipping him with her dishrag. 'Out! If I see you in hell, it'll be too soon!'

Lifting his hands in false innocence, Mr Newton leaves. The room is quiet, everyone eyeing one another.

'Do you suppose he'll turn us in?' one man asks no one in particular.

'Let him try!' growls Pete, a blacksmith.

'Hush, love – nothing he can do if you didn't lay with him,' Mother Mack replies to the first man, recomposing herself.

A fellow next to me asks, 'Has anyone heard from Gabe?'

'Still in prison,' replies another, sombre.

'Well, a lot of good it'll do us to mope about tonight – let's thank Mother Mack by buying some drinks! A bottle for my table!' calls out a man wearing a butcher's apron and lip stain.

The mood begins to pick up again. 'Would you like another drink?' I ask, turning to Henry.

'Actually,' he begins slowly, and my mind is a frenzy of worries. He's realised the danger we are in, and means to return to his comfort in the West End, he has lost interest in me, he has forgotten another engagement and must leave. He continues thoughtfully, 'It's easy to forget that there are so few opportunities for true companionship, that we can lose everything at any moment.' His eyes pierce into mine, stopping my breath. 'All I'd like right now is to go home with you.'

My heart flutters and, for a moment, I can't hear the crowds around us. Any awkwardness from earlier is forgotten – he does want me after all. With a fleeting kiss, I grab his hand and pull him through the crowd, out into the city. We let go of each other under the oil lamps, then clutch for one another in the darkness, nearly running through the quiet streets.

When we arrive at my shop I open the door carefully, peering around for Martha. Fortunately, the fire is low and all is still. I motion for Henry to be silent and he giggles, deftly removing his shoes and walking inside. Moonbeams light up my workbenches and he moves around them curiously, trying to see the pairs of in-progress stays laid out on them.

'This way,' I whisper as softly as I can, watching Martha's door all the while. He comes over and begins kissing me; it's all I can do to resist him. 'Upstairs – this moment.'

At last, I don't think of what may happen in the morning, or worry about hidden intentions. I just focus on him in my bed, tonight.

Now

I tramp downstairs into the kitchen. The smell of lye hangs in the air as Clara, the scullery maid, leans over a basin that's too large for her. A chorus of thuds from heavy pots against the sink and silver dishes set down on the table after polishing. There's no occasion for all this finery, it's just another day in the servants' quarters. I enjoy weaving through the chaos, seeing how long I can go unnoticed before someone tries to catch me in conversation. For as long as I've been here, I don't quite belong with these people. Not because of their status – I too must earn my keep – but because many of them work here from lack of imagination above all else. Their father was a footman, and so they became a footman. The maids are waiting for one of the men to marry them so they'll have their own home to mind and, otherwise, no one dreams of anything beyond the world of this manor. I suppose I cannot blame them entirely – we all need to make our living. But my situation is different – I am here by choice, not necessity.

Through another door is the linen room, where tablecloths and other serving linens are stored in great, immovable cabinets. On a table in this room I have laid out the bodice for one of Lady Elina's dresses and begun stitching it together. The sleeves have been particularly irksome, getting the correct space and dimensions in the shoulders for the silhouette I want to achieve. Mrs Ferrers, the housekeeper, sits in the prized place near the fire, counting table linens. I lower myself into a chair at the table, calculating how well the conical left sleeve currently attaches to the bodice and undoing the whip stitches I recently used to test the fit. I look over at Mrs Ferrers – there is a tall stack of linens in front of her, more than a usual evening calls for. 'Are those for tonight?'

'This weekend – Lady Elina said her husband has some friends coming to visit.' I nod, but am confused. Surely I would have heard of this before from—

'Rooke!' The valet pokes his head into the room, a note in his hand. 'Letter for you.'

I take the envelope, glancing at the paper – it's from London. I can feel Mrs Ferrers' eyes on me and immediately grow insecure. Carefully guarding my treasure like a devious bird, I hold the letter close to my chest to read. It's nothing secretive – only word from Mr McFarland about an incoming shipment of whalebones, but I touch the paper, feeling the grit of the capital on it, the dirt stuck to the ink. Checking my watch, I realise I could make the afternoon coach if I ran and be in town by nightfall. Of course, I won't – I have an appointment with Lady Elina in ten minutes, but I often take comfort in how accessible my true home remains. While the downstairs of the manor sometimes feels like a small village, I am always a little detached from the others partly due to my position in the household, but also because most leave after a few years and it's become difficult to pursue friendships. Perhaps that is why I still cling to my relationships in London so tightly after all these years, even as my connection to the city becomes more tenuous. At least I have my fantasies to console me.

A chime rings. I grab the bodice pieces and walk upstairs to find Her Ladyship.

—

'You see, Mr Rooke, the status quo has been designed that way by the very people who hold all of the power,' Lady Elina says, watching me circle her in the mirror. 'In time, the system will need to be overturned.'

'I understand, but how? Where do those at the top go, and would there be a change in government?' I surprise myself a little with the question, but there is no harm in making conversation while we are working. It's amusing to ponder these subjects with her.

'If only there was a simple answer to that,' she sighs. 'How do we choose our leaders? Does everybody get an equal say or is it only property-owning men, as in America? That simply perpetuates the system we already have, which is why the revolution in France terrifies our politicians here.'

These are potentially dangerous ideas, particularly for someone of my status to know about. Still, it is thrilling to realise that Lady Elina is not the cold, tiresome person I'd previously known, but rather someone bubbling with provocative ideas about reforming the world. I'm not sure how to respond, so I move behind her and pretend to focus on measuring between her shoulders. My mind slips to my upcoming visit to London – catching up on the changes I have missed, spotting some of the latest fashions, and hopefully grabbing a pork pie from Mrs Burley's shop. I am ready for the refreshing lift that comes from wandering through the busy streets heaving with artisans, labourers and intellectuals alike. Perhaps it will knock me out of the fog I have recently felt trapped within.

While I'm content for us both to muse silently, Lady Elina converses without any encouragement from me. 'Rousseau – the philosopher – asked how many pieces we might break government into. If businesses have their own power equal to that of citizens, could they take over the larger republic? What does "the will of the people" truly mean?'

I hope my face does not betray my confusion, but she has lost me. I don't wish to offend her, but it is vexing trying to follow her train of thought – my time is better spent focusing on my work. I measure her hips and jot the number down.

She turns around to face me, eyes alight just like they were a few weeks ago. I can't help but smile at her fervour. 'I've just begun reading a new publication by Olympe de Gouges,' she says, grabbing a small book from the table and showing it to me. 'It provides a much-needed perspective on where women belong in this new future we are envisioning.'

How can she know and read so much? I once imagined the books in her rooms had been there for generations and were merely decorative, but they must belong to her.

'I hope you do not mind my enthusiasm, but I believe you have an aptitude for this way of thinking,' she says.

I flush a little, dubiously flattered. Still, after so many years of monotony here, any sort of novelty is compelling. 'Your Ladyship,' I say, returning the book, 'we may need to reschedule our appointment next week. I think I must prioritise travelling to London to collect some new whalebone, figured silk, and other materials for you.' While her purview may be grand ideas about restructuring society, mine continues to be crafting the most resplendent gowns possible.

'Is that so? Very good…' she replies, but she avoids my eye and looks thoughtful. She walks over to her desk, her fingers grazing some of the papers stacked on it. I wait, in part because I have not been dismissed, but also because it's clear she has something more to say. At last, she turns back around. 'I wonder, Mr Rooke, whether you might consider doing me a favour on your upcoming trip.'

'Of course.'

'It's hardly anything, but perhaps you could post a letter for me, either at the coaching inn or once you arrive in town.'

'Certainly, ma'am, although may I ask why not give it to Mrs Ferrers instead?' The challenge is a little out of line but she shouldn't mind, given all her talk of equalising the classes.

'I do not wish for anyone in the household to know about this particular correspondence,' she replies carefully.

'I see,' I reply, though of course I do not.

'Including my husband.'

'Of course.' This is highly unusual, but being in her favour for something so trivial could prove useful. Besides, there isn't much in the way of entertainment in this household and I'm intrigued.

'Thank you,' she says, smiling. 'Let me know your departure date once you have made your plans and I will give you the letter then.'

She sits down at her desk and begins to work. Clearly dismissed, I collect my measuring paper, bodice pieces, and notepad before leaving her rooms.

Back downstairs, I wonder whom her mysterious correspondence is for – perhaps she has a clandestine lover? Or is she in some kind of legal trouble? If she does not want anyone else to know, it could be quite serious – perhaps a medical problem. I try to stop myself from getting too carried away – we all have our secrets to keep and, as I myself know, some of them are more dangerous than others.

After darkness falls and the house sinks into silence, I sit awake in my room, waiting. I crack my door open, peering down the corridor. Even though it's been quiet for a quarter of an hour, you never know who has decided to stay up late catching up with work – dusting the oft-forgotten rooms, getting an early start on scrubbing the fireplaces. This evening, the shadows are still. I sneak through the hall and make my way upstairs. The path is familiar past the old portraits and statues. Without a candle, these were once terrifying apparitions, but I have grown used to them by now.

I turn a corner, see a light under one of the doors. Still moving carefully, I creep forward and turn the handle. There's a warm fire at one end of the room and, at the other, a plush four-poster bed.

'There you are, my love,' says Henry.

The tension from my walk through the house evaporates and I go to him, our fingers intertwining silently as our lips meet.

Chapter Four

Now

It's early morning, the light just beginning to kiss the bottom of Henry's bedroom window. I roll over and run my fingers through his greying hair.

'Stay,' he mumbles.
'You know I can't.'
'Come and find me later?'
'Yes.'

He flips over to kiss me goodbye. My hand on his stomach – now softer and rounder than it used to be – before I reluctantly get up and search for my shift. I find it on the other side of the room, along with my breeches and wig. I check myself in a mirror, making sure I look presentable. The servants have already begun to wake and I can't arouse suspicion. Vest, jacket, stockings – all accounted for. With one last glance at my love, I carefully open the door and slide into the hall.

At first, coming here had been an adventure, a foray into the unknown. There was risk, yes – so many eyes upon us, staying alert at every moment, but I felt safe under Henry's protection. It was exciting to live in such a grand house, so different from anything I could have imagined growing up orphaned. I was sure it would take years to explore every room, to know them with the same familiarity as Henry did. Now I know exactly where to step, every squeaky floorboard to avoid, as I creep down the main staircase trying to keep my expression placid and nodding to a maid dusting the bannister.

I've learned that there is only room for two classes in an estate like Stonehurst Manor – master and servant. Though I am not quite the latter, I'm certainly no master, which leaves me belonging nowhere. Lacking direction does not suit me, but this is the path I have chosen to be closer to Henry. After so many years, he is my only family and we cannot imagine a life without each other. Besides, part of maturing is learning when to compromise.

I walk through the servants' quarters, hugging the wall and avoiding contact with others in case they can read the memory of last night in my eyes. The plain rooms and passages hum with an efficient energy. Henry and Lady Elina are away tonight, preferring to attend dinners and balls at neighbouring estates rather than entertain at the manor. It will be a quiet evening for me, spent in my own company.

I sit down in the linen room and pick up the pieces of Lady Elina's bodice at the far end of the table. Fifteen stitches per inch. I place my thimble on my finger and continue where I left off yesterday. Outside the door, I hear Mrs Ferrers speaking with Thomas, the valet, about a new footman due later today. 'We'll have to send a carriage to the coaching inn,' she says to him, then appears in the doorway.

'The new footman?' I smile. Walking in the countryside somehow requires more effort than walking in the city. Perhaps it is the muddier roads, the lack of diversions, or the patchwork of fields endlessly expanding around you, offering only the illusion of possibility. 'I can recall the first time I walked to the manor from town – I must have been twenty-four. I'd naively thought it would be an easy walk with all my luggage...' I realise she is watching me with furrowed confusion, so I stop speaking. She crosses the room to a cupboard, pulls out some white drapes. She has been at Stonehurst nearly as long as I have, and I think she mistrusts my tenure. I pray her severe expression does not indicate that she suspects anything between me and Henry. Without another word, she carries the drapes out the door.

I continue stitching the bodice, my hand already growing sore from the meticulous nature of the work. What does Lady Elina mean with this letter she wants me to deliver? Her recent shift in behaviour towards me is perplexing but, whatever the reason, she seems to have taken an interest in my mind. It's almost flattering, but I don't trust her entirely. We are all motivated to serve ourselves, are we not? For my part, I will probably continue reading the book she gave me because our discussions offer some much-needed novelty to my life here, but I must remain guarded.

'Ah, Thomas!' I startle at the sound of Henry's voice in the corridor, pricking my finger with the needle. 'Go to the stables and have my horse brought around.' I wonder where he's off to – perhaps simply taking a ride. I'm always on edge seeing him downstairs, among so many watchful eyes. He knows I often work in here, and momentarily he appears in the doorway. His coat is swept smoothly behind him and his shoe buckles gleam. Even here, where there are so few people of significance, he always looks his best. I admire him for it, though I suppose it's among his many responsibilities as the master of the house. 'Hello, Matthew,' he says, smiling and walking inside.

'Good morning, Mr Ashby,' I reply, the twinkle in his eye competing with my uneasiness about being caught by someone. It always feels unnatural to ignore the intimacy we've built up over the years and pretending we are simply acquaintances with hardly any knowledge of each other's inner thoughts has always been a struggle for me, if a necessary one.

'Working hard, I see,' he says, coming closer. He stood above me with that same teasing grin last night, until I pulled him down onto the bed again.

'Yes,' I respond softly. 'What have I missed upstairs?'

'Nothing at all. Oh, I received a letter from my father this morning – he's just returned from Antigua.'

After Henry's mother died, his father began taking regular trips to the West Indies. I'm surprised he has continued to travel so far at his age, but the old man has always insisted on remaining head of the family business. 'I'm sorry he's back on the same island as us,' I say sardonically, checking behind him to make sure no one is there to overhear my candour.

'Indeed,' Henry returns, following my gaze. 'He wants to come to supper next week, so I'm afraid he'll be a little closer than that.'

I sigh – his father pretends to visit for supper but always stays for several days and I have to make myself scarce. I've met him on and off through the years, occasionally passing each other in the corridors of the house. He always introduces himself over again, which is a relief, since it means he does not remember me. Henry is waiting for him to die so he can inherit everything and take charge of the family business. A bleak state of affairs, but I cannot pretend to understand this system they belong to. Henry assures me that once his father is gone we can be more free together, and I hope he is right.

'I'm heading to London in two days for some materials,' I say quietly. 'Perhaps I'll stay over a few nights.'

Footsteps in the hall grow louder and Henry steps back. We both pause, waiting, and they fade again. He speaks in a lowered voice, 'Come now, don't be cross with me. You know I never ask him – he always invites himself.'

'I know,' I reply. 'But I do miss the city. I haven't spent more than a day there since that disastrous trip two years ago.'

He laughs. 'That was entirely out of my control – who knew that Lord Finsborough would die and everyone would plunge into mourning?' He comes closer again. 'I shall miss you, even if you're only gone for one night. Don't leave me for too long.'

I can't help but smile – it still thrills me to be desired by him after all these years. Suddenly, a maid – Daisy – shuffles inside. 'Oh! Beg your pardon, sir.'

I look down to hide my flushed face, but Henry is cool and calm. 'That's quite all right. I'd better see about my horse. Good morning to you both,' and he saunters out the door.

I keep my focus on my work, avoiding meeting Daisy's eyes in case there is a question in them I cannot answer. I hear her open a drawer, push it closed, and then she is gone.

Then

Leaving Henry in bed, I sneak downstairs to make tea. My mind buzzes joyfully, whirling with the possibilities of how and when we can see each other again. I take a breath to calm my nerves – mustn't get ahead of myself. Carefully, I pour the water into my two best tea bowls and am gently carrying them towards the staircase when Martha emerges from her room, tucking her kerchief into her stays. 'Is that for me?' she asks with faint surprise.

'Yes,' I am forced to answer, passing her a bowl. 'There was leftover water, so I made one for you.'

She seems touched by this fictitious gesture and gently grips the bowl with her fingers at its edge, looking relaxed. 'Thank you, sir.'

'While I'm thinking about it,' I begin, unsure of how to get her out of the shop, 'you're very welcome to run out and purchase a couple of thimbles this morning. I recall you were having trouble stitching quickly.'

'No need,' she replies, and my heart sinks. She sidles around me to one of the benches and grabs a small piece of leather. When she brings it closer, I see she's sewn it into a triangular shape. She sticks it on her finger to show me. 'You see? I made my own with this scrap of leather. It fits much better than the metal thimbles do.'

'How inventive,' I reply, though of course she's not the first to do such a thing. It's all right for some work, but there's still the risk of the needle poking through and stabbing your finger. With the pace I stitch at and the force I tend to apply, I prefer the metal thimbles.

I try to avoid looking up at the ceiling, wondering if Henry is listening or growing impatient. I just need to get Martha out of the shop for a few minutes – as long as she doesn't see him walking down the stairs, it could be conceivable that he's just a friend stopping by for a visit.

'I'll be out today on calls to potential clients…' I start, but that won't do. I try again. 'Perhaps you could help with an important errand?' As I hoped, she tilts her head towards me eagerly. 'Would you pick up three yards of broadcloth from the shop?' This does not really pass as an important errand, but I try to add some intrigue. 'They're for a new client, a baroness!'

She grins. 'If only my mum knew I was making undergarments for a baroness! She'd be well pleased.'

'As long as you're discreet, you may inform her,' I reply, not wishing to spoil her fun.

A shadow passes across her face. 'It's not that, sir. I can't write and even if I could, she wouldn't be able to read my notes.'

I should have known. 'That's perfectly understandable,' I tell her, as the ceiling creaks. Martha looks up in surprise, but I try to distract her with a motion towards the front door. 'Tell Mr Blankenship the order is for me and he will charge my account,' I say, trying to remove any strain from my voice. 'Thank you, Martha.'

She nods, grabbing her cap from the workbench and fixing it to her head as she follows my gesture out the door. As soon as she is gone, I fly up the stairs to Henry. Luckily he's already dressed, perusing the notes he'd previously written that are stacked on my side table.

'I see you've kept my letters,' he says in a cheeky tone.

'They'll make good kindling later,' I joke. 'Now hurry downstairs as fast as you can.'

'What? But it's still morning—'

'There's no time, come along.'

'Very well!' he laughs.

I notice the slight stubble on his chin glinting almost golden in the sunlight, and nearly reach out to brush my fingertips against it. But that would be unwise – if I touch his face, we may never leave my room.

Martha should return in less than fifteen minutes, so we scurry out the door and down the alleyway towards Leadenhall.

—

Showing Henry around the market is like teaching an eager child how to play quoits – he is all curiosity and no talent. His manner and dress attract the attention of tradesmen, grocers, and vagrants alike and he seems perfectly happy to buy whatever anyone offers him.

'Don't be ridiculous – what are you going to do with an entire basket of pears?' I ask.

'I don't know, perhaps that sad-looking man would have one? And that child over there!'

He hurries off to spread his cheer. I look sideways at the woman who tricked him into buying her entire stock for the day. A part of me wants to protect him from being taken advantage of, but he seems to have plenty of money so why not share it with others if they are clever enough to ask for it?

Henry walks back to me, empty-handed. 'That little girl asked if she could keep the basket, presumably for her ribbons or toys,' he said. 'Better than me carrying it around all morning!' He's so happy exploring my world, I decide not to tell him that she doesn't have ribbons; she'll use the basket to carry laundry for her mother.

We continue walking west. I want more than anything to hold his hand and lean against him, but of course I can't. We pass Mr Blankenship's shop. 'Ah!' I cry. 'This is where I buy some of the fabrics that you saw on my workbenches.'

'Really?' he asks, peering in the windows. 'How remarkable – do they cut it for your designs right there in the shop, or do you do that yourself?'

'I have scissors,' I laugh.

He smiles, bashful or embarrassed at his ignorance. 'I'm sorry, I'm… I'm just fascinated by the work that you do. I wish I understood it better.'

I hold his gaze. 'It's not the physical demands of the work that are unique – those are quite straightforward, really. It's the imaginative element, creating something utterly unusual, that I find compelling.' I reach out, touch the embroidery on his jacket sleeves. 'Although you made this suit here in London, the embroidery was done in Lyon. This silver-gilt thread is commonly used there.' I let my fingers hang on his sleeve just long enough for my knuckles to brush the inside of his wrist. A hint of colour spreads across his cheeks.

There's a commotion up the road. I begin to notice that everyone on the street is walking in the same direction. Henry and I follow, finding ourselves at the back of a large crowd near the Royal Exchange.

Standing on my toes, I can just see the front where broadsheets are flying from hands like pigeons over the rooftops above. 'Thomas Collins verdict! *Guilty!*' someone yells. There's a heat to the crowd, a tipping point coming nearer.

'Let's leave,' Henry says.

We edge our way backward and out of the crush. A discarded paper is stamped into the ground near a wall, so I pick it up. Large block letters read:

THOMAS COLLINS FOUND GUILTY OF SODOMY

My heart pounds and my stomach twists. I can still feel Henry's kisses on my back, arms, and neck like they've been imprinted onto my skin. My clothes, once a practical barrier against the elements, now feel like armour I must hide behind. I skim the article, but it contains no surprises. I feel Henry standing nervously next to me, edging away in increments. Our eyes meet: he looks caught. I understand how he feels.

'What will happen to him?' he asks.

All I can do is glance down, checking the details. I swallow. 'Hanging. Next Thursday.'

We don't make a sound, the air sucked from the street. For a moment neither of us move, but then Henry takes the paper from my hand and scrunches it up into a ball. He turns away, not meeting my eye. As he walks down the road, I see the ball drop gently from his hand.

Should I follow him, try to discuss what has happened? There's a vibration under my skin, some kind of energy that needs direction. I realise I too need time to myself. It's not that I'm surprised by stories like Mr Collins', but each one wears on my spirit just a little more. We spend so much time in our minds, living in worlds of our own creation, that it is painful when reality snaps back into place. Slowly, I make my way through the crowd to the safety and quiet of my shop. Or so I had hoped.

'Morning! Have you been fitting Mrs Daullers?' Martha asks as soon as I walk in.

In the excitement of having Henry here, I had forgotten that I need to call on Mrs Daullers today. I take off my coat and put the kettle on the fire. 'Yes,' I lie. 'She'll be a straightforward case.' I should be able to fit her later this afternoon and Martha will be none the wiser, not that it's her place to question me about clients anyway.

Martha smooths the fabric she was stitching when I walked in. 'What d'you think? Oh, and I put the broadcloth for the baroness over there.'

I note the neatly folded pile on a nearby workbench, then meander over to inspect her work. Small, even stitches all the way down – impressive. She's improved since I hired her and I begin to feel a small swell of pride before reminding myself that consistent stitching is nothing significant in this trade. Any other apprentice would be the same. 'Very nice,' I tell her, turning around to draw up some designs for Mrs Daullers – I may as well bring a few ideas to her since I'll have to stop by later.

'Sir, there are also the eyelets on this one,' Martha calls, holding up a nearly finished pair of stays. 'Are these all right?'

'You know there's no need for me to inspect every piece you've worked on,' I begin, but then I see the eyelets. Pristine, even edges; tight, strong structure. I hold the panel up to get a better look. 'These are remarkable.'

Martha blushes. 'Thank you. I was very careful as I was going around them.'

She's certainly an excellent worker, but I don't wish to praise her too heavily or she may stop trying. 'Yes, well. Good job.' In just a month, she has proven herself a real asset to the shop – in part due to my training, but also because she's applied herself. In time I might be able to give her more responsibilities as I take on additional clients.

She gives me a nervous look, like she's about to reveal something. 'Since you feel that way, I was wondering… if it might be beneficial, or suit your needs, sir… for me to work independently on Mrs Daullers' stays when the time comes? You said yourself they would be a simple pair to make.'

This is an unacceptable, presumptuous request and for a moment, I'm too taken aback to reply. Her audacity makes me wonder if she heard me and Henry last night. Is she merely suspicious, or does she have a credible threat against me that she will use if I deny her? I tread carefully.

'You haven't been my apprentice for very long. You don't know how to work with gold thread, how to select fabric – you don't even know where to cut if I don't draw out the pattern.' I may have edged too close towards injury – her brows cinch sharply together.

'You said I was doing good work. You said—'

'Yes, your work has been satisfactory and you are a fast learner. I appreciate the initiative you've taken,' I add, not wanting to forget her extra help when I was out with Henry. 'But what you are asking is, quite frankly, laughable given the skills required.'

Her eyes are flat, her mouth a small line. 'If that's how you feel, then I'm sorry I asked. But, sir, women are starting to take on more staymaking work, and I might want my own shop one day. I'd ask you to start training me properly, not just using me for basic needlework.'

Now I do laugh. 'Women staymakers? How could they possibly? I mean no offence, Martha, but women's hands are too weak and they haven't the eye for design.'

She stands up, needle in her hand. I see it glint in the afternoon light.

'I'm going out for a walk.' She storms past me and pulls the door open.

'Leave the needle,' I say, 'in case you decide not to come back.'

As she stares at me, aghast, I feel I've gone too far but it's too late to apologise now. If she does return, I will find some way to be contrite – perhaps an afternoon off. After she's left and the door closes with its characteristic jingle, my emotions release in waves of anguish, dread, but also relief. Henry and I are still safe.

Chapter Five

Now

Lady Elina's letter sits firmly within my breast pocket as the coach to London jostles its passengers violently. Across from me sit a clerk, a priest, and a young woman, who keeps her eyes planted firmly out the window. The floor of the coach is covered in a thin layer of mud from everyone's boots – I brace myself against the seat to avoid smashing anyone's toes.

I go over the list of materials I need to collect – whalebone, brocade, figured silk, double linen thread in bright yellow. First I must post Lady Elina's letter, then check in on Mr Blankenship, pick up the whalebone from Davis McFarland, and finally treat myself to one of Mrs Burley's pies if I have time.

I stay on the coach until we reach the Black Lion at Water Lane, where the priest and young woman also get out. I watch them walk – were they together this whole time? – until their paths split, the priest making his way towards the ships and the woman heading to the inn. I cast a lingering glance over the great expanse of the Thames, its shores promising either adventure to faraway lands or simply a trip to Southwark, then walk away from the river and towards the tipsy wooden homes of the East End.

My visceral impression of the city may be familiar, but the sights are all new. Fresh coats of paint in bright greens and oranges, new brickwork in unexpected places. But the heart of these streets has not changed – the constant push and pull between the river and Londoners as merchants and traders unload and restock barrels of wine, sacks of grain, sugar, and countless wares. The city sucks up everything from the Thames and redistributes it, but the ships are never left hungry for long.

Heading up Ludgate Hill, I peer down narrow yards and courts to see the stables and workshops churning with life. In one, a young man brushes his horse down while someone else hooks a fresh one up to a cab. Down a different alley, sheets of leather skins hang to dry, the stench of tanning agents assaulting anyone who walks past. Looking up, I see steam from the laundries and kitchens drifting out into the grey sky. Each person I pass is like a cog, keeping the city moving until the day's work is over.

I glance at the address on Lady Elina's letter – 24 Paternoster Row. Why, that's just around the corner – I can deliver it myself. The pace of the city is hurried and efficient – I feel as though I will disrupt the flow of the traffic as I check building numbers to find the right one. Surely I am not the only person new to this street today? I read the sign on the door – John Josephson, yes, that's correct – and push it open.

Immediately, the outside scuffle is barely audible and my eyes take a moment to adjust to the dark, wood-panelled lobby. I look around, unsure which route to take. There's no one in this antechamber, just a flight of stairs and passages to my right and left. Hesitantly, I choose a direction and begin walking. I squint down the corridor, hoping to see a labelled door or any other indication that I'm heading the right way. It's dim, the oil lamps fading in and out, and just as I decide to turn back and try the other direction, a door opens. I can't help but startle.

'Excuse me, I didn't realise anyone was here,' says the man in the doorway, regaining his composure more quickly than I do.

'I'm terribly sorry, I'm looking for John Josephson,' I explain.

He gestures towards the room he just came out of. 'He's just through there, but if you're looking for the publishing house, I might be able to help you?'

'Oh, I...' I fumble, removing the letter from my jacket. '...I'm just dropping this off.'

He takes the letter and looks at it, presumably checking the return address because he asks me what the frank is.

'Oh, no, I'm not a messenger. I...' I hesitate, not sure how to describe myself or Lady Elina. By this point he has opened the note and begun reading it.

'Ah yes, of course – Mr E. Ashby! I'm thrilled to make your acquaintance after all these months!'

He reaches out and gives my hand a hearty shake, but I don't feel sufficiently recovered. 'Ah,' is all I can muster up.

'Your work is extraordinary, your ideas just what the public wants to read,' he says. 'I'm delighted you've accepted our offer and we can begin with the book!'

I re-button my coat as I take a step back. No wonder Lady Elina insisted on keeping this a secret – Henry would not want his wife publishing anything, much less a political treatise. He would regard it as outrageous and, more importantly, so would his father. But how to respond to this man? If I correct him, will I ruin her chances? Perhaps I should give them no contemplation, yet I do.

'Yes, well...' I say, 'I'm looking forward to it too, but I must be going. I had a short window to drop this off before making my way home to Surrey.'

The man's eyebrows flick up in surprise. 'Are you quite sure? You must come inside for just a few minutes!'

I've already stepped back from him, trying to extricate myself as quickly as possible before more damage is done. 'No, really... I'm afraid I must be going.'

He sounds disappointed but encouraging when he answers, 'Of course, Mr Ashby. We'll look forward to your next chapters in a few weeks.'

An awkward moment as we both turn in the same direction.

'Please, after you,' he tells me, and I make my way back into the spring afternoon. I blink in the sunlight, wondering what to tell Lady Elina. How long has this been going on? Has she published other materials? I did not realise these ideas were so important to her that she would write them down, much less that they would be desired for publication. And now I am mixed up in her scheme – should I tell Henry?

—

My errands complete and new materials in tow, there's just enough time to head towards Bishopsgate and see one last person. I hasten down the street, swooping and leaning to avoid the ebb and flow of traffic. Turning into the old familiar alleyway, I rap upon the door and then, feeling congenial, I push it open. 'Mrs Powell?' I call.

Martha is around the workbench with her arms out to me in an instant. 'Oh, Mr Rooke! How well you look!'

'It's only because I'm in London and seeing your smiling face,' I answer, which may well be the truth. All worries of Stonehurst Manor and my life there fall away, for I am home.

'Let me put the kettle on,' she says, bending over the simple fireplace.

While she busies herself with tea leaves and bowls, I survey the workshop. Stays in every phase of production are neatly laid out across the stations. I miss the cosy bustle of others working by my side – if I ever returned to London, perhaps I would be back within these very walls, stitching with Martha and… I double-check the empty stations. 'Where are your workers?' I ask.

'They've got a curfew to keep every night,' she says.

'Ah, of course. The downside of employing orphans,' I jest.

She hands me a steaming bowl. 'I like training them so they'll have a way of earning a living. Makes me feel useful.'

I sit at one of the benches – we never did have a proper table and chairs for meals – and watch her stack a pile of linen cuttings on top of each other, tidying charcoal pencils and scissors back to their resting places for the night. She catches me watching her and smiles. At one time, our roles were reversed, but she has been in charge now for longer than I ever was. It's quite a thought, somehow I had never considered it before.

'And what brings you to town this time?' she enquires.

'Picking up some silk and whalebone, in addition to an errand for…' I drift off, thinking it best not to say anything else. I change the subject. 'Is your family out?'

'George is still at the factory,' she replies, sitting down at last, 'and the children are upstairs.'

'Well, go on – let's see them! It's been long enough.'

She laughs. 'You say that now – just you wait,' but she leans towards the staircase and calls out, 'Oy – Georgie! Bess! Come downstairs!'

The sound of stools scraping against the floor – perhaps being knocked over – and little shoes scampering across the room and down the stairs. Within seconds, there they are – the sweetest and rosiest faces you might imagine. Bess carries a stuffed toy – perhaps a lion, though it is well worn and difficult to say.

'Georgie, tuck your shirt in,' Martha tells him. 'Look who's here!'

'Hello! Do you remember me?' I ask them, reaching into my jacket for the sweets I plucked from Mrs Ferrers' kitchen before leaving this morning. 'Here you go.'

'Thankee, sir,' they reply. 'Mama, can we go out and watch Bill light the street lamps?'

'Tomorrow, my loves,' she replies, scooping little Bess up and giving her a hug.

'They've grown so much,' I say, watching her with them. 'What do you feed them?'

She puts Bess down and laughs. The children dart around the room, using my legs to hide from each other, and eventually settle under one of the benches with a book. Martha turns back to me. 'Will you stay for supper?'

'Thought I'd stay the night if you'll have me.'

'Excellent! You can work on some tabs for me while I get the food ready.'

It wasn't the couple of days I had hoped to spend in the capital, but I do want to return to Henry before his father arrives. As invigorating as it is to be in London again, there is something missing that I can't quite place. Perhaps I had anticipated the trip for so long, I idealised the city and was not prepared for some of the changes I found. Or maybe I miss the friendships I had when I was younger, the exuberant and joyful crowds at Mother Mack's. But Martha is talking.

'...just some leather lining,' as she passes me a pair of stays. They're very light in my hands – shorter, as is becoming the custom, and fewer bones.

'Silhouettes continue to soften, don't they?' I ask.

'Indeed. Fashions keep changing, we must follow,' she replies, chopping some turnips and carrots. ''Course, there's only so many modifications in our control as staymakers – the dressmakers are having quite a time of it, from what I gather. Well, you know how it is!'

'I'm not sure I do. Out in Surrey, I often feel as though I'm playing catch-up.' I reach across the workbench, poking through several spools of thread. When I find the white linen, I run it through a cake of beeswax, then thread a nearby needle and fold the thin piece of leather in on itself, so I can begin attaching it to the tabs on the bottom of the stays with a whip stitch. 'Do you find it exciting, with such dramatic changes happening?'

She wipes her hands on her apron, tosses the vegetables into a pot on the fire. When she looks over to answer me, she chides, 'Bess, get down from there!'

I turn around and see Bess has climbed onto one of the workbenches and is reaching for a pincushion. 'Pillow!' she says.

'No, my darling.' Martha picks her up and places her on her hip, then turns back to me. 'I've got enough challenges in my life, as you can see,' she laughs. 'But yes, I suppose it's nice for this work to evolve. Keeps me alert.' She smiles, wipes some sweat from Bess' forehead. 'Speaking of changes, you hear that Bartlett's shop has been taken over by competition from Miss Hewley?'

'You don't say?'

She nods. 'Another shop by women – seems like there's more of us than the men at this point.'

'You must have inspired them.' I try to smile but am concentrating on stitching the leather around the curve of the tab whilst keeping it smooth.

She sits down on the other side of the bench opposite me. 'To be honest, I think the ladies are beginning to prefer us to the older men. Take that pair of stays – you see the scalloped cups at the front?' I flip the stays around and am amazed to see two separate scoops for the breasts. It's wholly unique from the usual single line they occupy on a fashionable woman's shape, unlike anything I've seen before. Martha seems satisfied with my surprise and nods to prove her point. 'How can a lady expect a man to measure her comfortably for those?'

I chuckle a little. 'Staymakers have always had to be delicate conducting our business. You've seen the cartoons accusing us of stealing wives away from their negligent husbands, but of course there's no truth to them. Besides, it's only a body.' Nevertheless, I take a close look at the shell-like shapes, the folds required to set them into the main stays. Lady Elina has not asked me to make her anything resembling this newer fashion yet, but I'd like to be ready.

Martha shrugs. 'Well, I'm just saying what the preferences seem to be right now.' Bess leans over her arm and she sets her back down on the floor.

I smile meekly, my mind making quick calculations. I had always planned a return to London at some point, but my time at the manor has stretched on without end and I begin to wonder whether I've missed my window to come back and pick up my work as before. It's not the first time I've felt powerless to break free of the tide and firmly take control of my life's course.

'Don't look so forlorn!' Martha laughs. 'You never know what the future may hold.'

I nod, but cannot help feeling as though my days of new opportunity have settled in the past.

She picks up a panel of fabric and begins punching holes in it using her awl. When the doorbell jingles a few minutes later, George finds us there, working side by side.

'What year have I stumbled upon?' he asks with a hearty laugh. Georgie and Bess run up to him and he's forced to walk into the room with a child attached to each leg.

'Let your father sit down,' says Martha, pulling them off.

We gather around the hearth and exchange stories of the last year. I don't have much to share but describe what the changing seasons have brought to life in Stonehurst, the first spring bulbs beginning to poke out from the hard soil. George begins to share a humorous tale about a run-in with a maccaroni. 'Didn't you tell him this already?' he laughs, handing me a plate of boiled vegetables and chicken. 'I thought you wrote to each other?'

Martha dabs at the corners of her mouth. 'We do, but it's usually about the shop and finances, not silly stories. Anyway,' she continues, 'George couldn't stop staring at the man.'

'I swear, his wig reached the upstairs windows!' he howls. I laugh along with them, though it has been so long since I've been at a social occasion where I might see anyone of fashion, ridiculous or tasteful, that I would welcome the chance to be back in such a world again. I glance towards the stairs leading to the quarters that were once mine so many years ago. The countless times Henry and I sneaked up those steps to avoid Martha, the hours I spent poring over his letters by candlelight. How different the workshop is now, under Martha's care. How different everything is.

'Are you tired?' Martha asks me. 'You've had a long day with the journey in.'

'I'm all right,' I reply. 'Just a bit thoughtful.' I try to smile reassuringly, and it seems to work.

In no time, supper is over and George plays with the children while Martha and I sit by the fire. She inclines her head towards me. 'I've been wanting to ask you – I hope it isn't a difficult subject…'

'Martha,' I reply, 'I should hope you know by now that you have nothing to fear from me.'

She nods. 'Well, we've been able to save a little money recently,' she begins, 'and I wanted to ask about buying the remainder of the business from you.'

I don't reply at first. I can't pretend it's a tremendous surprise, but something about the suddenness of her question catches me unprepared. In addition to our earlier conversation about changes in the industry, it is too many new developments for me.

Martha waits patiently. 'You don't have to answer right away,' she begins, 'I just wanted to let you know our situation and open the conversation.'

'Of course,' I reply. 'I'm sure we can come to some sort of arrangement.' I rub my forehead, where a dull pain has begun to creep in. I am not ready to let go of my shop just yet, not completely.

She reaches over and clasps my hand. 'Thank you, Matthew. You've been good to us and we're very grateful.'

I chuckle a little, putting my hand on top of hers. 'You've done it all yourself.' And it's true – she has always worked hard and redoubled her efforts when needed. What have I really done for her apart from the occasional, too-often suppressed, kindness?

'I mean it,' she insists. 'I don't know where I'd be without you, without your employment when I first arrived in London… I shudder to think of it.' Looking at her earnest face and family playing behind her, my heart blooms. Perhaps my inclination to cling to the past simply reflects an uncertainty about my own future.

Once worn out, Bess and Georgie go to bed in what I always think of as Martha's room at the back. After we've had a round of drinks and are sufficiently exhausted ourselves, Martha, George, and I retire too. They head upstairs and I stretch out in front of the hearth, embers glowing with a warmth stretching back many years.

Chapter Six

Then

London in winter is my favourite time of year. The air is invigorating, oil lamps wink along the roads, and the nights, where I find comfort, are longer. Many clients flee to the countryside but there are enough and, besides, there is merriment to be had. In the clean, crisp air, delicious scents of fruit pudding and spiced wassail travel easily, but I hurry through them at a quick clip. Under my best wig, my hair is tied back with a fine black ribbon. I brace myself against the frosty air with the nicest embroidered coat I own – green wool with pale flowers and buttons made from river shells.

The snow lands on my polished shoes and its chill has just begun to permeate my feet as I approach the Strand. Waiting for me at St Mary's is Henry and, as soon as I see him, a rush of joy expels any sense of the cold. His broad grin is full of anticipation, and his eyes stay fixed on mine. If only I could catch his hand, tug him along to show my eagerness, but that would be a foolish risk to take.

'Where are we going?' he laughs. 'Somewhere festive, I hope.'

'Somewhere magical.' We dash through the streets, sliding on snow through crowds in vibrant cloaks and furs. Some ladies wear bright pink and green hoods pulled up over their hair, while those with more robust coiffure leave theirs down. Filigree fasteners on men's cloaks sparkle in the moon and lamplight.

We return to Mother Mack's coffee house. I always forget how unimposing and small it looks from the street when I visit. 'But you've taken me here before!' Henry pouts. 'I was hoping to go somewhere new.'

'Don't worry – you haven't seen it quite like this.'

We step through the door and are greeted with a rush of heat and laughter immediately upon passing over the threshold. Butchers and bandits alike drink gin by the fire and from the corner comes a boisterous, out-of-key Christmas carol. I lock eyes with the barkeeper and he nods.

Around the back, up two flights of stairs, and down a corridor is where we belong tonight. At an unassuming door, I turn around and face Henry, his eyes alight with curiosity. 'Are you ready?' I smile, now free to squeeze his hand.

'You're awfully eager! Let's see what this is about.'

I push the door aside to reveal what might be a startling scene to some. A large room with high ceilings and wooden panels, lined with garlands and holly boughs. In one corner, a group of fiddlers play – in another, a table decorated with perhaps the largest punchbowl known to mankind. Between the corners, a motley group of men dance an allemande.

'Why, many of them are wearing dresses!' Henry exclaims, pleasantly surprised.

'Would you like to try it?' I ask and, upon his grin, extend the bag I brought with us. His eyes twinkle playfully and he nods.

One corner of the room has been curtained off – we duck behind it so Henry can change. The music is dampened back here, but we still hear the fiddlers going. There isn't much space, so we stand close together. I unroll the skirts, then reach back into the bag for the stays and bodice. I had to guess at the measurements, but luckily Henry and I are roughly the same size. The fabric is nicer than I can afford, but I made an arrangement with a neighbour. Her chequered silk taffeta will feel soft against his skin. I help Henry out of his jacket and vest, carefully folding and setting them aside. He looks a bit nervous, his hands fumbling with his breeches before slipping them off and standing to face me in his shift. I take a deep breath. I open a pair of stays – a practice pair I made years ago – and wrap them around him. I run the cord through each eyelet, minding his frame as I go. His shoulder blades peek through the top of his shift and I brush my lips against the back of his neck. He swallows, looks around at me.

'Here...' I smile, holding the skirt open so he can step inside. He gently puts his hand on my shoulder for balance as he stands on one foot. I pull it up to his waist and fasten it, then find the bodice with its bright ruffled sleeves. Delicately, I help him into it, holding his wrist in my hand as he stretches each arm through, then fastening up the front. His lips are already stained, but I add a bow to his neck as a final flourish.

'How do I look?' he asks, his face growing rosy.

'Like you belong in court! But Mother Mack's will have to do.'

He turns to face me, looks me up and down. 'Aren't you changing?'

'No,' I reply. While some men find it liberating to dress up in skirts and bodices, I have tried it in the past and it does not suit me. I pull him around the curtain and onto the dance floor. We face each other and clasp opposite hands, then I turn and reach behind me to meet his right hand. The tempo is a little faster than I'm used to. I spin him, then after three steps he spins me. When we both step the wrong way and break apart, we laugh. 'Why don't I get some drinks for us?' I ask him.

'Don't be gone too long,' he calls after me.

I cross the room to a table, where Mother Mack doles out the negus. 'Nice to see you're still cavorting with that pretty lad,' she says, handing me two glasses as I place a tuppence on the table.

Although I've known her for years, I feel a little shy disclosing too much about Henry. 'Yes, it's been a few months now.'

Bill Lemington, a baker who dresses up in fine women's robes and is known as the Duchess of Dunstan, stumbles backward into the table, laughing at something across the room. 'Oy, duchess!' Mother Mack calls. 'Mind you don't spill all your drink on my floors or I'll give you a spanking worse then Primrose Peggy later tonight!' She cackles at herself, looks back to me. 'I've got some pies in the back, love, if you want any.'

I stare, unsure whether she's being literal or is hiding something else – or someone else – in the back room.

She sees my expression and laughs again. 'It's not like that – don't you think I know my own business? There just ain't enough for everyone.'

I laugh, relieved. 'If I know you, there's plenty to go around – you just want us each to believe we're your favourite.'

She shrugs, jolly. 'Lady of mystery, that's me.'

Years ago, Mother Mack told me how she'd come to own this coffee house. After one too many drunken nights with the publican downstairs, they'd decided to marry and combine her boarding rooms with his kitchen. I asked her once why she chose to pursue clientele like me when she might instead serve a less criminal class.

'It's London, we're all criminals in some way,' was her initial reply. She'd then looked away and added in a softer voice, 'I had a brother who also preferred the company of men – Caleb was his name. He worked down on the river, pushing punts back and forth.' Her eyes shone with the memory. 'Such strong shoulders. He didn't know how to swim even though he worked on the water. Always had a friend he was partial to – sometimes a different fellow every week. Such a lot of potential, Caleb had. Making good money, educating himself after hours so he could move into a respectable profession.' Her face darkened. 'But word spread that he was a bit different. He started noticing people following him, dangerous men. One evening at work, someone he thought was a customer pushed him into the river halfway across. He managed to stay afloat enough to avoid drowning, but the tide took him a couple miles downriver before he could come ashore. After that, he decided it was safest to go abroad, have a fresh start. So he boarded a ship for New Scotland. I know he's not gone completely, but it breaks my heart to never see him again.' She cleared her throat, pressed a hand to her chest. 'I just hope he's all right. Caleb was a spark of light and this city treated him like a maggot, so I aim to bring a bit of his brightness back to it.'

The fiddlers finish their song and everyone gives a hearty cheer. A couple of men even stamp their boots on the floor.

Mother Mack gives me a little smile, nods in Henry's direction. 'You'd best bring those drinks back to your girl.'

Henry is talking to the Duchess of Dunstan when I find him. He still seems a little nervous – shoulders uneven and eyes darting – but he laughs easily at her gesticulations. I join them and nod along to the duchess' stories about early mornings at the bakery. Too many feature rodents and I steal an embarrassed glance at Henry, who looks remarkably enchanted and forgiving. I hope he doesn't think we all tolerate mice in our shops.

Later in the night, after everyone's feet begin to grow tired from the dancing, Primrose Peggy comes out in a nightdress, bloated belly underneath. 'Oh, the pains, I think the baby's coming!'

Everyone crowds around him. 'What's going on?' Henry asks, bemused.

'It's just a bit of theatrics,' I say, looping my arm around his. 'Shall we go watch, Your Ladyship?'

We move to the front of the crowd. The duchess is back, performing her midwife duties. 'I need hot water! And where's my bag of herbs?'

'Between your legs!' someone yells to a swell of laughter.

'Oh my days, the pain is excruciating!' claims Peggy, who is a soap boiler by trade, but one of the best actors in the bunch.

'There, there, won't be long now,' the duchess says, flicking some oil at him. She makes a big show of sticking her head under Peggy's dress and calls out, 'I can see the head! Get ready to be a mother!'

'I think I may faint,' says a man on the other side of Henry.

With a final embellished scream from Peggy, the duchess reaches up under his dress to reveal: a wheel of cheese. The crowd erupts with deep-throated laughter as Mother Mack rushes forward. 'Now, now, let's get this molly baby baptised so we can add it to the table!'

After such an entertaining intermission, the fiddlers strike up again and we're ready for more dancing. In the middle of a minuet, Henry accidentally steps on my foot.

'Sorry – I'm not used to following.'

'That's all right. You can lead if you'd like.'

'Actually, I'm not sure I want to wear this dress any more.'

Tenderly, I cup my fingers around his ear. 'You look so beautiful, but if you'd be more comfortable in your own clothes—'

'It's not that.' A mischievous grin. 'I don't really want to wear anything right now.'

The rhythmic thump of boots is drowned out by my own heartbeat. 'Kiss me and I'll take you home,' I tell him. With the cold weather keeping Martha in the workshop most evenings, I've become accustomed to staying with Henry at his house in town.

Pressing my lips against his, I step backward, pulling him towards the curtain. His warm breath spills down my throat and I want more, so kiss him again. I gasp in pleasure – despite our differences, this connection we share has only grown stronger with time. There are whoops and cracks from men nearby and Henry trips over his skirts as he pushes towards me. We both topple over and burst into a fit of laughter on the wooden floor.

'Go,' I tell him, still in stitches and handing him his clothes. I know I won't be able to keep my hands off him anyway.

The doors to Mother Mack's fly open and we dash outside, not even bothering to fasten our coats. We laugh, giddy from the punch and dancing – our hands fumble towards each other as we dash down the street.

It's late and we're being so loud, it takes me several minutes to notice the group of men following behind us. I thought one of them murmured 'detestable sodomites' as we passed, but could not be sure and decided to ignore it. Yet we've turned a corner and they are still looming on the periphery of my vision. I try not to behave too differently but whisper to Henry, 'We may need to scamper.'

'What? Why?' He takes a lopsided look over his shoulder and, alerted, the men begin chasing us.

Immediately, my pulse quickens and my thoughts crystallise with a desperate need to keep Henry safe. 'Come on!' I tell him, breaking into a run. I pull his arm as I take a sharp right into a narrow mews, then a left on to an alley. In the still night, I can hear the men's footsteps behind. The negus slows down my thoughts, but I try to remember what's at stake. If they catch us, they'll beat us before turning us over to the authorities – or worse.

Following the twisting alley, we turn left and come out at Seven Dials. I spin around, terror laced tight across every inch of my skin. The streets blur together and I choose randomly, then keep going, throwing a quick glance over my shoulder to see if the men have followed. Luckily, Henry is a strong athlete and has no trouble keeping up. His skin is too perfect for cut lips and bruises – if they do catch up, I decide to hurl myself at them so he can escape. I take panicked turns through Soho – Walker's Court to Peter Street to Husband Street – until we cut through Golden Square and I begin to relax.

Henry pants beside me. 'What the dickens?' he asks.

'They were dangerous,' I say. 'We shouldn't slow down too much.' Our breath heaves out of us in great white clouds. 'It's been a long time since I've had to lose someone like that.'

'I'm sure I could have made some sort of arrangement with them if it had been necessary.'

'As if they'd have given you the chance. Better to stay in control of the situation.' For as long as I can remember, there have been whispers of men pulled from the street, beaten and left for dead, or never seen again. Perhaps these men tonight would not have been so extreme, but it is impossible to know for certain and not worth the risk of finding out.

Conversation falters and we walk at a clipped pace, not daring to speak or draw any sort of attention to ourselves. The minutes eke along slowly, but at last we reach a frost-covered St James's Square. Henry walks up to his front door while I linger several paces behind, trying to look as dignified as possible so as not to arouse any suspicion from his footman. We cross the threshold and I release a sigh of relief, the warmth of his home already enveloping me. The footman takes our coats and escorts us through to the drawing room. 'Thank you, Anderson. You may retire for the night,' Henry tells him.

Once we're alone, I kneel before the fireplace, hoping its warmth will help me relax. Henry goes to a cabinet and pours two glasses of wine. This routine has begun to grow comfortably familiar and my heartbeat slows at last. Even in the short time that we have been together, these easy evenings simply taking in each other's company have become integral to the rest of my life, providing balance and pleasure where there was previously none. While I am always a little on edge around the household staff, Henry dismisses them with ease and has assured me there is nothing to worry about – when his parents departed for Surrey they took most of the servants with them, leaving him with only a handful of people to manage. As his employees, he promises that they don't question his proclivities, like not being disturbed in the morning. It's difficult to know how long we can carry on like this but I can't bear to imagine the end of such a magical time.

He collapses on a nearby sofa and I sit beside him before putting my arm around his waist. He pulls an unopened letter out of his pocket, taps it against his thigh. 'Who's that from?' I ask.

'My father. I've had it all afternoon.'

'Aren't you going to open it?'

He hesitates. 'Why would he be writing now? It can't be good news.'

'Well,' I reply, 'if that's the case, better to face it head-on and earlier rather than later.'

He smiles slyly. 'That wasn't your attitude when we were running from those men.'

I tighten up, still fearful of the direction our night might have taken. 'That was different, as you well know.'

He slides his finger under the seal to break it. His eyes briefly scan the writing before he reads aloud: 'Dearest son, we are looking forward to seeing you at Stonehurst for Christmas next week. The manor is quiet and wants a youthful presence. Your mother and I saw Miss Quorrley on our afternoon walk and were surprised to learn that she is still unattached. With such an estate to inherit and her pleasant demeanour, she would make a fine match. We expect her to call next week when you are home. Your loving father.'

I feel terribly for him – faced with the pressure to marry not out of desire, but out of duty. He must eventually succumb to that responsibility, and what will happen to us then? I try not to think about it – far better to enjoy tonight without worrying about what tomorrow will bring. He slumps down on the sofa and buries his face in my shoulder.

'You see why I didn't want to open it?' he asks, nearly spilling his wine before I take his glass and set it on the table.

'I am sorry. But it does no good to think on it tonight – why, perhaps this Miss Quorrley will be ill next week and you won't have to see her. Or it will rain and she will not wish to travel for the visit.'

'She has a carriage, Matthew, and anyway I doubt there will be a tempest,' he snips. I had forgotten that people do not walk everywhere in the countryside. As if to counter our dismal mood, the fire pops and crackles pleasantly in its hearth. I stroke his hair with my fingers, trying to be a comfort. He sits up suddenly. 'You could come home with me – as my guest. Then we could be together, even if I do have to see their precious *Miss Quorrley*.' He raises his voice as he says her name.

'We've discussed this,' I sigh. 'How would it look to bring someone home for such a holiday with no prior notice? We can't raise even the slightest suspicion.' As if his parents would dine with someone from my class any day of the week, much less at Christmas.

'It isn't fair,' he complains.

'No, but it is life and death.' I squeeze his hand in emphasis.

He leans back against me, watching the fire. His fingers trace my knuckles pensively. After a moment: 'Are you sure? I've never known anyone to be punished for it. That man in the paper—'

'Did exactly what we did. He was just like us.'

'Well,' Henry snorts, 'he was a brewer.'

I stand up and let him fall onto the sofa. 'A tradesman like me! How can you say such a thing?'

Through the gloom of his own misery, comprehension sets in. He drops to the ground and hurries over on his knees, scooping his hands around my legs and pressing his cheek against my thigh. 'I'm sorry, it was terrible.' He sits back on his heels, palms open and looking up at me with sorrowful, helpless eyes. 'You know how ugly I can be when I'm not thinking properly, yet you love me anyway.'

The word explodes in my ears like a firework. I lose focus, my breath caught in my throat. For a moment I don't register time or space as I realise he's right. 'Yes,' I murmur, clamouring down to meet him on the carpet. 'Yes, I do love you,' grabbing and kissing him fiercely. As we begin pulling each other's clothes off, Henry takes the letter from his father, crumples it, and throws it into the fire.

Chapter Seven

Now

Henry's office at the manor is as large as the first staymaking shop I apprenticed to. His desk is perpetually adorned with papers – mostly correspondence for his father's business. I don't bother to knock any more, merely check that no one sees me open his door.

'Hello,' he says warmly. 'What a wonderful surprise. How was your trip to London?'

'Invigorating as ever, but it wasn't half as fun without you there.'

He's pleased about that. 'We'll go away together soon, I promise.'

'You always say that.'

'And I always mean it! Sometimes I'm just pulled in too many directions.'

I remember what that was like, the strain between seeing Henry and finishing my work when the shop was busier than ever. I made my choice and for so long it felt like the right path to take, but lately I have felt just how constrained and limited my life has become as a result.

'I was thinking a trip to Bath might be just the thing.'

I walk behind his desk and wrap my arms around him. 'That sounds lovely.' I pull back, teasing him. 'But it won't happen.'

He scoffs. 'I'm a man of my word!'

'We haven't had a trip away together in two years.'

'Yes, I know. But we're happy here, aren't we?'

Are we? In some ways, it is bliss living with the man I love. But my existence here is overlooked by the household and taken for granted by Henry, not to mention the enduring threat of being caught together. I look out the window at the dainty white blossoms appearing on the blackthorn trees around the lawn. The sun briefly peeks between thick clouds before disappearing again. There was a time when my life had a greater impact and affected more than just one person. That freedom and feeling of being valuable is difficult to forget.

But there is something else on my mind this afternoon. If I can only figure out how to phrase it. 'Lady Elina' – I still cannot call her his wife – 'what kind of character does she have?'

'Well, she reads too much for her own good. I keep telling her she should take up a hobby more befitting a lady – embroidery or some such, but she refuses.'

I ignore what could be construed as an insult to me, suddenly feeling protective of her. 'It's not really for you to say how she spends her days, is it?'

He looks up from studying a letter on his desk, startled by this strange remark. 'I suppose I don't really mind, so long as she stays out of trouble. Why are you asking about her character?'

I stumble over my words, trying to be clearer without revealing too much. 'I'm not really, I just mean… well, is she the sort to become violently angry or hold a grudge?'

'Heavens, how should I know? You're aware I avoid her as much as I can.'

'But you have been married to her for nearly twenty years.'

He sighs. 'I suppose she's a bit cold, but she seems in control of her temper, if that's what you're worried about. Matthew, what are you really asking?'

I could tell him the truth – what happened at the publisher's office, my fear of Lady Elina's reaction. But something stops me. I cannot put my finger on it – perhaps a sense of intrigue, or sympathy with her. It's certainly not out of loyalty, even if she has changed her behaviour towards me. I can tell Henry anytime I like – there's no sense hurrying it, especially before I've spoken to her. 'I ordered the wrong fabric from London,' I say, 'for her dress at Lord Newington's summer ball – it's not too different, but I wasn't sure if she'd be upset.'

He goes back to his letter, clearly disinterested. 'I'm sure it will be fine.'

Can lying be so easy as that? I suppose I am accustomed to hiding things from other people, but less so with Henry. Guilt picks at the back of my throat, but I remind myself that I can tell him the truth another time. Besides, he has very little regard for how she occupies herself. Our business concluded, I kiss him goodbye and depart. As I open the door, I catch the eye of a footman down the corridor. 'Thank you, sir,' I call into Henry's office to cover my tracks. Occasionally I will make a waistcoat or simple shift for Henry, to justify my frequent visits to his office. The staff understand that we have known each other for years and have a friendship mingled with my employment here, but I always worry about fully convincing them since Henry usually draws such sharp lines between himself and his domestics.

I force my feet to take me upstairs to Lady Elina's rooms, still dreading the interaction. Outside her door, I take a breath to steady myself. Shoulders down, eyes down. I knock.

'Is that Mr Rooke? Come in.'

She is on the ladder by her bookcase, reaching for something on the top shelf. Loose curls tumble down her back, pulled away from her face by a thick white ribbon. She peers over her shoulder as I enter her rooms and close the door.

'Are you having a pleasant day?' she asks.

'Quite pleasant, thank you.'

She gets down from the ladder, book in hand. 'I suppose life in the countryside is a bit dull in comparison to the diversions of London.'

'Well... yes, a bit. But of course there is much to keep me occupied here.'

She gestures towards the fireplace. 'Won't you have a seat?'

'Thank you, but I don't think I'll be long,' I say, then immediately wonder if I've come across too harshly. But why would I mind? Henry will let me stay here no matter what she says – why do I care about causing her distress?

'Very well,' she answers carefully, resting her free hand on the back of an armchair. 'I wanted to thank you for – well, for the favour you did posting that letter. It contained rather sensitive information.'

It's my turn to speak, but all I hear is my heart pounding. My ears feel warm, my hands clammy. I clear my throat. 'About that letter. I have something to... well...'

'What is it?' she asks, a hint of alarm creeping into her voice. 'Were you not able to send it?'

'I was – I recognised the address and decided to take it there myself. It's reached its destination, but... well...'

Reassured, she tilts her head as if trying to see me from a different perspective. 'Mr Rooke, please try to compose yourself. I only want to know what's happened.'

'Yes – quite so.' I take a deep breath and try to say everything in one go. 'The man I delivered the letter to thought I was you, which is to say, I know you are planning to be published, and that you intentionally hid your sex from your publisher. Unfortunately, they now believe you are not only a man, but me specifically.'

Her face pales, she takes a step back. She doesn't look at me and I feel even worse than before.

'If it's any consolation,' I say, 'they seem very keen on your work. They said it's just what the public wants to read.'

Initially, I'm not sure that she's heard me. She is still looking at the floor, her mouth slack. At last, in a low voice, she murmurs, 'I will need some time to consider the implications of this. You may go.'

Then

Candles twinkle in the windows of Berkeley Street, though it's barely evening. Dusk arrives quickly these days, hushing the city even as most of us must carry on with our work. As the seasons have turned and the new year has begun, Henry and I have closed ourselves off in his London home in a private paradise all our own. I dine there whenever I can, so long as work does not interfere – usually several nights each week. Sometimes I stay the night, but am mindful of not arousing Martha's suspicions.

I hurry along in the brisk air, Lady MacIntyre's stays wrapped in paper and tucked under my arm. The smell of smoke and burnt sugar drifts through the street – someone is roasting chestnuts to sell.

The iron gate is already ajar, so I push through and tap the knocker. The butler opens the door and I hold out the package. 'Delivery for Her Ladyship.'

'Aren't you the staymaker?' he enquires. 'Lady MacIntyre requested that you come in to ensure the stays fit correctly.'

I lift my eyebrows in surprise, but don't say anything. She's an important client and one that I'd like to keep, but we've already done our final fitting. It is highly unlikely that she would ask for any alterations at this point, though I would welcome the opportunity to charge her a higher fee.

The butler shows me up the staircase to Lady MacIntyre's rooms. She is beside the vanity in her shift and quilted petticoat, a maid brushing her hair. 'Mr Rooke!' she says, looking at me in her mirror. 'Thank you for coming up. I wasn't sure after our last fitting… whether they would still fit.'

She's a bit older, perhaps forty, and perfectly composed – clearly comfortable with her elevated position and social status above everyone in the room. I sense an opportunity for flattery. 'Why, Your Ladyship is as slender as ever! I would not be surprised if we have to lace these stays up tighter than planned.'

She laughs lightly – 'How kind you are' – before standing and crossing the room. Her maid removes her petticoat so she's just in her shift. Carefully, I set the package I've brought onto a nearby chair, then unwrap it and pick up her stays – unlaced and in one long piece. The slight weight of them in my hands, individual whalebones pressing against my fingertips, the soft silk brocade shining in the firelight. I always take pride in my creations, but I've outdone myself with these.

She lifts her arms and I wrap the stays around her, bringing the ends together at her back so I can begin the spiral lacing. I adjust as I go – a slight twist here, a tug there – until I step away to get her opinion. Of course, they fit perfectly.

'Laced and tied?'

'Yes, Your Ladyship.'

'I can't believe how light they are! Yet, still supportive.' She passes her hand across her stomach, feeling the silk. 'Impressive work. Watkins,' she says suddenly, addressing her lady's maid, 'will you check what Simpson is serving for dessert tonight?'

'Yes, ma'am.' Her maid gives a slight bow and leaves.

I hesitate – presenting the bill is always a bit awkward and I desperately hope to secure another order from her. 'I'm pleased you're happy with my design,' I begin. 'I do hope you'll keep my services in mind for any stays you might need in the future.'

'Indeed I will,' she replies, and I can't help but smile. She looks down at the stays, almost caressing herself. 'The support is… well, it's like being held in a lover's embrace.' She laughs a little to herself. 'Forgive me – do you ever get lonely, Mr Rooke?'

What's this, now? I must proceed carefully. 'It is difficult to be lonely in London, Your Ladyship.'

She crosses the room towards me – I'm surprised to realise that I'd been slowly backing away from her. I smile politely as I stumble into her vanity. Cosmetic dishes and ivory brushes clatter and I cringe, trying to straighten them whilst keeping an eye on her.

'You mentioned your services,' she says, reaching out and brushing imaginary lint off my jacket – I checked myself meticulously before knocking on her door only twenty minutes ago.

'My *staymaking* services,' I reply emphatically.

'I'm sure a man like you has an array of talents to suit your clients.' She grips my jacket more tightly now. 'After all, you're in your prime, such a lust for life...' She leans forward and on instinct I step sideways, my stomach clenched.

'I'm sorry, Your Ladyship – I really must be going.' I don't dare to look at her again as I make for the door. Luckily, no one is in the hall and I manage to compose myself before seeing the butler again on my way through the front gate.

What a disaster. I review what happened, ashamed of how awkward I was – but how could I have behaved differently? It happened so quickly – now that it's too late, moments flash into my mind and I wince, wishing I had taken control of the situation in some way. I've missed the second payment on those stays, but perhaps I can send Martha back in a day or two to collect it. She has been doing good work, her stitching consistent and even. She's given me no reason not to trust her, and would appreciate the new responsibility. Unless I've irreparably offended Lady MacIntyre and she refuses to pay entirely.

Icy snow crunches under my feet and I long to take a coach back to the workshop so I can get there faster, but it seems wasteful to spend the money. Every delectable scent seems to accost me directly: roast beef, pork pie, baking bread. My stomach tugs and contracts, but I press through the market without buying anything and turn homeward. The atmosphere changes as the buildings become tighter – there's a familiar snugness, the air's frosty edge dissipates with the crowds of people milling about.

I trudge through the door exhausted, register Martha watching me from across the room. Must she always be here? Of course, it's good for the shop that stitching is carried out even when I am away, but right now I need to be alone with my thoughts.

'Sir,' she asks as I hang up my coat, wig, and hat, 'could you inspect these channels I've done? Is the backstitching even enough?'

Dragging my hand through my hair and stifling a sigh, I weave through the workbenches and over to her. The warmth from the shop makes its way into my limbs until even my ears are no longer freezing. I pick up the stays, squinting to see her stitching in the low light. 'You've done very well, Martha.'

She beams. 'Oh, I'm glad, sir. I did some extra practice in my spare time.'

I run my finger along the even stitches, no gaps in sight. 'These should hold well.' I return them to her, a thought catching in the back of my mind. 'Your time is limited and your work is improving – I don't expect you to spend your spare moments labouring. You must dirty your boots and experience the city.'

She opens the stays out onto the table, smoothing them as she does. 'Thank you, but I'm not one to squander an opportunity. I want to become as good as you – I've still got my eyes on having my own shop one day.'

I consider her – the earnest, eager expression that quickly shifts focus onto the channels she is sewing, her small hand forcing the needle through several layers of fabric, neck craned as she examines the line. She has been under my employ long enough that I owe her something more than menial tasks. 'Martha,' I begin, 'I'm going to teach you how to read and write.'

With a fluid motion, her face shoots back up to meet mine. 'Really, sir?'

'Well, if you'd like me to.'

'Oh yes, I would. It will be a great help to order supplies and follow the reports on popular fashions.' She rubs her hands together with anticipation.

I spin around to my drafting table and grab some paper and a pencil. As I reach for them, I remember Lady MacIntyre's hand coming towards my jacket. But I mustn't think of that right now, nothing can be gained from it. Blinking the image away, I turn back to face Martha. 'Right

– we'll begin with words for materials to help with placing orders, but the very first step is to learn the letters.'

I write them out for her – upper and lower case – then slide the paper across the table.

'Why don't you start by copying those out?'

As she does, I take her through the sounds for each. 'It's awfully complicated,' she sighs.

'Yes, I suppose it is.' I was lucky to learn when I was a boy – my first employer taught me and I can hardly remember the painful early lessons any more. 'Here, I'll finish these channels while you practise.' I slide the panels of fabric closer and continue her even backstitch. As I do so, my thoughts drift back to Lady MacIntyre – should I have acted differently? I have worked so hard to get her calibre of clientele and she was the first step on my ladder to the nobility ranks, excluding the baroness I made up for Martha two months ago. Now all that work will be wasted. I wonder if she will tell her friends what happened – if their expectations are similar to hers, it seems likely that she will. If they are not, her simplest course of action is silence, which does not promote my shop as I had hoped. I had forgotten that her class is accustomed to behaving as they like and the rest of us must face the consequences of their actions, no matter how skilled we are. Supposing she feels truly insulted, she could say anything about me and ruin my reputation forever. I am powerless. After about an hour, the panels are finished so I tie off the thread and put my needle away, taking myself upstairs to bed alone.

Chapter Eight

Now

Gold ruffles. White lace. Turquoise silk. I delicately lift and fold the robe into a manageable bundle, then push the door open and carefully make my way upstairs to Lady Elina's rooms.

Her door is ajar, and I brace myself before going in. I clear my throat, watching to gauge her temperament. In the month since I told her about the mishap at her publisher's, she has hardly spoken at our fittings. It's more akin to how our interactions were in years past but, after the lively engagement of the last few months, our relationship now feels hollow and tense. I wish it did not bother me, but recently it's as though I've been coming up for air and the stillness between us has plunged my spirits back down again.

Today, she does not give much away. 'Mr Rooke – is that the dress for Lord Newington's summer ball?'

'It is, Your Ladyship. Final fitting.' I have a few surprises with this one which I hope she will find pleasing. I've taken pains to make it as comfortable for her as possible.

'You may leave it with Anne,' she says coolly, craning her neck to indicate her lady's maid standing in the corner.

Anne approaches to take the dress from me, but I tilt away from her and walk towards Lady Elina. This must end – if I can apologise to her, perhaps we can restore the budding warmth between us. 'Your Ladyship, I would ask to stay here to take notes on any changes you require.'

'I will write them down for you,' she replies.

I pause – should I leave things as they are? No, I cannot. I lean in, speak more softly. 'Please let me stay. I have made some changes to this particular gown that I believe you will find agreeable.'

She watches my face, considers this request. She looks at the robe delicately laid out across my arms. 'Very well,' she breathes. She stands, removes her dressing gown and waits in her shift.

Anne hurries forward and wraps her in the stays I recently completed to go with this dress, lacing them up with expert speed. I hand Anne the skirts first, then the bodice, which shimmers with the silver spangles I painstakingly sewed onto the sleeves one by one. I watch the delicate motions Anne's work requires – gentle touches on Lady Elina's abdomen, holding her wrist to stretch out her arm, smoothing wrinkles in the fabric. I wonder if these are the only times Lady Elina has physical contact with another person and am suddenly sorry for her.

She looks at herself in the mirror. 'I like the square neckline,' she tells me.

'Try walking around in it, Your Ladyship. I made some unconventional adjustments to lighten the weight of the skirts.'

She paces around the room – crossing her bookshelves and desk, around the bed, and back towards her mirrors. Although her silhouette is straight and poised, her shoulders appear relaxed and she seems to move easily. 'Yes,' she says, a bit surprised. 'I do notice the difference.' She twirls, picks up her skirts, and kicks her feet out one at a time. I smile, watching her.

'I hope it will help you negotiate your way around a room with more ease,' I say. 'I've designed it to inspire confidence – the colour is taken from your selected essays by Madame de Genlis,' I gesture towards the shelf housing her favourite books, 'and the spangles are meant to dazzle and disarm your adversaries in conversation.'

She tips her face down towards the bodice, laughs a little in recognition. 'Thank you – your efforts do not go unnoticed.' She turns to Anne. 'Will you wait outside while I speak to Mr Rooke alone for a moment, please?'

It's a simple request and she says it in a carefree way – it's clear Anne doesn't think twice before walking through the door. My relief is chequered with anticipation, the hairs on the back of my neck raise a little. We will have the chance to speak plainly, and I must ensure she comprehends my apology. As the door closes, I brace myself and turn back towards Lady Elina. 'I hope you understand how contrite I—'

'I've been reflecting,' she cuts me off, 'on our earlier conversations.' She wears a calculating expression, eyes fixed on mine. 'My debating society is hosting an event in London next month – it's really more of a gathering between friends – and I would like you to join as my guest.'

Going to London with her, attending an event? Part of me would prefer having the house to myself with Henry, even though we are never truly alone here and there is always a risk of being caught by the servants. Yet my interest is piqued by the mystery inherent to her invitation – what exactly happens at a debating society? Do they host fervent discussions? Given my misstep at her publisher's, am I obliged to say yes? If I do attend, what will be expected of me? Perhaps it would be wise to remain at the manor – after all, I have never spent more than an hour alone in Lady Elina's company.

'Oh,' she adds before I can answer, 'I don't know whether this influences you, but I would prefer it if we kept the nature of the trip from my husband.'

Another secret? My stomach tightens with fear and guilt – how can I continue hiding our interactions from Henry? And yet, if I told him now, Lady Elina might wonder at the nature of his and my relationship. There is something compelling about sharing a secret with her, stepping into her world of ideas and equality. 'It's a kind invitation,' I tell her. 'I would be honoured to accompany you.'

She beams triumphantly. 'I think you will enjoy it. I always find my mind expanded by these parties and would love to bring your perspective into my circle of friends. I will let you know the details as the day approaches.'

'Very well, Your Ladyship.'

She smooths her skirts thoughtfully, watching herself in the mirror. 'Would you ask Anne to come back and help me out of this? I don't wish to wrinkle it.' As I open the door, I turn over my shoulder and look at her. 'Thank you again, Mr Rooke.'

Crossing the foyer on the way back to my room, I pass Henry's valet. 'Letter arrived for you just now,' he says, sifting through the cluster in his hand before passing me a small folded paper.

'Thank you,' I reply, glancing down and immediately recognising Martha's handwriting. I return to my room and close the door, walking towards the window to read her letter by the light of the fresh spring sun.

The Three

Then

While I've grown more comfortable in Henry's London home with each passing week, the constant presence of servants during the day always puts me on edge. This man – Paterson, I believe – helps me step into my silk breeches and fastens the clasps under my knees to keep my stockings up. Henry very generously bought this suit for me, the newest fashion from Paris. He's also lent me silver cuff buttons and shoe buckles inset with rubies, which should match the deep scarlet of my coat and help me blend in with his peers.

I stare in the mirror and think of Henry, down the corridor with his own suit being ceremoniously fastened to him. We have opted for contrasting colours tonight – while my coat and breeches are scarlet and my waistcoat is gold, his outfit will be the reverse. I'm sure no one will notice but it amused us when we thought of the idea.

Outside the window, spring has already begun to turn, the scent of fresh flowers in the square outside Henry's house as muggy air clings to the buildings in the East End. The past few months have been a blur – I've had luck with some new clients and, after full days at work, I rush over to Henry's for supper and affection. Sometimes I'll spend the night, but then it's a race across the city the next morning so I can return to drawing designs and stitching channels.

Paterson helps me into my waistcoat, quite unnecessarily. I'm about to button it up myself, but he steps around and begins doing it for me so I hold my arms midway in the air, feeling foolish. When he's done, I sit down and he helps me with my shoes, adding the silver and ruby buckles, which I must admire – they do make my pumps look much more impressive.

'Are you ready for your wig, sir?' he asks. Was that a slight sneer on his lips? He doesn't know my station, but perhaps guesses that I am below Henry – what man of this class doesn't have his own shoe buckles?

'I'd just like to check in with Mr Ashby,' I reply, standing and walking down the hall as confidently as I can.

I rap my knuckles on Henry's door. 'Yes,' he beckons.

He's sitting back with a drape over his shirt while yet another servant shaves his face.

'How's the suit – hasn't changed since you last tried it on, I hope?'

'It's marvellous,' I reply. 'Fits like... well, like it was designed for me.'

'Ha! Well, you know all about that.'

'I'm nearly finished, so just wanted to see how far you'd got. Perhaps I'll wait on my wig for a moment.'

'Yes, I'm sorry. I had a letter from my father that I needed to respond to. Why don't you wait in here with me for a few minutes?' His shave completed, he tosses the drape to his servant and waves him away. 'Leave us.'

I've never grown accustomed to how abrupt he can be with them while always so gentle to me. When the door closes, I walk over and take Henry's hand, pressing my lips to his palm and nibbling at his thumb.

'Is everything all right with your father?'

'Hmm? Yes, fine.' But he's distracted. I reach forward, turning his face towards mine. We both smile knowingly but, instead of kissing him, I grab the foundation from his table and begin dabbing it on his face. He laughs at this and seems to relax. As I dip my finger into the foundation and bring it to his cheek, he catches my hand. 'When you think of the two of us... how far ahead do you imagine? Can we sustain this?'

'Oh.' The air is sucked out of my chest – is it already time for this conversation? 'I suppose I haven't given it much thought. I don't make many assumptions about the future.'

'You do if it's your trade,' he replies with a faint smile.

He's right. I put the foundation down and pace the floor. 'I have... learned not to expect very much when forming attachments. The way the world is makes it difficult. At least with you, I do have love.'

'Yes, that's what I was thinking,' he says, seeming encouraged. 'I don't want this to end, I don't want our love fading to nothing because circumstances dictate it must.'

A swelling in my chest pushes out the words, 'Nor do I.'

He stands, clasping my hands. 'Well, I've devised a plan for us. Would you like to hear it?'

I'm still catching up from the sharp turn the conversation has taken. 'All right.'

'We must marry, you see? If we married women, perhaps two friends who were often in each other's company, that would give us the freedom to carry on above suspicion.'

I don't quite know what to make of this. I've never considered marriage before, knowing that for someone like me it is largely a financial proposition. Anyone with more money would be uninterested and anyone with less would be incapable of making me happy. 'It's an intriguing thought,' I say, buying time.

'It's unassailable!' he says energetically. 'We could still see each other whenever we liked, go on trips together... we could carry on like this for the rest of our lives.'

His sentiment is so sincere, I find myself melting a little. But I suddenly remember: 'No woman in your circle would want to marry the likes of me.'

'You haven't seen the marriage market. Can you imagine these women's terror – ending up unmarried and childless? What else can their lives consist of? Besides, love triumphs over station. You carry yourself respectably and can be charming when you want – there are women with enough money that those are the significant qualities they will care about.'

I'm still not sure what to make of this idea, but Henry's imagination has taken off without me.

'Why, tonight I believe we could meet Constance Hartwell and her sister, Amelia. The chance to marry off two of his daughters at once could be just enough to persuade their ageing father.'

'Whatever you think is best,' I say, deciding not to worry about this plan until it grows more serious. 'I'd better go and finish getting dressed.'

'Yes – make sure Paterson doesn't skimp on the wig powder! I ordered extra for tonight.'

'All right,' I chuckle.

A few hours later, we saunter up the path to the Ranelagh pleasure gardens, which are much transformed from previous daytime visits. The setting sun casts a golden glow across the gates and an orchestra plays gentle music, which wafts through the trees and carries the scent of jasmine with it. Henry and I cross the lawn, past fiery torches and acrobats performing exploits. I feel my cheeks flush. Luckily, I have enough foundation and rouge painted on to keep my nerves secret from the members of high society mingling around us.

A man walks past with champagne glasses on a silver tray. Henry takes one and I follow his lead. There are tents set up with tables inside where counts and dukes sit, eating the fruit heaped upon them and chortling amongst their company. We follow along the pebble path, passing flirtatious demireps and the men too weak to resist them. More acrobats, including a man who slides a sword down his throat. I pause in amazement, momentarily forgetting everything else.

We sip our champagne and my confidence grows as I notice nods of admiration in our direction from passers-by. But as a group of people step aside, I spot Lady MacIntyre and my blood stops. We lock eyes. She whispers to her husband, and they begin walking over to us. I suck in my breath, glancing at Henry. 'I'm sorry, this may be awkward.'

He looks quizzical. 'Whatever would be the matter—' But she has already floated up to us.

'Mr Rooke!' she says warmly. 'How lovely to see you here!'

I'm taken aback by how friendly she is. 'The pleasure is all mine, Lady MacIntyre. This is Mr Ashby of Stonehurst Manor.'

She nods to him, then looks back at me. 'I'm sure you'd prefer not to focus on your working life on an evening like this, but it may reassure you to see that your labour does not go unappreciated,' she says, gesturing towards her torso. Underneath her bodice, I can see the finely detailed stomacher I designed to go with her stays for this outfit. I don't look for too long, assuming that's what she wants.

'I'm pleased you're happy with it,' I reply.

Henry nods towards her husband. 'It's nice to see you again, Lord MacIntyre.'

I do a double take – he knows them? How?

'Young Henry,' replies Lord MacIntyre, 'I trust your father is well?'

'Thank you, he is.'

'Did I hear he was in the Americas?'

'Yes, due back next month.'

'A fine man,' says Lord MacIntyre in admiration.

'Mr Rooke, I will be in need of your services again when the king returns and the summer courtier parties begin,' says Lady MacIntyre. My stomach clenches.

'Of course, I will be happy to oblige Your Ladyship.'

To my relief, her husband waves to someone else and they begin to back away. 'Until then,' she tells me, running a finger along her lower lip. I look away, pretending to fish debris out of my glass.

'That wasn't awkward,' says Henry. 'Well, apart from her husband's ostentatious esteem for my father.'

'Never mind,' I reply. I can handle Lady MacIntyre, though I could do without the stress of seeing her. In the months since she accosted me, I sent Martha to retrieve her final payment but have otherwise heard nothing. I doubt I will, despite what she's said. I should use tonight's ball to meet potential clients so I can keep the shop busy enough to turn her away if she does request another order.

As I shake off the pall cast by the MacIntyres, we carry on walking and admiring the splendour. At the back of the lawn is a small pond, clusters of revellers around it in little groups. I barely hear the orchestra any more and sip my champagne. Henry touches my arm gently, giving me goosebumps of pleasure.

'You see those two ladies?' he asks as we change direction. 'They are the sisters I was telling you about.'

'Oh,' I return, trying to hide my disappointment.

'Just give it a chance, Matthew,' he says. 'Be open-minded.'

The sisters smile appealingly as we catch up with them. 'Miss Hartwell, you look lovely as ever,' says Henry by way of greeting. 'And Miss Amelia, it has been far too long.' He kisses their hands in turn, which I must remind myself is normal, expected behaviour. The surge of jealousy catches me by surprise, but I flash my teeth to hide my grimace and dip into a bow as he says, 'This is my friend Mr Rooke, an exclusive designer of ladies' clothing and eligible bachelor.' This induces a blush and giggle from the women.

'Pleased to make your acquaintance,' I say. 'It is clear that beauty runs from your family…' Wait, that's not right. 'I mean, that it runs *in* your family. My apologies.' My second humiliation of the evening – this was not the experience I'd hoped to have at my first ball.

Miss Hartwell laughs good-naturedly. 'That's quite all right. What sort of ladies' fashion do you design, Mr Rooke?'

It's kind of her to be so cordial, and I try to answer with ease. 'Mostly stays. There is great demand and opportunity in London, as you can imagine.'

'Oh yes, and what tremendous work that must be! All those stitches on the channels!'

'It does involve a lot of sewing.'

'And a lot of time in ladies' dressing rooms,' adds the younger sister.

'Amelia!' chides Miss Hartwell.

'Benefit of the trade, if you ask me,' says Henry jovially, and I feel a sudden flash of anger.

'How scandalous you are!' Miss Hartwell returns flirtatiously.

I recover myself. 'It's really not as glamourous as all that. Typically there are servants bustling about and of course the lady is always wearing a shift.'

'Oh, come now!' says Henry, eyeing me up. 'We're just having a bit of fun.'

'Of course we would never dream of insulting your professionalism,' says Amelia.

She gives me a giddy smile, which Henry notices. 'Miss Hartwell,' he says, turning to the older sister, 'your glass is empty. Can I escort you to the refreshment tent?' In an instant, they walk away together but not before he gives me a meaningful look and gestures towards the younger sister. I sigh to myself and look down at my own empty glass.

'Tell me, Miss Amelia, are you from London?'

'Heavens no! Our family home is in Somerset, but we come to London for the seasonal balls and to see the latest fashions from Paris.'

'Of course. There is much to take in.'

'Yes, it's a remarkable city, although awfully dirty for my taste.' Her attention begins to drift as she searches the faces around us. 'Still, it's convenient to have everyone so close and easy to call upon.'

'That's true.'

She fans herself – the slight breeze ruffles her brunette curls. 'I suppose you don't have much time for social calls yourself, with all the work you have to do. Or do you have staff who handle most of it?'

A clever tactic to glean a better sense of my worth. 'I do have some assistance, which allows me to strike a pleasing balance between work and society.'

Her eyes narrow almost imperceptibly, suspicious of this response. I shift my weight from one foot to the other, trying to think of something else to say. Fortunately, she sees someone she knows behind me and gives them a small wave. 'Well, it was a pleasure meeting you, Mr Rooke.' She smiles sweetly and glides away.

'I... certainly, and you as well.' I cannot believe how ill-prepared I am when it comes to flirting with women, despite working closely with them for years and learning to please them with my designs. Embers of acrimony towards Henry still smoulder in my chest and pair with this latest embarrassment. How can this plan of his possibly work? While he can attract Miss Hartwell, her sister clearly has no interest in marrying someone like me.

Watching Amelia leave, I allow my eyes to scan the sprawling lawn dotted with clusters of revellers, their voices ringing out and echoing for miles. Henry is nowhere to be seen, so I begin walking in search of him.

The crowd is thicker now and I carefully weave between lofty, coiffed hair and swinging glasses of wine attached to animated hands. I spot a golden jacket and impeccable wig, but the man turns and it is not Henry. Looking around at the swell of faces, I decide I won't find him immediately and may as well work my way back towards the musicians. I turn down a path and listen for stringed instruments, but all I can hear is a woman pissing loudly behind a nearby tree.

I suppose my evening is no different from the stories – like so many who have come before me, I attended this ball with high hopes of romance, expecting the wondrous magic to wash over me, but all too quickly find that the man I want to dance with has his attention captured by someone else.

I carry on, pebbles crunching under my polished shoes and past a group of naval officers singing 'Rule Britannia'. As the chorus begins, they jostle each other and start a wild, violent sort of dance that mainly involves them kicking at the air and each other. No one else in the vicinity seems to mind, but I find it loathsome.

I catch an eerie musical note on the warm evening air. It's just a whisper, but I follow it back towards the garden entrance and into the rotunda. There's a dense crowd of people, but I loop around the large skirts and wigs until I find an open place along the back wall. In the centre of the room, a young boy plays the pianoforte. He can't be more than ten years old and his pale face is surprisingly placid as he delicately plays. There is no accompaniment, only the pianoforte, and the notes ring through the room with such joy and precision that I can't help being moved. A calmness comes over me, and I feel the rest of the room held in attention, barely drawing breath as we all focus on the child before us. The notes waft overhead, transforming the boisterous, debaucherous party into an elevated affair. My gaze traces the outlines of the people in front of me, reading their backs. Do I belong in this crowd, or will I always be an outsider?

For now I am a simple observer, and that will do. As the boy continues to play, I turn towards the door and make my way outside.

'Clever little thing, isn't he?' asks a woman leaning against the door frame. She has a lilting northern accent that's almost musical itself and appears to be alone. She's fashionably dressed – plunging neckline and a gown made of maroon lampas with a silver fleur-de-lis design featured, yet the sleeves are uncharacteristically plain.

'Extraordinary.'

'Must take an awful lot of practice to be so good at that age.'

'Yes, I suppose you're right.'

Out of her pocket, she pulls a long clay pipe and box of tobacco, which she offers to me. I shake my head – she shrugs and lights it. She's certainly a bit unusual, but clearly takes pains to look her best. Perhaps she is in need of new stays.

'I'm a staymaker by trade,' I say, 'so I only have the time to enjoy music created by others.'

At this, her eyes widen gleefully. 'What luck that we should meet! I need a set of stays on a quick turnaround for some upcoming travel to the Americas. I thought I'd have to settle for one of the standard shops, but I'd rather have them made custom since I'll be sitting for long periods of time.'

This is a fortuitous turn for the evening to take. 'My workshop is a little busy, but I'm sure I could make room.'

'If you could, I'd be very grateful. Of course I'll pay an additional fee for the rush.'

'Perhaps I could draw up some designs and measure you next week?'

She puffs out a quick cloud of smoke. 'That would be wonderful, though we can discuss the designs in person too. They should be fashionable, of course, but by no means traditional.'

'You don't strike me as a very traditional type.'

She laughs. 'You've noticed? I'm staying with the Horne family on Gerrard Street, managed to discard their company after the first drink this evening. But they're very friendly – stop by any afternoon next week.'

'I will, Miss...?'

'Maes. Good night, staymaker,' she says with a final puff of her pipe, making her way inside the rotunda.

The sky is velvety black now, though, from the yells and laughter across the gardens, plenty of people are still enjoying themselves. As increasing numbers of bodies tumble horizontally onto the cool, damp grass, I stride across the lawn and make towards the exit. 'Matthew...' A familiar hand on my arm. I turn to look at Henry. 'Are we retiring to my house?' he asks.

I tilt my head, musing. I can draw up the designs for Miss Maes easily enough, but the side of Henry I've seen this evening has left me reconsidering what I can expect from him. 'Thank you for tonight – it's been an entirely new experience. Magical in so many ways.'

'I'm glad,' he says, looking around and covertly clasping my hand.

'But,' I pull away, 'I have some work to begin, and must go home to my shop tonight.'

'Oh,' he replies, crestfallen. 'Right, well... if you must.'

I don't want him to feel completely dejected. 'I'll write to you tomorrow.'

'Yes, yes...' He looks pensive. I want to tell him that he can come with me, but know it's best if I take the night to myself.

'Are you going to stay?' I ask. 'I'm making my way to the boats – I'll see how far east they will take me.'

He's lost in thought for a moment. I give him some time before gently placing my hand on his shoulder.

'Good night.'

'Here,' he murmurs, pulling his purse from a pocket and handing me a sixpence coin. 'You were my guest tonight – it's only fair I pay for your way home.'

I hesitate to accept the money – it feels transactional and cold. But Henry is always generous, and it's easier to take it than to spend ten minutes debating the matter. I thank him, then exit the gardens and make my way towards the river, where a number of boats are waiting to take their merry guests back to London. As we pull away from the shore, I watch the reflections from the garden torches drip like gold into the river. Will there always be this divide between me and Henry, our backgrounds too disparate to come together in any significant way? How can we hope for a shared future if we cannot even attend a sumptuous gathering comfortably? Watching the darkened city glide past does nothing to answer my questions – London's shores are silent and distant.

Chapter Nine

Now

'Isn't it invigorating?' Lady Elina calls from over her shoulder. I hustle, trying to keep up with her as we dart between Londoners going about their days. The road is crowded and carriages ramble past, kicking up dust. 'I come here so rarely, but always enjoy my visits. Do you think if we cut through here—'

'I wouldn't, Your Ladyship,' I reply. 'That way goes straight to the river and we don't want that.'

'No, I suppose not. Although it would be delightful if the debating society were to meet in the hull of one of those great ships, I rather think we would miss the victuals of Mr Phelps' kitchen. Right, then.' We carry on down Cockspur Street and up the Hay Market.

We turn off the main road into a quieter street. I look around, trying to pretend I haven't been to this part of town since my early twenties instead of the reality: two summers ago with Henry. We stayed in his home on St James's Square for two weeks and he worked while I went for walks and visited Martha. Most evenings, we fought about what to do – go to his friends' dinner parties or, my preference, somewhere we might be anonymous. I could never stay upset with him for long – so much of love is balancing between self-protection and an unquenching desire for the other person, and giving in to Henry can be addicting. In truth, it was a relief when Lord Finsborough was accidentally shot on a hunting trip and Henry's circle stopped making plans.

Lady Elina stops in front of a house made of enormous grey bricks. 'Now, you mustn't be intimidated,' she says, turning to me. 'You have every right to be here and will provide a valuable perspective to these men and women.'

She spins back around and knocks on the door. A footman pulls it open and she immediately steps forward. 'Lady Elina to see Mr Phelps,' she says breezily, marching ahead. I can only follow behind, too nervous to meet the man's eyes.

She doesn't wait to be directed, but instinctively walks down the powder-blue hall and into a drawing room on the left. I remove my hat, glancing at the silver sconces and sumptuous vases of fresh flowers as I follow.

The room is a large rectangular shape, with high ceilings and walls a herby-green colour. In its centre, a semi-circle of dark wooden chairs is arranged and several men and women are seated. They stand when they see us enter.

'Lady Elina, delighted you could join us,' says one man, stepping forward. 'And your, er, acquaintance?'

'Mr Matthew Rooke,' she replies as I attempt to smooth my features into an expression of resting intelligence. 'A staymaker and, well, my personal dressmaker.' Her fumble makes it clear that she doesn't quite know how to introduce me to these friends of hers – perhaps she is more comfortable thinking about equality than putting her ideas into action. It makes me more aware of my place outside the group – I must do my best to fit in.

'Please find a seat,' says the man, presumably Mr Phelps and the owner of this grand home. 'We have a special guest joining—' The doorbell chimes and he startles. 'Oh! That might be him now, just give me a moment to check.'

He hurries out of the room while Lady Elina and I find chairs. She smiles and waves to a few of the other members. Everyone shares the same air of animation and alertness that I've come to associate with her – the man next to me smiles and says hello before the woman sitting in front of him turns around and asks him a question. The room buzzes with their energy and the hum of their voices, though judging by the location and everyone's dress, I am the only tradesman. I don't understand how this assembly will unfold, nor what is expected of me. 'Do you know who this guest is?' I ask, leaning towards Lady Elina.

'Not as such. It's customary for guest speakers to join at these rendezvous – typically someone with specialised knowledge to offer.'

I nod, wondering if I will be able to follow along with the debate.

Mr Phelps returns, followed by a tall Black man dressed in a crisp blue jacket and breeches. 'This is Mr John Stuart.'

'You may call me Ottobah Cugoano,' the man says, addressing the room.

'Oh yes, of course,' says Mr Phelps. 'That is the name you published your abolitionist work under. My apologies. We're very pleased to have you with us today so we can discuss the impact of your work and what remains to be done.'

'Thank you,' Mr Cugoano returns as Mr Phelps finds a seat and stares at him eagerly.

Mr Cugoano looks calmly around the room, clearly accustomed to speaking in such a setting. He stands tall, highlighting some fine embroidery work on his lapels. When he begins talking, his speech is slow and deliberate.

'Our greatest task at this moment in time is to release African men and women from the chains of slavery. Many Britons believe this feat has already been accomplished, but it is not the case – although a Black person may not be taken by force and sold on British land, white British inhabitants may bring Africans on to these shores as enslaved persons and the government allows it. We must demand a higher moral code – why should it be illegal to enslave a white British citizen, but not a Black one?'

Everyone leans forward a little when he speaks, and my thoughts swirl as I listen. Of course I have heard about some of the cruel conditions enslaved people are kept under in the West Indies and Americas, but this is the first time I've been in the room with someone who has survived them. Henry's father has lately made plans to become much closer to the plantations in question. I have not considered it before, but find myself agreeing with Mr Cugoano's point about the differences in how the law treats Black and white people.

He continues. 'Let me tell you about my early life. I was playing in a field with other boys and girls when we were captured and taken by force to a ship a day's journey away. Many of us tried to escape, but cutlasses and pistols threatened death. Once in Grenada, I was sold to plantation owners, who treated me very badly indeed. Please remember, I was only a child when I saw my countrymen whipped until their knees buckled and the skin fell off their backs. It was barbarous, and my little mind filled with horror and indignation.'

The room is silent – no one coughs or adjusts their postures. I glance over at Lady Elina, see tears suspended in her eyes, and am filled with relief that she feels the same way I do.

'There is much wrong with our present forms of government, where some are protected but others are not. How can enlightened nations sit still while this torrent of oppression rolls on? Do the values of individual liberty and natural rights apply to all of us, or a selected few?'

Lady Elina leans forward towards Mr Cugoano. 'Of course, the law only reflects the rights of those in power! We see this divide when it comes to women's rights also – as Mary Wollstonecraft wrote, marriage imprisons women and turns them into slaves.'

'With respect, it is not quite the same,' says Mr Cugoano.

She raises her eyebrows in surprise. 'Marriage robs women of their property, not to mention their bodily sovereignty. We are compelled to work in the shadows, if at all.'

'That may be, but are you forced to work against your will? Slavery is only enacted against Black men and women; there is a punitive line drawn solely from the colour of one's skin. It is this line that I speak of ending.'

Irrationally, I interject before I can stop myself: 'Sir, this lady is well informed on the issues and has insight into the hardships of marriage for women.'

'No, Mr Rooke,' she says, putting her hand out. 'I thank you, but this is an area of political discourse where my knowledge is lacking. Education is precisely why Mr Cugoano speaks to societies like this one, and I am a willing learner.'

'If you wish to educate yourself further, consider the work of abolitionists like Olaudah Equiano or those in the Clapham Sect.'

Lady Elina nods, pulling a pencil and small notebook from her pocket to write his recommendations down.

I sit back, stung by how quickly I was dismissed. But I respect Lady Elina for not holding a grudge against Mr Cugoano – it is a lesson I will try to learn as well. When I reflect on why I jumped to defend her so impulsively, I cannot see the logic in it – it was an entirely emotional response. I hope I have not humiliated myself in front of these intellectuals.

After a thoughtful pause, Mr Cugoano continues. 'While the revolution in France may attempt to restore common rights to those within her borders, I would urge you to remember that the evils of slavery are still practised in its colonies just as they are around the world. In fact, British law protects opulent slaveholders who place their fellow men in bondage.'

'One must wonder whether complete abolishment is the correct course of action,' begins an older man, rubbing his chin. 'Think of the financial ramifications and how far down the ladder they might be felt.'

'But Mr Andrews, is it right to expect labour for no pay? We would not stand for such treatment ourselves,' Lady Elina challenges.

'Of course not, which is why I understand the need to abolish slavery on our shores. But these individuals are not without compensation.'

I steal a glance at Mr Cugoano to gauge his reaction, but his face rests in its same composed expression as he watches Mr Andrews, who continues.

'If plantation owners had to pay a living wage, we would see a cost increase for products that are already dear – sugar, cotton. Other jobs down the production line could be lost. I believe considering the larger societal cost makes this proposition more complex than it at first appears.'

I think of my own trade – fabric is already expensive, and it would be difficult for smaller businesses to put forth the money to purchase it before receiving payment from their clients. It could reshape the way business is done, but the industry is always changing and reacting to new technologies and fashions. At the end of the day, it would be a small adjustment to make in exchange for fair treatment across all points of production.

I notice that many of us in the room are watching Mr Cugoano, waiting for him to make an unassailable counterargument to Mr Andrews and claim the victory. But he stares back at us in expectation.

His eyes meet mine. *Well?* He raises his eyebrows – a challenge.

I take a deep breath, then turn to the man. 'Mr Andrews, you seem to know a great deal about the production line on British plantations. I must wonder if perhaps you are allowing your financial interests to blind you to the moral merits of Mr Cugoano's argument.'

'Now, see here—'

'You are Willis Andrews of the British Tobacco Company?' I ask. I remember Henry complaining of convoluted negotiations over Atlantic shipping with this company last year.

Mr Andrews' face has gone scarlet. 'You are new here, perhaps you don't understand how to behave with civility.'

I open my mouth to respond, but Lady Elina's voice rings out: 'Do not speak down to my friend.'

Our host has finally found himself and intercedes. 'Everyone, please! We are here to encourage intelligent debate, and that is precisely what we are having. No arguments need to be taken personally; after all, the aim of this society is to consider how best to help all levels of our community. Everyone has made excellent points in this regard.'

I nearly reply that it is impossible not to take this particular discussion personally when a man who has been subjected to the system of slavery is standing in our midst, but I look at Lady Elina and can see that she agrees with me. *We will discuss this in further detail*, her expression says.

'Let us take respite from this debate in the form of some tea,' Mr Phelps continues. 'Mr Cugoano, please.' The two of them walk to the back of the room, where a table of tea and cakes has been laid.

'I see you are honouring us with fruits of the Empire,' Mr Cugoano says wryly.

'Oh – quite – ahem – would you like a biscuit?' asks Mr Phelps nervously.

Lady Elina and I stand, but hang back from the others. I begin quietly. 'I apologise if I went too far—'

'Not at all, Mr Rooke – you were a credit to yourself. There is much work to do in educating the public on the evils and ramifications of slavery. I myself can improve by engaging more fully with this pressing issue, particularly as it applies to emerging ideas about individual liberty.'

'I must commend you for your generosity of spirit,' I reply. 'It is not so easy for me to see where my knowledge falls short. Although I'm aware I am in a box, I cannot see the edges of it.'

She nods. 'It requires a great deal of comfort with oneself to recognise how much is left to learn. Growing up overseas, I witnessed heartbreaking inequality and felt inspired to advocate for change. It was through an assortment of reading that I began to understand the value of remaining open to new ideas. As Socrates recognised, the more we learn, the more we realise how little we know.'

I have never known someone who carries the wisdom of great thinkers in their mind everywhere they go. But beyond an increasing admiration for Lady Elina's intellect or the exhilaration of partaking in a lively debate is a warmer feeling, the imprint of remembering that she came to my defence and called me her friend.

Then

I plunge down the Strand, rushing to the West End to meet Miss Maes. People pass by, eyes forward and fixed on an unknown point far ahead. I try to imagine a future where Henry's plan works and we both marry the Hartwell sisters – it's true that we may see each other often, perhaps even spend the night in one another's homes, but never in the other's bed. We might pretend to go for a walk in the woods of his estate and pass a few hours in an abandoned hunting cabin, but always returning to our wives within the afternoon. I turn right, away from the river. What Henry is trying to promise is permanency, but in reality he can only offer brief moments of tenderness stolen behind closed doors. Is our love so easy to diminish and reduce to a tawdry secret? Besides which, I could never leave London and live in the countryside! I am not used to compromising and I suspect he is not either. There must be another way.

I push on through Leicester Fields and up the road to Gerrard Street. I know the Hornes' home by reputation and spot it immediately. A footman lets me in and directs me to a drawing room on the right. It's a sunny day and the long curtains are open to let the light in. I clutch my hussif of measuring paper, pins, notepaper, thimble, and thread tight against my side and peer around, trying not to be too conspicuous. Stepping from the comfort of my London streets into unfamiliar rooms always puts me slightly on edge – I know that the opulence and finery designed to seduce visitors is not meant for me.

Presently, the footman is back and announces Miss Horne and Miss Maes. They walk into the room, skirts rustling and hair most likely refreshed from whichever social event they attended last night. Immediately, Miss Maes rushes forward with a smile.

'I'm so pleased you found me!'

'It's lovely to meet you, Mr Rooke,' her friend begins in a high, prim voice. 'Won't you take a seat?'

I begin to sit down on the sofa she gestures to, but Miss Maes cuts me off. 'Mr Rooke is a staymaker who has come to measure me. I imagine his job will be easier if we withdraw to my room?' She smirks a little and I chuckle amiably.

'Quite right,' replies Miss Horne with crisp neutrality, sweeping back towards the door and gesturing. 'Please come along.'

We steer around the corner and up the staircase, where Miss Maes' room is the first on the left. She opens the door confidently and steps inside, leaving me to follow. I notice that Miss Horne appears determined to join us, which of course makes no difference to me. She seems severe in contrast to Miss Maes' light-hearted manner – perhaps her role is more guardian than friend.

The room is simply decorated, though all furnishings appear to be of high quality. Miss Maes crosses to a trunk on the other side of the room, pulls out a pair of stays, and brings them over to me.

'These are my favourite pair – they've formed to my shape now and are sublimely comfortable.'

I set my hussif on a nearby chair, then pick up the stays so I can examine them. The lining is worn and frayed in spots, and the laces at the back are discoloured. 'I can see you wear them often. Would you like me to refresh them with a new linen lining? It won't take any additional time.'

She beams. 'Would you? How marvellous.'

I look over the individual panels comprising the stays, checking for irregular shapes and cuts, but see nothing unusual. 'Shall we begin? Just leave your shift on, please.'

She begins unlacing her jacket and loosening her skirts. Miss Horne steps forward to help her, but she brushes her aside. 'You needn't stay for this, Fanny,' she tells her. 'I know you have letters to write.'

'Are you quite sure?' Miss Horne asks.

Miss Maes almost rolls her eyes but remains polite in her reply. 'Of course! I'll be right here when you're done.'

Miss Horne nods, turns towards me for the briefest moment, then strides out of the room, closing the door behind her.

Upon her departure, Miss Maes seems to relax and unties her skirts and bodice without ceremony. 'I'd like to order two sets of stays from you,' she says, twisting around to face me.

'May I help?' I ask, reaching for her sleeves and gently shaking them down her arms.

'Thank you,' she replies. 'I mentioned I am travelling and need to depart as swiftly as possible – what is the earliest you could complete two pairs?'

Two sets of stays at once is an excellent order, especially with the additional fee to expedite their production. A month's worth of living expenses in one spurt, though it won't be easy.

'If I really hurry, I can complete them in one week,' I say. Martha won't be pleased, but it will be a good learning experience for her.

I help Miss Maes out of her bodice and stays, setting them on a nearby chair, then pick up her skirts when she steps out of them. She stands, shoulders back, and faces me in her shift. Yet there's a change in her, something askew between us that wasn't there earlier. Her boisterous confidence has quieted and she avoids meeting my eye. Has she never been in a state of undress in front of a man before, even a staymaker or dressmaker? Perhaps she just needs a moment – I turn around and get my measuring paper and notebook.

She's still looking at the floor when I walk back over. I extend the measuring paper and encircle her waist, make a note of the circumference: thirty inches. I measure the centre of her chest down her front, towards the slight curve of her abdomen. It isn't until I bring the measuring paper around her hips that I feel something unexpected. I write down the measurement: thirty-eight inches, but add a star next to it.

I clear my throat. 'Miss Maes, are you...' I can't finish the question – it's too insulting to imply to an unmarried woman of her social station, or any station. I try again. 'Perhaps you would prefer that these stays do not extend down quite so far?'

She purses her lips, watching me struggle before looking down and touching a hand to her abdomen. 'I don't know,' she murmurs. 'That's why I need to leave sooner rather than later. I'd like to arrive in America before...' She doesn't complete her sentence, but I can imagine. Before it becomes obvious that she is pregnant, before her family gets word, before she's had a chance to start anew.

I try to think how best to help her. 'I could add additional lacing at the sides so you could let them out as needed.' Of course, that would look unusual for someone not pregnant and anyone dressing her might be suspicious. 'Or use less boning. Are you travelling with anyone?'

The Three

She shakes her head. 'I still have time,' she says, almost to herself. But we both know her moment of escape will pass only too quickly. She must be terrified about what could happen, how difficult it will be even if her plan works perfectly, but her expression is composed and determined. 'What you might do is make one pair of stays as usual, and try the side lacing on the other.'

I bow my head in consent and complete my measurements. In any case, she will need the support of high-quality stays once she has the baby and is carrying it around. 'What do you hope to do in the Americas?' I enquire.

She smiles. 'I have some money set aside, and land is cheap there. I plan to move to a small town, build a cabin for myself, and live off the land.'

'My goodness, but you're brave. Don't you worry how you'll manage all that on your own?'

She does not meet my eye for a moment, perhaps overwhelmed by her plan. Then she faces me again, leaning in a little. 'Is this convincing? At first, I'll say that my husband is in the navy, then pretend he's been killed. That should be enough to keep people from asking questions. Perhaps, after a time, I will find someone who will love me and my child.'

I nod, still in awe of her dignity in the midst of such difficulty. 'I hope it goes smoothly for you.' Such a scenario would probably be her best chance at success, particularly in the colonies where there might be more opportunities born of necessity, and plentiful bachelors.

I gather my measuring paper and fold it inside my sketchbook, then turn to a new page and jot down what we've discussed.

'I will line these with wool and linen – do you have any preference for the outer fabric? A dark brocade, perhaps? A simple ribbed silk?'

She tilts her head, considering with a faint smile. 'I'm tempted to order something colourful and outlandish. But my travel dress is black, so it's probably best to use simple black silk on the exterior of the stays.'

I nod, but try to push her a little since she seems to want something more lively. 'A luscious pine or aubergine could still complement the black dress while offering a hint of colour?'

Almost wistful for a moment, she shakes her head and sounds more stern when she replies, 'No. I should avoid attracting attention while I'm travelling.'

After making a note of her preference, I stick the pencil into my pocket. 'I shall get started right away so we can finish these as quickly as possible.'

'Thank you,' she says, a bit tense. 'You are sure it won't take more than one week? My friend does not know of my plans to leave and I'd like to be gone before she does.'

I head for the door. 'I promise it won't be longer than that.'

Clearly relieved, she smiles and gives me a small wave. 'Thank you, Mr Rooke. And good day.'

I hurry downstairs and out of the dark entryway, into the bright afternoon streets. The spring air is crisp and full of new possibilities, but I have work to do.

When I return to the shop and explain the situation to Martha, she glowers at me from behind her workstation. 'One week? One week to make two fresh stays, along with all that we've already got to do?'

'She's paying extra for the rush, and we'll both work on it – you've nothing to worry about.'

She shakes her head, perched over the stays she is currently sewing, stitching the final trim around the bottom. She holds the lining steady, moving quickly with a backstitch, her leather thimble bobbing out from under the stays every so often. Watching her, I can tell she has more to say.

'Well, what is it?'

She doesn't stop, trying to prove her point about how busy we are. As if I didn't already know that. I wait for her to continue, trying to hide my impatience. At last: 'I noticed Mr McFarland looked low on silks and cottons – might be best to run out this afternoon for more supplies.'

I nod. 'Let me put my designs together first so we don't purchase more than is necessary.'

I pull out my notebook and lay a fresh sheet of paper on my workbench, then begin sketching.

–

The elegant shops of Piccadilly always display their colourful wares in a crisp, clever way as if to remind you that they only sell the finest materials. I admire the windows but hurry past, on my way to Henry's for a quick lunch. He wants my help drafting a letter to his parents, asking them to suspend their demand that he marry within the year. He's only asking for my benefit, but his sister recently had another son and perhaps that will afford him some flexibility with his future. I'm not optimistic, nor can I imagine both of us marrying and living out the rest of our days in the countryside with our wives. Every day we spent away from each other would be agony. And how would I earn a living? Since seeing Miss Maes, I've begun to half wonder if Henry and I wouldn't be better off running away to another country too, whether to the Americas or somewhere even further away. I think of the taut skin of his chest, picturing each hair, every freckle, and counting down the minutes until I can bring my mouth to them again.

There's an interruption to the usual business of the street. Normally, people and carriages pass back and forth with a pleasant energy, clipping along with purpose yet ultimately calm in demeanour. But this afternoon, there is an edge to the way people move and I sense tension in the air. I begin following the scent of unease down the street, the crowd getting denser as I go further west. Like a lodestone, I feel pulled past stalls selling wilted lettuce and flowers, towards Hyde Park. Hawkers press broadsheets at me, but they barely register on the periphery of my mind. It is one of those times when I can read the street by feeling, and sense that something important is coming.

As I reach the park, there's a commotion in the road. I move aside as a crowd follows a cluster of guards leading a blindfolded man in a horse-drawn cart through the crush of people. 'Please God, spare me...' the man moans as they pass. They must be taking him to Tyburn to be hanged. I wonder what offence he has committed, or been accused of committing. The government enjoys the public spectacle of these hangings, believing it deters others from criminal temptation. I have gone to a few but did not see the appeal in watching. Still, there is something about the prisoner that intrigues me, so I turn and follow along on the outskirts of the procession.

White crocus flowers splash across the field in great clusters as far as the eye can see. Despite the fresh spring afternoon, there's heat in the air – a sense of anger about whatever injustice this man committed. 'Filthy piece of scum!' someone yells over my shoulder. They are bloodthirsty, clapping each other on the back and occasionally throwing rocks at the prisoner, though their aim is haphazard at best. My blood throbs in response to the crowd's perilous momentum.

As the street widens and we come to the turnpike, the crowd begins to chant, 'Hang the rogue, hang the rogue.' Fear tints my curiosity and I step back, aware that the energy could crest at any moment and violence may erupt. My pulse rings through my ears with a terrified, rapid beat.

The noose already around his neck, the guards deliver their captive to the gallows. A constable calls above the crowd, who drop their voices to a murmur. 'Mr Richard Arnold, you have been found guilty of the crime of sodomy and will be punished by public hanging. Have you any remaining confession to make?'

All sound and motion ceases. Perhaps the man makes his reply, perhaps not. I can no longer feel the crowd of bodies surrounding me, whether they are still yelling or pushing in for a closer look. Space and time settle – it's as though I am, somehow, surrounded by emptiness. Perhaps one day the man standing at the gallows will be me. Perhaps it will be Henry.

The drop is not far, the prolonged strangle takes about five minutes. As the man sputters and kicks his legs, the crowd of Londoners cheer.

Chapter Ten

Now

Lady Elina's door stands before me, imposing and impenetrable. Henry once told me it was made from a nearby oak tree chopped down a hundred years ago. I hope my creations will endure that long – they're certainly built to – but will there be any desire to maintain them? If fashions change and the cuts are no longer in style, I doubt it. Dressmaking can be a fickle business. Some might say there is value in the immediacy of their use, that beauty of any sort is always ephemeral. But I wonder if there is not more value in creating something that will last through time, that *can* last. Surely that is more difficult to do than recreating what is popular in the present moment.

That Mr Cugoano, for instance. There are plenty of people who do not care about the consequences of slavery and his path forward is difficult. But if he is on the right side of history, his work will be remembered. Perhaps even Lady Elina, with her forthcoming book, will leave her mark on future generations of thinkers. For the first time I begin to understand the value of legacy, of passing down something of benefit to those who come after us.

I rap my knuckles on the oak door and announce myself. 'It's Mr Rooke, you called for me?'

When I enter, she is at her usual thoughtful position in front of her bookshelves, arms akimbo atop skirts of iridescent green, like a ground beetle's wings. She turns and meets my gaze.

'Mr Rooke,' she breathes, 'won't you please have a seat?'

There is something disarming and yet appealing about her. I hesitate only briefly before sinking into a nearby chair. Am I in trouble? I can't imagine what for. Lady Elina and I have been a fixed presence on the periphery of each other's lives for years, but something has begun changing between us these past few months. I can't quite pinpoint what it is – perhaps a mutual fascination that keeps us returning to each other's company. Or a shared awakening to new possibilities that only the two of us can offer one another.

She takes a seat opposite me, looking unsure. Is she nervous? No, she always calculates her conversations. She has trusted me before with the letter to her publishers, although I could have handled it better. Perhaps she will entrust me again.

She looks to the side, avoiding my gaze, then shakes her head and returns my stare. 'I hardly know where to begin...' Her hands open and close in a pulsing rhythm. So she *is* nervous. 'Well, you know my passion for the issues affecting our everyday citizens.'

I nod, though it's clear she will press forward whether I acknowledge her or not.

'You recall too that I write my opinions down, and there are those who find them worthy of publication?' she adds. 'Well, as it happens I have had a letter from my publisher and... and I find myself in the position of asking you for a – great personal favour.'

I feel my eyebrows lift – I understand her character better than I might have hoped. I lean forward, waiting to hear what she will ask.

'For the first time since working with them, my publishers would like me to come into London and promote my latest work,' she says. 'As they are already under the impression that you are Mr E. Ashby, and as it is very difficult for a woman's work to be taken seriously, I am asking you to attend in my place.' I sit, unconscious that I am staring at her in stunned silence until she says, 'Mr Rooke? It will be an opportunity to return to London for a day or two, which I know you always enjoy.'

'I...' I do not have the knowledge to pose as her. The experience was difficult enough when it was for five minutes in the corridor at her publisher's office. I have never spoken before a crowd of strangers, especially intellectuals ready to challenge anything I might say. 'Your Ladyship, I cannot—'

'I agree the situation is not ideal for either of us,' she interrupts, now calm. 'But I believe you are capable. I've noticed your spark when discussing these matters, and I believe I can train you to speak with a convincing level of expertise on the subject. I do not think you will be asked very detailed questions.'

My eyes go wide. 'I would have to answer questions?' Her request grows worse by the moment.

She carries on, entirely composed now that she has overcome her initial entreaty. 'I imagine as much. You will speak to the Reformers Corresponding Society on the basic arguments of my book, then there will be questions and debate. Not that you will need to debate too fiercely – simply stay on the talking points I will provide.'

'If this is punishment for the way I behaved—'

'Not at all, Mr Rooke!' She clasps my arm beseechingly. 'While I was once frustrated by what happened when you took my letter to John Josephson's, it was not your fault and, in all likelihood, for the best.' She leans back again, smiles at me. 'You were wonderful at the debating society, speaking with both confidence and kindness.'

'I cannot take credit for your work, Your Ladyship – all the time and effort you've put into it.'

'These men will not give credence to my work if they think the ideas are from a woman. It is one thing to take a fashionable interest in the news of the day, but to write as I do... even my radical friends do not know. Please, Mr Rooke – I ask you because I must, and because I believe you can help me.'

She looks away, clearly disappointed by her inability to work within the system her sex prohibits her from. I imagine the steps before this, where she has fallen short – no formal education as her brothers would have received, no training at the behest of an illuminated thinker in her field. Signing her letters and articles with just a first initial, knowing that putting her full name would mean destroying their chances of reaching the audience who deserve to read them. I cannot help but feel her injury deeply – I may not be the daughter of an earl, but at least I can take credit for my own designs and work.

'Of course, of course I must help.'

Her cheeks redden, perhaps with relief or embarrassment, then she smiles and takes my hand. 'Thank you,' she says with shining eyes. 'We will begin our work immediately.'

I sit back, flush with exuberance at helping someone I care about, but it isn't long before the thought creeps into the back of my mind: should I tell Henry? How can I keep this from him?

As I leave Lady Elina's rooms, a stack of books under my arm, I pass him coming up the stairs. 'Oh – hello!' Henry says, cheerful. 'She's got you dressing the books now, eh?'

I'm a little flustered to run into him so quickly, but I know he doesn't expect a witty response so simply tilt my head to the side.

He continues, 'I actually had something I wanted to chat to you about – won't you follow me to my office?'

I turn back up the stairs and shadow him along the corridor, using the pause to steady myself and put on a veneer of nonchalance. Suits of armour stare down at me menacingly, ready to protect the Ashby family from any threat past or present. As we cross the main staircase, I briefly glimpse a prized portrait by Sir Joshua Reynolds that Henry recently acquired. He opens his office door and I close it behind me. Our usual custom, the motions now second nature.

I walk over to him and he lovingly places his hands on my shoulders. 'I've managed to arrange a holiday for us to Bath,' he says.

It's been a long time since our last trip. While there is always some risk in going about together in society, we can be anonymous in a larger city and carefully enjoy a few meals and sports in each other's company. Perhaps going away is what we need, a change of scenery to refresh our perspectives on each other. 'How wonderful! Are you sure it won't be too public though?' From my understanding, Bath is the sort of place one goes to be seen.

'Not at all – everyone there is so concerned with standing out, they don't notice what others are up to. Besides, it won't be until the autumn.'

'Well, if you're sure. I've always wanted to visit and take the waters.'

'Yes, I know! It worked out that an associate was going to be in town, so it made sense to line up a quick jaunt without my wife.'

We've been intertwining our fingers as we talk, but I pull back now. Of course he has another reason for going away, he always does. I'm only added on to the trip as a convenience.

Henry reads my expression. 'Don't be upset. I've been waiting for an opportunity like this to come along so we could have some time together.'

'How can we be together when you'll be off with... whomever you're meeting this time?'

'Maurice Gerrald – good fellow. I'll only meet with him one day – the rest of the trip will be dedicated to you.' He leans forward, kissing me.

It feels good to give in to him, so I do. But a sense of unease prickles at the back of my neck. 'Do you ever worry,' I begin, 'that change will come and, when it does, you'll be on the wrong side of history?'

'What in heavens do you mean?' Henry asks. 'Of course not. Oh, it will be such a relief to be away from Elina for a few days – she's been so demanding lately, wanting to attend dinners and even local balls with artisans and commoners.'

I watch him, perplexed. I've begun to notice that these passing comments from him, once easy to commiserate with, now strike me as arrogant. Surely it isn't how he really feels – he simply does not always think before speaking. I try to nudge him in the right direction. 'It must be rather difficult for her here, with so little control over who she sees and where she goes.'

He scoffs. 'You've complained about her enough, how she's dismissive of your dressmaking skills and has no opinions about her own clothing.'

'That was years ago.' As Lady Elina has been talking to me about the inequalities in France and our own English societies and particularly with this latest request, I've found myself beginning to sympathise with the more difficult aspects of her life. 'She's – she's much improved lately.'

'Good. In any case, the trip to Bath will be a welcome reprieve for all of us.' He turns his attention back to the papers on his desk, and I watch him for just a moment before heading downstairs. There is so much he does not see.

Then

Martha sidles around my workbench and peers at the paper next to me. 'Four yards em-er-ald silk broc-ade, ten yards broad-cloth, one... skein of yellow linen thread, two bod-kins.'

'Very good,' I respond, setting my needle down and taking a moment to stretch my hand and roll my wrist. She has been working hard at learning to read and her effort shows. I reach for my purse and pull out some coins so she can purchase the materials.

She bustles to her room to finish getting ready. I barely look up from my work until she calls out, 'Have you got a spare handkerchief?'

I pull the one I'm wearing from around my neck in a quick motion, holding it up with one hand as I draft a pattern with the other until she hurries back around the room to grab it. 'Don't forget to check the yardage of the brocade,' I tell her. 'And beeswax for the linen thread.'

'I still think I could convince Mrs Hatchfield to use wool externally,' Martha returns.

'She's not your client, and you haven't earned that privilege yet.' We are growing comfortable in our routine, but I must still be firm with her or she'll run me out of the place and take over.

She gives herself a quick once-over in the mirror, then waves goodbye and hurries out the door. As she does, Henry hustles inside with a tight jaw and stern look on his face. My eyes widen and my neck tightens, watching how Martha will react, but she merely takes a second glance at him as he rushes past, then carries on down the alley.

Henry barely looks around as he storms in, even though the shop is in a state of disarray. Half-completed stays wait for fresh supplies before they can be finished, cuttings of panels for less urgent orders are almost discarded at the end of a bench. Pins, thread clippings, and fabric scraps adorn the floor. It's not how I usually keep things, but we've been so busy trying to push through the extra orders this week for Miss Maes. It doesn't help that every time I thread a needle, I see that noose settling around Mr Arnold's neck. But Henry is too agitated for any distraction – he tears a letter from his pocket. 'From my parents,' he says.

Nerves suddenly push through my weariness. I stand and lean against my workbench for support as he spins around me and reads aloud.

'They say: "Of course you must marry, and sooner is best. The estate demands an heir and you cannot disappoint us. Think of all the workers who depend on you." What nonsense! If those workers weren't on our land, they'd find somewhere else to live.'

He's upset, so I don't bother to correct him. 'You cannot pretend to be surprised that they feel this way?' Disappointment sears my throat.

'No,' he sighs bitterly. 'No, I knew this would be their reply. I simply allowed myself to hope...' He takes a breath and his face becomes resolved and hardened. 'But no matter. We will just have to follow my original plan.'

Now it is my turn to sigh. 'The Hartwell sisters.'

And so serveral days later, I find myself on an outing with my lover, the woman he is courting, her sister, and their chaperone. With Miss

Maes' order due so soon, I can't justify being away from the workshop, but I was too weak to resist Henry's injured tone when he asked. I haven't had time to think about what the letter from his parents really means for us, whether there will be a way to recover, so I simply agreed when Henry suggested an hour or two of shopping at the market for ribbons. He has urged me to be charming and I try to avoid meeting his eye, but it is difficult.

'I must find the perfect lace pieces for my summer frock,' says Constance as she examines the curved trims and filigrees.

'Oh, but these are so lovely!' cries Amelia, fingering a yellow silk ribbon.

The two are so different, I can't help but insert myself. 'If I may ask, what kind of fabric is your dress made of? And where do you envision the ribbon going? Silk will hold its colour and shape whether worn in the hair or around the waist, while lace must be more carefully considered.'

Henry's jaw tightens nervously but the women seem enchanted. 'Oh yes, we must not forget that we have an expert in our midst!' says Constance.

'I apologise if I've imposed myself,' I reply, trying to walk back my interjection. I did not catch the chaperone's name but can feel her eyes suspiciously judging my every move. 'Sometimes the winds of enthusiasm carry me beyond socially acceptable behaviour.'

'That's quite all right,' says Amelia in an icy tone. I tense, aware of our shared misery in this ridiculous situation. For Henry's sake I must try to enchant her so I offer a smile, though I cannot imagine it looks convincing.

Her sister is more generous. 'Mr Rooke, we are delighted to have someone with your knowledge on an outing such as this. You are up to date on all the fashions from Paris and an indispensable member of this party!' She and Henry are the only ones who appear to be enjoying themselves. Constance giggles easily at every small thing – perhaps she truly is so carefree, or she has a talent for hiding her troubles. Henry is animated, engaged and charming as usual. Am I the only one who wants to scream? 'Indeed, it is a wonder Mr Ashby can be so ignorant on these matters,' Constance teases, holding a pearl button up to Henry's coat. I cross my arms and clench my fists as I watch her.

'Yes, how do you stay such close friends when one of you has no interest in fashion?' Amelia laughs lightly.

My mind clouds as my eyes slowly find Henry's. The ladies wait for one of us to say something. I stutter, 'We share a fondness for…'

'…Theatre!' Henry interjects with a smile. 'We met at the Theatre Royal last year and both adore the comedic arts.'

I try to relax and the Hartwells turn their attention to a tray of fasteners. 'These will go well with my bonnet,' says Amelia, fingering some large ivory buttons.

'I suppose I must follow the Parisian trends for my work,' I say. 'Perhaps I would not care for fashion otherwise.' After all, clothing tells the story of a place and time more than it highlights an individual's character. What we wear is only a choice insofar as it is made within the limited confines of acceptable fashion at a particular moment.

Constance turns her attention from Henry and smiles at me. 'We must all stay informed, otherwise we might be taken advantage of by our dressmakers and spend far more than is necessary!' Everyone chuckles.

'And your staymakers too?' I ask, which silences the party. 'I must confess, I am surprised it does not bother you that I must work to earn my living.'

Henry glares at me, as angry as I have ever seen him. I know I've gone too far, but I can no longer stand the sick feeling in my stomach. Besides, he is too naive if he thinks my station is appropriate for a woman like Amelia Hartwell. I know it isn't – she can barely stand my company while her sister pursues Henry.

'Come now, don't be down on yourself. You're a highly skilled artisan,' he responds carefully, angling his body so the women can't see his facial expression. He gives me a scolding look, then blithely transitions as he turns back around. 'There are many respectable ways to make one's fortune now. Why, I've seen at least six families of craftsmen move on to my street in the last year!'

His words ring hollow in my ears. There is still so much work to do on Miss Maes' stays. Leather lining, outer silk. They will be finished in time – I just need a day to focus on them. It is a pity she will be leaving town after this order, as I could use another stable client. I will leave my card with her friend and cast my hopes for future orders on to her.

The sisters have the good grace to feign interest over a display of handkerchiefs – I don't even bother throwing them a glance, but face

Henry head-on. 'I suppose it's a matter of values, then. I find myself pitying those who do not need to work, for they have never learned to live with a sense of purpose and this lack of guidance displays itself in an unbecoming manner.'

He squares his shoulders. 'Surely you don't mean that.'

My thoughts stumble, blocked by jealousy and frustration. I look into Henry's eyes, see the tenderness and hurt in them, and realise no, of course I do not mean anything. Our situation is not his fault, and my provocations do nothing to help.

'I rather like these,' says Constance, holding up a silk ribbon in robin's-egg blue and a yellow lace ruffle. She either thinks we've ceased talking or has decided to ignore our conversation.

'Oh, how lovely!' says her sister.

Henry widens his eyes at me, indicating that I utter my approval too. My anger flares up again, but I resign myself to a prudent response. 'Most excellent choices – I'm sure you will enjoy wearing them this season.'

'Allow me to purchase them for you,' Henry tells her.

'How kind!' She beams at both of us.

I take a moment to collect myself as she hands the ribbons to Henry. He turns back around to walk towards the shopkeeper behind me, but imperceptibly pauses as he passes and gives me a look. There is more to discuss.

The ladies admire their new ribbons one last time, then everyone makes for the door. I lag behind, guilt beginning to challenge whether I should have acted as I did. Much as it stings to watch Henry courting someone, it's no excuse for being cruel. I blink and see Mr Arnold's boots kicking and then spasming intermittently in the empty air. Everything is slipping away – Henry, control over my shop responsibilities, my sense of belonging in London. I don't want to lose any of this, but do I have a choice?

I must apologise to the Hartwells, for Henry's sake if nothing else. If this plan of his is successful, I wonder if it would ever occur to him to apologise to me for the pain he has inflicted. Does he understand how much it costs me to watch him with Constance Hartwell, how much more it will cost both of us if he does marry her? I remember when he stormed into my shop just two days ago, the lines of concern on his face, how taut his jaw was. Of course he understands. The edges of my jealousy begin to wane and the heaviness in my chest lightens.

Outside the haberdashery, I turn to the group. 'This has been a lovely afternoon, though I do apologise for losing my temper earlier.' I meet the eyes of Amelia, Constance and, finally, save my most apologetic look for Henry.

'Of course, Mr Rooke,' says Constance sincerely, putting her hand on my arm. Amelia merely smiles and nods demurely, then says her goodbyes to Henry. They are so polite, almost to a fault. Is this who they are, or do they have something to hide?

Before I can take this thought any further, Henry opens a carriage door and helps the ladies inside. We stand next to each other, smiling falsely and waving dramatically as they drive away. When they round a corner, the tension between us starts to ease and he turns to face me. 'Thank you for apologising,' he says, leaning forward as if to take my hand.

I want to melt into him, but there is nothing more to say here on the street. We must each consider this plan of his and whether it will be possible, assuming Amelia would allow it, which is by no means certain. If she does, perhaps I can control my jealousy in the future or better bear my aching heart. Perhaps not. There is too much to do at my shop and not enough time with Henry now, so I simply reply, 'You're welcome.'

He knows I am preoccupied with work this week and gives me a strained smile. 'Let us write soon.'

I make my way back across the city. As I tread further east, each step brings a new worry about my shop – Mrs Daullers has placed another order, but when will I find the time to measure her again? There is also the stomacher to finish on our latest pair of stays for Mrs Hatchfield. New orders arrive every day, with some ladies even writing from their country homes. Still I wonder whether we will bring in enough money this month to pay our debts. If we are running late on an order, we cannot collect payment until it is finished.

I open the workshop door and survey the hum of activity in the shop since I stepped out to meet Henry and the Hartwells. At least Martha and I have remained focused and improved our efficiency as the new orders have piled up. I sit down at the workbench across from her. She snips a piece of thread, waxes it, and sews panels together before passing them to me for boning and lining. As time passes, my eyes grow sore and my fingertips ache with every whalebone shoved into place, but it will be worth it when orders die down again and we can take a break.

Martha has gone from strength to strength – I would not be surprised to find that she could do the work nearly as well as me if given the opportunity. Perhaps during a slower period, I could consider a short holiday with Henry. I check a design, measure, and begin a new running stitch along the front of these stays – I hardly remember who they're for, though the name is written on the pattern. What if the work does not let up – what if this success is permanent? It's difficult to imagine. Perhaps I would need to hire a few more workers and Martha could take on more responsibility, which I'm sure she would enjoy.

I shake out my hand and finish the boning, then reach for a strip of leather to sew along the top and bottom of the stays, but my hand grabs at the air. I get up and walk to the back of the shop where we have whole pieces of fabric laid out. I take a pair of heavy scissors and cut a thin strip of white leather, no wider than an inch, then return to my bench.

'Sir?' Martha calls from across the room.

'What is it?'

She's examining some papers – designs for Miss Maes, if I had to guess. 'These call for wool lining and black silk for the outer panels.'

'Yes, and?'

'We don't have any black silk here.'

I look out the window – dusk. The shops will still be open. 'Right, one of us will have to run out.'

She looks down nervously. 'I haven't seen black silk in the shops recently.'

I remember that these stays must be completed in the next two days so Miss Maes can make her escape across the Atlantic. 'I'll go. Continue sewing the primary panels so we can finish these when I return with the fabric.'

There's no time for this setback, but I must press forward. Martha nods, understanding the urgency of the situation, and I don't bother grabbing a wig or retying my hair before rushing out the door.

I first head to Mr Blankenship's shop – it's close by and I suspect he will work a little harder to find what I need, since I'm a loyal customer.

I press my hand against his glass door and push inside. As usual, he's right behind the counter. 'Mr Rooke! What a pleasant surprise.'

'My friend,' I attempt flattery, 'I'm in a slight rush – would you happen to have any black silk in the shop today?'

'Not something you ordered?' he asks.

'I'm afraid not.'

He furrows his brow and turns around, goes into his back room. He's gone for a while and, as the minutes tick past, I grow anxious. I glance through the shelves in the front room, rolls of linen blends laid out upon them. He returns from the back and I'm elated for half a second before seeing he is empty-handed.

'I'm terribly sorry – wish I could help, but we appear to be completely out. I have a few yards of a navy-blue silk, if that would suffice?'

I know it will not, so I thank him and hurry outside to the next shop I can think of.

Three hours and countless shops later, I'm no closer to finding the black silk required for Miss Maes' stays. How could I have left this to the last minute, what was I thinking? This affair with Henry is making me lose focus at a crucial time when I can ill afford it. He does not understand why I cannot be available in the middle of the workday, how hard I try to earn a basic living. I trudge down Gracechurch Street, eyes cast down, wondering what to do next. I could use a different colour of silk, but would need Miss Maes' approval first, and I shudder to think about the look on her face when she hears about my mistake. I could ask her for more time, but I know she does not have it. I curse my stupidity and myopia, turning down a side street and heading back to my shop. Tears sting my eyes – I'm backed into a corner. How will I find a way out of this?

Chapter Eleven

Now

I am in Lady Elina's rooms, sitting at a table with a stack of blank paper in front of me. My right hand is poised, quill hovering above a pot of ink, ready to work. For a fleeting second, I wonder what Henry would think if he saw me like this, looking so studious, before remembering that he mustn't find out. Now that I've settled into the idea, I'm looking forward to the prospect of posing as Lady Elina – not the act itself so much as learning how to do so. I was surprised at how intrigued I was by the discussion at the debating society and felt myself swept away by the possibilities of the conversation. Perhaps I have a knack for this, as she has suggested.

Several feet away, Lady Elina reaches up and pulls a book from her shelves. She taps its cover thoughtfully, then glances up again and takes another book down. Walking back towards me, she sweeps her skirts to the side and sits in the chair opposite.

'I think we should begin with John Locke.'

Carefully, I write down 'John Loque' on my paper, then glance at the book she is holding and correct my spelling. She flips through its pages and stops halfway through.

'He introduces the idea that there is a sort of contract between people and their governments. Essentially, there are rules that we must all follow or society crumbles. A straightforward example would be committing murder – without a law against killing each other, you might be stabbed at any point without recourse.'

I nod, this makes sense. Then, I remember Mr Arnold. The horror and shock of his gruesome death has not diminished over the years. 'But the government is allowed to kill people. So the rules do not apply equally.'

'That's right. The argument is that the government only kills someone when they have broken the law, which is in everyone's shared interests.'

'But suppose some laws are unfair?' Selfishly, I think first of myself, then remember Mr Cugoano and the treatment of those who are enslaved.

She beams at me, perhaps a little too generously. 'You have an inquisitive mind, Mr Rooke! Locke would answer that there is a certain level of agreement between our government and the people, which gives it legitimacy.'

I write down 'legitimate government', blinking my eyes to remain focused.

'Now, the aim of a legitimate government is to preserve the rights of its citizens.' She speaks quickly, with increasing zeal. 'I admit I take issue with whether this is actually what it does, for the reasons we've just discussed about unfair laws and which side to take when we consider public good versus individual rights. In any case, Locke uses this concept of the legitimate government to highlight the conditions under which rebellion might be appropriate.'

I catch her last sentence, but cannot understand how she reached it. I do not wish to appear idle or stupid, but know that I cannot imitate her without a thorough understanding of her knowledge. 'I'm sorry, Your Ladyship. Could you repeat that last part?'

Momentarily carried away by her enthusiasm, she pauses and searches my face. 'It's not essential,' she says. 'I was trying to build your foundation of political theory, but can see it will be too much to learn in the time we have. Let us jump ahead to the debates being had today.'

'Are you sure? It sounded important.'

'I think,' she begins, pressing her index finger under her chin, 'the best thing to do will be to move forward to contemporary subjects and then we can go back for historical context as needed.'

I nod, slouching back into my chair. She stands, puts the books back on the shelf, and crosses the room to her desk, where she picks up several pamphlets resting on it. I feel embarrassed that I could not keep up and shift in my seat.

She hands me the pamphlets with an imploring expression. I glance down at them, catch 'Vindication' and 'Burke', then look back up at her. 'In some ways, I am building on what thinkers like Ms Wollstonecraft have begun arguing – that our institutions have overstepped the mark and common citizens deserve a voice in how they are governed.'

I nod – this is a familiar pattern of thought.

'But I would like to take the argument further,' she continues, 'to ensure that women are equally included in this new world we are dreaming of building, and consider the ways our lives interlock by necessity – even if it means adjusting our present notions of individuality.'

I lean back, confused again. 'I understand that women's roles in some levels of society are equal to that of men,' which has certainly been my experience in the staymaking trade, 'but do you really imagine them taking an equal role in government?'

'Why, yes, Mr Rooke! It's a matter of moral principle as well as logic. As women integrate further into society, we will also require representation within the government to uphold our interests.'

'But if everyone has the same interests, then won't they be taken care of by those their male peers elect?'

She sighs and begins to sound impatient. 'You are not grasping the philosophical principle at the root of the argument. We are living through a time when more specific representation is demanded of government, not a generalised approach.'

I feel myself growing defensive and am tempted to remind her that it is me doing her the favour. 'I'm sorry, but it's a lot to grasp when you change subjects so quickly.'

'I am trying to distil these points as clearly as possible, but they are complicated and you will need to remain focused.'

Shame spreads up my cheeks. I look down, trying to bite my tongue, but before I do: 'How can you advocate for equal representation when you need a man to pose as you to your publisher and readers?'

She snaps up and is across the room in half a second. She cranes her neck upward and does not look at me. Immediately I know I've gone too far and want to apologise, but I feel suspended with fear, unable to move or breathe.

The air is electric and full. I cannot unclench the tension in my body, but I see Lady Elina's shoulders begin to rise and fall in slow, controlled breaths. Finally, she speaks to the painting hanging near her shoulder. 'My husband would never allow this publication to go forward if he knew about it. It is all very well to discuss my ideas at the debating society, but they will not carry the necessary weight for publication if they are seen to come from a woman. I must work within the system available while I fight for something better. You are doing me a favour for which I am very grateful, but I did not say it would be an easy task.'

I try to speak, but my throat is muggy. I clear it, then stand up. 'I'm sorry.'

She turns towards me and smiles her forgiveness, holding her hand out. I grasp it softly. 'And I apologise for my tone. Indeed, the difficulty of our endeavour makes this favour all the greater. I will not forget it.'

We carry on for another hour, each a little tentative and acquiescent so as not to deepen the bruises we have given each other.

'I do miss being in London, at the forefront of these debates,' she sighs at one point, smiling politely at me. 'You must miss the city too.'

I lift my brow in recognition of her sentiment, wanting to be honest but aware I must not say too much about the circumstances that brought me here. Henry and his control over every aspect of life at Stonehurst Manor hangs over both of us. 'Yes, the pulse of culture, the hum of so many different people from all walks of life in one place – it is difficult to forget.'

She smiles in understanding. 'I'm pleased we will both have a chance to return for this presentation of my work, even if it is nerve-wrecking for each of us in different ways.' Her expression shifts and her eyes search mine with curiosity. 'Why do you not return permanently? You are a talented dressmaker, surely you would not have trouble finding work.'

My blood slows, my limbs grow numb, and I take a breath to steady my voice. I knew she would ask about this again. Although I hope she cannot read my expression, how can I close myself off from her completely? 'I am not sure that remains the case,' I reply honestly, using the truth to muster as much confidence as possible. 'Besides, I am content at Stonehurst. There is a different kind of challenge living and working here, and challenges are how we grow.'

'That's true,' she replies. 'Still, it was good of you to leave London when Mr Ashby asked you to, all those years ago. I have never understood your friendship, but then I suppose there is so little about my husband that I can comprehend.'

It seems my heart has stopped completely. Lying to her has become more difficult as our friendship has deepened, but it is unthinkable that she should ever learn the truth – it would mean death for both me and Henry. 'He has been a loyal friend and patron,' I say deliberately, 'but always mindful of the difference in our stations.' I hope to flatter her but also change the subject: 'Unlike the way you have recently treated me, which is far warmer.'

She smiles at this. 'I do hope you will think of me as a friend and equal. You may always speak your mind plainly with me, for I have extensive training in the art of accepting criticism.' It's a warm sentiment, even if inaccurate. I will never be her equal as far as our social positions go, just as she will never be my equal in Henry's esteem.

When she suggests we stop for the afternoon shortly after this, I'm all too grateful to leave her rooms. I can still feel my cheeks burning – with embarrassment? Indignation? Compassion? Guilt? It is difficult to say. I think of how easy it would be to walk into Henry's office and tell him everything, and yet I cannot. Beyond his fury at his wife for attempting to publish a political discourse, I sense he would not understand why I went along with it for so long. He would abhor me for keeping her secret and detest the work itself, since his politics are more conventional. I will have to withhold this from him, just as I have hidden our love from her for all these years. We are all locked in a precarious balance, but it is a matter of survival.

–

The following week, I round a corner into the dining room and I nearly bump into a maid, Daisy, polishing flatware for the evening's meal. 'Excuse—' I start to say, then pause as I notice the fork she's holding. It's the King's Hourglass set. 'Is that for tonight?' I enquire.

'It is.'

This can only mean one thing. As nonchalantly as possible, I continue through the other side of the room, into the lounge, then double back and sneak towards Henry's office. Luckily the door is already ajar so I can slip through it quickly and walk straight up to his desk to demand: 'Is your father coming to dinner tonight?'

Henry looks up, not startled but a little bemused. 'Yes, didn't I tell you?'

'You most certainly did not.'

'Well,' he leans back in his chair, 'now you know, so what's the trouble?'

'You know perfectly well that I ask for advance notice so I can make myself scarce when he comes to visit. I'm far too anxious around him.'

I try to stay out of the way when Henry has guests, allowing him to shine on his own. It's also useful to keep away from Mrs Ferrers and her staff during these dinners – the servants always have a nervous hum about them when Mr Ashby Senior visits. It's understandable, for the man's brash nature knows no limits and one always has the sense his temper is moments from flaring up. His manner of speaking is abrupt and to the point; he rarely softens himself to suit the company. Despite slipping into the background, I find myself intimidated by him on the rare occasion we are in the same room. I don't know whether he dislikes me, tolerates me, or is completely indifferent. The first few times we met he kept forgetting who I was, which I suppose is as good a sign as one might hope for.

'I think it's charming.' Henry smiles.

'Why didn't you tell me?'

'It was organised at the last moment!'

I don't quite believe him – he never takes responsibility when he forgets something. He hides behind his position of power in the house, using a veneer of lofty disengagement to seem above suspicion. All the same, I know there's nothing I can do but forgive him. What good does it do to get upset over these trivial things? 'It's fine – I'll just keep to myself for a few days.'

'He's only coming for dinner, Matthew.'

'That may be, but you are always disagreeable after he visits.'

I can see he wants to respond, but bites his tongue. He pushes his shoulders down in determination. 'Don't worry, my love, we still have our visit to Bath in two months and then we can focus entirely on each other.'

Hasn't he lied enough for one conversation? This trip will not happen, I can feel it. 'Yes,' I return, mustering up a half-hearted smile. 'Well, I'd better be on my way downstairs.'

'Come now, Matthew—' he begins, but I do not want to keep bickering over what we cannot change. I spin around on my heel and leave his office.

With no time to make arrangements, I decide to spend the evening in my room and study Lady Elina's notes on equal rights. The wind has picked up and rain sprays the window. I smooth the wool blanket on my bed and begin to sit down, when there's a knock at my door.

'What is it, Mrs Ferrers?' I call, getting up. But when I open the door, Lady Elina is on the other side.

'Oh good, you're reading the Diderot,' she says, seeing it on my bed.

I cannot respond, still stunned to see her here at this time of the evening. It is unprecedented, but I recover after a moment. 'How... how can I help, Your Ladyship?'

She quickly turns her focus back to me, fixing me in place with an intense expression. 'I would like to invite you to dine with me and Henry this evening – given your friendship and his father's visit, it would be nice to have another person at the table for conversation.'

This is one of my worst nightmares, trapped in a room with Henry's father and no opportunity for escape. I try to keep my tone light as I reply, 'I really don't think it's wise, Your Ladyship. You know I do not dine with the family and I am not well acquainted with Mr Ashby's father.'

'Goodness, after all these years?' she muses, and my skin prickles nervously before she adds, 'I do envy you.'

I chuckle good-naturedly, then move to close my door. 'Have a good evening, ma'am.'

'Oh, please Mr Rooke – it is dreadfully dull when the two of them get going and then I have no one to talk to.'

I'm surprised she cannot participate – although she does not interfere with the way the manor is run, she certainly has the knowledge for it. 'I am sorry they leave you unmoored within their conversations.'

'Indeed, I would so enjoy having a friend at the table – someone warm, who understands me. You appreciate how quiet my life in Stonehurst is... I won't pretend it isn't useful at times, but one does miss regular company.'

I remember that her family is still abroad and has never visited. Like me, Henry is her only family here and yet she is bound by her duty to him and his father in a way that I have mercifully avoided. The sand grains of my empathy tumble until I feel myself giving in. 'Very well... how much time do I have?'

She beams with gratitude. 'Twenty minutes. Thank you – I'm sure we will all have a delightful time together.' She steps back over the threshold, then turns around and murmurs, 'Remember not to mention anything of our lessons.'

I nod, and she grins in delight at our shared confidence.

The short notice is a blessing in a way because it dampens my opportunity to become nervous. As soon as Elina is out the door, I change into a fresh shift, find my nicest pair of breeches and my shirt with the most ruffles. A waistcoat to match the breeches and a contrasting coat in bright emerald should make me presentable enough. There isn't time to shine my buckles, but they'll be under the table most of the night. A fresh tie for my hair, powder for my wig and face, and I'm as ready as possible under the circumstances. I traverse the house towards the family's quarters.

'...All the way from Tunis!' I hear Henry chortle from the doorway to the drawing room. He turns around, sees me, and his smile strains at the edges. Lady Elina must have told him that she invited me, but that does not mean interacting in front of her and his father will be easy for us. 'Ah, Mr Rooke. Delighted you'll be joining us this evening,' he says as I awkwardly cross the threshold. The familiar room now seems fuzzy and strange, but I take one last breath and plunge inside. Henry, his father, and Lady Elina are all standing around the card table with glasses of wine. I hope my nervous smile comes off as cordial and walk over to them. Henry pats my shoulder and I feel my expression crack. 'Father, you remember Lady Elina's dressmaker, Mr Rooke?'

The old gentleman furrows his thick eyebrows and stares at me. 'Let me see, Mr Rooke... were you here at Christmas?'

'I was, sir, but I didn't dine with you.'

'Well, it's very good to meet you now,' he replies. I avoid Henry's gaze, afraid I will lose my composure. Through the windows, I catch a flash of lightning.

'I believe supper is ready – shall we make our way in?' Lady Elina asks, gesturing towards the dining room to the right. We shuffle inside – I'm careful to let the others in ahead of me, not knowing where to sit – and take our seats around the long table. As we do, a rumble of thunder rolls through the room. I feel so small and far away from everyone – this is nothing like the table in the kitchen, which is half the size and serves three times as many people.

The Three

This is one of the few times Henry, Lady Elina, and I have all been in the same room together. I must strike a balance between them without letting either of them catch on to my connection with the other. And then, of course, there is Henry's father. His eyes follow every small movement, calculating and cruel. When he speaks, he is without mercy.

The kitchen staff place bowls of pale green soup in front of us. Do the butler's eyes linger on me for just a second longer than necessary? The other servants must wonder why I am seated here this evening, even if they cannot agrue with it. I lean over the soup and sniff, catching a strong scent of mint.

'Did you have a chance to go over the estimates I sent over last week?' Henry asks his father genially.

'Oh, let us begin with more intriguing topics!' Lady Elina intercedes in a warm tone. 'Did you hear that the king of France has fled?'

'He should if he knows what's good for him,' Henry's father mumbles. 'It's only a matter of time before those bloodthirsty rebels set upon him.'

'I think they're quite brave,' Lady Elina returns. 'Don't you agree, Mr Rooke?'

I pause with my spoon in mid-air, glancing down the table at her. She smiles in the expectant, engaged way she always has when we are discussing these topics in her rooms. Henry's expression is curious and curt, his brow furrowed. 'Of... of course, Your Ladyship,' I respond. 'They endeavour to write a new future for their country.'

'Indeed!' She beams. 'And I believe they will show Britain the path forward.'

Henry's father gulps down his wine. 'We are well aware of your senseless liberal proclivities and the weak-minded ministers you use them to befriend.'

Elina is about to answer him when the door opens and trays of supper are served. Pigeon pie, blanched runner beans, and boiled turnips with butter. Another flash of lightning makes the shadows of tree branches bolt across the wall through the windows. I swallow, then gingerly pick up my fork and knife.

Henry attempts to sweep aside any awkwardness. 'Anyway, I think you'll be pleased with the numbers I sent last week. With the favourable weather this season, many of our farmers are expecting a high yield.'

'I have everything in hand,' his father says. 'I'd rather discuss your legacy.'

Henry, Lady Elina, and I all sit a bit straighter, though none of us look at each other. I feel the air shift between us all, and I'm sure the old man does too.

He continues. 'You will need to name an heir at some point, since you have none of your own and wouldn't wish to create any trouble with the rest of the family.'

'I know that perfectly well,' Henry returns, a bit terse.

'Especially if you've got a bastard running around somewhere in one of the houses in town.'

'Father.'

'Men in our family have never had trouble producing an heir until now,' the old man says with a sideways glance at Lady Elina. I see her face flush red, but her jaw is fixed shut.

'You've no right to speak to my wife like this under our own roof—'

'But it's still my roof, boy.'

The wind picks up and black leaves reach out from the darkness outside to tap against the windows. Henry tries again. 'I have tried to make up for my... shortcomings... by studying the estate and have made great strides. Just last year, we brought in an extra six per cent.'

'Don't take credit for my work. It's as if you're still the same naive boy you were when you first returned to the manor after your London years. What would your mother think if she were still alive?' He sits back in his chair, takes a drink. His eyes seem to pin Henry in place. 'You'll produce an heir if you want to collect your inheritance, and that's final.' Now he slowly turns towards my side of the table, as if just remembering my presence. The candles flicker, distorting everyone's features. I feel his eyes creep over my hands, coat, and face. 'I hope you can forgive our little family disagreements, Mr Rooke,' he says with a sickening grin. 'Though why I'm expected to share the table with a dressmaker at all is beyond me.'

'He is here as my guest,' Lady Elina says with more force than expected. Loudly, she picks up her cutlery and continues eating.

My throat solidifies, my hands tremble just a little. I look over at Henry, trying to share the pain this man has imposed upon us. But he looks straight ahead, frozen. At last, he sighs and keeps eating as well. I want to melt into my chair and onto the floor. I take a deep breath, then

The Three

pick up the elegant silver fork Daisy had been cleaning this morning – it feels impossibly heavy in my hand. I move some turnips around my plate, but cannot take a bite.

Chapter Twelve

Then

The bell jingles merrily, contrasting with my low spirits. Martha turns around expectantly – her eyes fall when she spots my empty hands. I do notice that she doesn't seem surprised.

'No luck?'

All I can do is shake my head. I walk to my bench and pull a different set of stays across so I can add shoulder straps to them. Martha is still watching me.

'What are we going to do?'

'I haven't decided yet,' I return. 'Let me think a moment.'

She returns to her work and we carry on in silence. I run through various scenarios in my mind, trying to determine the next step to take. I blink my eyes to keep them focused, then realise Martha has left her bench. I startle to see her standing in front of me, pinning her bodice and smoothing her apron to go out.

'Where—?'

'I've had an idea, but I need to check,' she says before spinning around and running out the door.

Perhaps thirty minutes later, she's back and carrying a small package. My chest swells in anticipation and she doesn't leave me waiting – she approaches my workbench, sets the package down, and opens it to reveal about two yards of pristine black silk.

Every question jumps from my mouth in one second. 'Ho… wh… wher…?'

'I noticed yesterday that Mrs Bettes' laundry had this drying outside and wondered if she could be convinced to sell it.'

'How much?'

She pauses briefly, pursing her lips. 'One pound.'

I breathe out – twice what we usually pay for such fabric, and it almost negates any profit from this job. Still, it is worthwhile to complete the work we set out to do. 'Martha,' I cannot hide the admiration in my voice, 'that was very resourceful of you, well done.'

She doesn't blush like usual when receiving a compliment, just bows her head and swiftly returns to her station. 'I'm glad I was able to help.'

It's now dark but we still have hours of work ahead of us. I add some coal to the fire and light a few candles, then stretch my fingers and back before sitting down again and pressing on.

—

After an exhausting week and four new clients satisfied, I return to Gerrard Street to deliver Miss Maes' stays. I knock on the door with a little urgency – as if delivering the stays a few seconds earlier will make any difference. The footman opens the door and I immediately sense something is wrong.

'I'm here to see Miss Maes,' I tell him.

'I'm afraid she's not here,' he responds.

I try to suppress a wave of annoyance – she had said she would be home now and I was hoping to collect the remainder of my payment this afternoon. 'Do you know when she'll return?'

He hesitates and I see a quick calculation behind his eyes. 'I'm afraid I do not.'

Something is amiss and he is trying to keep it hidden from me. I hazard a guess and ask in a low voice, 'Has she departed early?'

This seems to win his confidence and he leans forward, keeping his grip firmly on the door. 'Only an hour ago, Miss Horne demanded she take her things and leave.'

'Good heavens! Where has she gone?'

He shrugs. 'Didn't get a carriage from here – I don't think it was offered to her. Last I saw she'd picked up her bags and walked that way.' He points eastward down the pavement, then looks at the package of wrapped stays under my arm. 'Shall I... take that for you?'

My mind whirls – where could she be? Only an hour gone and carrying her own luggage, she can't have travelled far. 'No, thank you,' I tell the footman. 'I will try to find her.'

I begin walking east down the pavement, stitching together a map of the city in my imagination as I go. At the end of this street is the Golden Swan – might she have stopped there to rent lodgings? A quarter mile away is St Martin's Lane – perhaps she will seek refuge in the church there? Half a mile away is... of course, the Thames!

I leap across the street and find a carriage. 'Billingsgate!' I tell the driver. She was already planning to leave within a matter of days and if Miss Horne kicked her out, surely she would go straight to the river to begin her journey.

Once at the docks, I look for a departures board or someone to ask about upcoming passage to the Americas. As I spin around to get my bearings, I spot her by some miracle, emerging from a building and lugging her bags behind her. Her face is flushed and her hair is limp with sweat.

'Oh, Mr Rooke!' she exclaims when she sees me.

'Is everything all right?' I enquire, rushing forward and grabbing a large leather case next to her.

Together, we stumble towards the river before pausing for a break. 'I can't believe you found me!' she pants. 'Miss Horne found out about my plans to leave and when she demanded to know why, I told her the truth. She kicked me out immediately.' She tugs her handkerchief down from around her neck and dabs her temples.

'Have you booked passage for this afternoon, then?'

She nods. Her demeanour is as valiant as usual, but she must feel the rejection by her friend most dearly. After all, she was once staying in her home and now their last words to each other will forever be of bitterness and anger.

'I am sorry Miss Horne was not more understanding.' I do not know what else to say, so extend the wrapped stays out to her. 'I brought these for you.'

She takes the package from my outstretched hand and opens one of her bags to place it inside. A cool breeze comes off the water and presses my coat against my knee. She stands and sighs. 'What a mess. I can't really blame her, but I wish the whole thing had never happened.'

I nod. There are real perils to falling in love and it can be a matter of life and death, as I know myself. Relations with a woman have never been something I've had to worry about, but of course the threat of pregnancy would be petrifying. 'Without wanting to be impertinent, would it not be easier to give the child away or demand marriage from the father? Do you really want to start fresh in a new country with no friends and a child to care for?' I feel self-conscious – hopefully she understands I am asking out of genuine concern.

She looks over at me, squinting in the afternoon sun. 'I know it won't be easy, but I welcome the chance to begin afresh,' she says. 'Better to start over in a new land than be weighed down by the constrictions of conventionality. I do not fear being different or mocked, only being limited.'

I cannot imagine such a dramatic departure from my life here – in addition to Henry and my shop keeping me happy and busy, I would never leave London by choice. The most dynamic city in the world, for a humble cabin in the American woods? There's all the adventure one needs right here. 'I'm glad you're able to go and live on your terms.'

'Thank you.'

I look out at the Thames, row upon row of ships waiting to depart. They're so close, you could walk from one deck to another. 'When do you leave? Would you like me to stay with you until it is time to depart?'

'You needn't trouble yourself, Mr Rooke,' she responds with a smile. 'I will find a wherryman to help me with my luggage and bring me on board.'

I nod admiringly, then frown in deliberation over what I must ask. 'I do not wish to be awkward, but if I could just get the rest of my payment?'

'My goodness, of course! How could I forget something so important?' she says, fumbling with a pocket in her skirt. She pulls out a couple of small coins, then looks confused and tries the other side. 'Just a moment,' she says, bending back over her travelling case and sorting through her effects. 'I know I've got more in here somewhere... the passage was more than I'd been led to believe, but I wanted to be safe in my own quarters...'

She pulls out a book, flips through its pages with increasing urgency. I sneak a glance at her face, which has begun to turn pink. I feel my own cheeks flush and look down at my shoes, not wishing to embarrass her. I cannot help myself. 'Miss Maes,' I say, 'it's all right.'

'No, Mr Rooke, you've spent time and effort on these, not to mention the cost of the materials. I won't have you thinking I ordered them without intending to pay.'

'It's no trouble,' I tell her, wincing a little inside as I remember the black silk. 'I hope your adventure is a success.' Can she feel my sincerity? I do admire her bravery – the journey is dangerous and the risks are high. But she's certainly determined and perhaps that, with some luck, will see her through the worst of her challenges.

She seems to understand, shaking her head a little. 'I can never repay your kindness.' She gives me a warm smile and clasps my hand. 'Thank you.'

I leave her on the quayside and walk back up the hill towards the Tower. Bells from a nearby church begin to toll. Quarter to four – I pick up my pace and look for a carriage to take me west again. I have an appointment with Henry that I can't be late for.

Exhausted from my second time crossing the city today, I nearly roll out of the carriage in front of the Hartwells' rented home. When I ring the bell, I am ushered into a square drawing room with high lavender walls. Sitting on the sofa is Henry, with Constance next to him. Amelia is across from them, and all three turn their faces up in anticipation as I am shown in. I gulp some air and try to smile. 'Good afternoon! Apologies if I am late – I took an unforeseen trip to the Pool.'

'How thrilling,' says Amelia in a flat tone.

'Do be seated, Mr Rooke.' Constance gestures to the place on the sofa next to Amelia. As I sit, the lavender walls seem to close in on me and I try to focus on Amelia filling my bowl of tea. I attempt a grin, then raise the delicate china to my lips carefully, dreading somehow breaking it and upsetting the party. Across from me, Henry and Constance giggle softly. My heart pangs, but I try to ignore it.

Amelia wears a bright blue chintz gown with a floral design. It's trimmed with saffron-yellow bows, very fashionable. She sits straight, her stays resting square in the centre of her frame. But none of this matters – her voice drifts back into my periphery. '…the cause of your adventure to the London Pool?'

I take a breath, aware she is judging my every word.

'A friend's voyage was more sudden than I expected, that is all.' I can feel Henry's attention on me, his curiosity piqued by the word 'friend', and suppress a smile.

Amelia nods, then wafts her tea with a sigh. 'Orange blossom is such a fitting flavour for springtime, don't you agree?'

'Oh yes. It's a delightful flavour.'

She seems pleased about this, but continues looking at me, waiting for additional conversation. What can I ask this woman I have no interest in?

'Tell me, Miss Amelia, when do you return to Somerset?'

She looks towards her sister and Henry. 'In just three days, I'm afraid.'

Am I to withstand another three days of this agony? What would it be like to carry on with this sort of conversation every day, watching Henry with his wife across the table? My breath is shallow, my cravat suffocating. I resign myself to the obvious reply: 'Well, I shall be very sorry to see you leave London.'

She turns her attention back to me with a cold stare. 'You don't mean that.'

I nearly fall backward from such a sharp, direct statement. Focusing on retaining my composure, I set down my tea bowl a little too hard – everyone looks at me when they hear the clatter.

'Apologies – it seems the tea is so strong, it has a mind of its own!' I say, attempting to recover. Henry grins nervously, then returns his attentions to Constance.

I turn to Amelia, trying to understand what she hides beneath her aloof expression. She watches her sister and Henry with an almost hungry look in her eyes, the hint of a smile every time they laugh together. Whatever secret she is guarding, I do not think it has to do with me.

I lean in and speak in a low voice. 'Are you nervous about going home?'

Her eyes fly to meet mine and she takes a breath, calculating. She folds her hands over each other nervously. 'My sister has been close to an officer stationed there,' she says softly, 'but his fortunes are not great enough to marry. Nevertheless, she has grown very attached to him.'

This is quite a confession. 'Why would you share this information with me?' Perhaps she senses a hesitation from Henry and wishes to do away with the charade.

'It is imperative that Mr Ashby offers his hand to her before we leave for Somerset,' she urges in a whisper. 'I worry she will return to Mr Edwards if she does not have a new commitment arranged.'

'I see.' While I understand her concern, I do not expect Henry to consider proposing so soon. We are still getting to know these women and it's equally possible he won't propose at all. But Amelia seems to genuinely fear what her sister may do, so I try to sound reassuring when I add, 'I will speak to him.'

She breathes a sigh of relief, her posture relaxing slightly. 'Thank you. Would you like a biscuit?' she asks, gesturing to a plate a little awkwardly, but with more wamth than before. I shake my head, my thoughts already turning to the future when I can be free of this stifling home.

Later, Henry and I wave goodbye to the Hartwells as his carriage pulls away from their front door. 'I think that went very well,' he tells me, pushing back into his seat and closing his eyes. Is he more fond of Constance than I realised? I bite my tongue, knowing I must wait until we have more privacy to speak.

Martha is on errands this afternoon, so the coach drops us at the end of my alley. We pass through the shop door and I don't wait for the bell to cease its jingle before finding a bottle of gin and pouring us two glasses. I set Henry's down in front of him. 'It was very difficult to watch you with Miss Hartwell. Flirting, touching her arm… it was agonising.'

He reaches up to gently clasp my wrist, slides his palm down until our fingers weave together. 'You know I don't mean it – I wish it were you.'

I sit down across from him, Amelia's words swirling in my mind. 'I am not sure this plan is wise… perhaps… perhaps there is another way.'

He looks at me quizzically, then shakes his head. 'I'm afraid there is not. I will propose to Miss Hartwell, which will then allow you to offer your hand to her sister.'

'What? So soon?' I am startled – weren't we simply trying on this option? I never imagined he would move forward so quickly.

'This is what we must do to be together,' he tells me with resignation.

My heart begins pounding faster. 'We *won't* be together – we'll be mere acquaintances who sneak into each other's rooms a few times a year.'

'No! We'll see each other all the time – dinners, cards, hunting parties. Even if…' he stammers. 'Even if we're not together like we are now, we'll still be part of each other's lives.'

My pulse quickens with a sudden realisation and I cannot hold it back. 'It will be an incomplete life. Our love will not survive it.'

His hand tightens over my fingers. 'What are you saying?'

I feel helpless, the truth dropped on top of me without any exertion required at all. I must do him the honour of meeting his eyes. 'I can't do it. I cannot marry her.'

For an eternity, neither of us move. Even the dust previously dancing in the sunbeams appears to stand still. There's tension between us, a connection about to break. I try to savour these last moments before it does.

Henry sucks in his breath. 'So you're abandoning me. You would have me face this life alone?'

'I would have you stay here, with me. We might carve out some kind of happiness together.'

He stands, pressing his hands against his wig. 'You know that's impossible. Abandon my family – my responsibilities? Without them, what am I?'

'You're mine,' I plead, but I know he won't change his mind. 'I simply cannot live so much of my life as a lie.'

'And that's what I'm doing, is it?'

Paralysis creeps over me. 'You know what you must do. I'm sorry that I cannot follow your example.'

He looks at me, more than a little petulant. 'It's easy for you to take such a stand with nothing at stake – your parents are dead and you have no estate to provide for.'

His fury comes quick and easy, and a rush of anger swells in my chest to meet it. 'I see – I'm not as important as you, is that what you're saying?'

'I'm saying I have a place within society that I must consider – my decisions are not merely my own, but impact other people – so perhaps yes, you are less important. I think you would feel the weight of this more heavily if you were of my station.'

His expression is unlike anything I have seen on him before, twisted and ugly. He might hate the words as soon as they are out of his mouth, but I no longer care. I step up close to him, jutting my chin out. 'You are not as significant as you imagine. My decisions do not impact other people? Look at where you are standing! My life threads through countless others and there are many whose existence I financially sustain.'

He snorts. 'What does this place bring in – five hundred a year?'

White-hot ire explodes in my mind but my tone is steady. 'Get out. I don't want you in my shop, my bed, or my heart any longer.'

This knocks him speechless. He stumbles backward a little, but regains his grace and confidence as he reaches the door. 'Very well.' He saunters out.

Suddenly exhausted, I sit down at a workbench. My chest is tight, my throat closes up. I stifle a sob with the back of my hand, trying to choke down the forces bubbling up inside me. Blood thunders in my ears, so I don't hear the door creak open or the footsteps behind me until Martha's face appears.

'Sir?' she asks tentatively. 'That man… was he… are you…?'

I don't need to ask her if she's seen and heard everything – I already know the answer. I slowly turn towards her. Will she betray me?

Chapter Thirteen

Now

The grass is tall and sweet from a summer of healthy rain. Lady Elina throws a blanket down in front of me, points at one end: 'You can set the books down there.' As I do she sits down, turns her face up towards the sun. 'It's so lovely to be outdoors for a change.'

I join her on the blanket – it doesn't seem necessary to wait to be invited at this point. We've continued meeting since the awkward, painful dinner with Henry's father and it is infinitely more pleasant to be here with her now, both of us away from our Stonehurst responsibilities. The house is barely visible through the grove of trees and birds chirp sweetly. I take in the woodland surrounding us, admiring the different shades of green, before my eyes fall back to the materials we've brought out with us. I'm about to ask which book she wants to start with when she opens her eyes and blinks at me.

'Let's begin. What did you make of Kant's *Critique of Practical Reason*?'

She always has a way of making me feel put on the spot, like I'm already behind in our conversation. Yet I know that she genuinely wants to hear my thoughts, and there is something exhilarating about it. My nerves creep in, but I remind myself that I must try to speak with confidence if I'm to represent her in London next week. How has the time passed so quickly? 'I liked what he said about personal freedom but many of his finer points were lost on me.'

She nods and speaks brightly. 'That's quite all right, Mr Rooke. We needn't go too far into the details – I just wanted you to see how he writes about the law and individuality.'

I nod. Speaking with her and asking questions does much more to assist my comprehension of the books than the authors themselves do.

'We are beginning to see the tides of conversation turning,' she continues, 'and there is increasing interest in granting rights to more individuals. But who will still be excluded in this new world order, and what of interdependency?'

'Interdependency?'

'Yes,' she replies enthusiastically. 'It was you and Mr Cugoano who helped me see that our rights are collective, not merely individual. As I have worked on my own theories, I've realised that we must account for collective responsibility too.'

I squint, hoping I am still following along. 'But won't we accomplish that by opening up individual rights for everyone?'

She sighs and picks at her dress, a patterned Indian chintz I made last year. 'I hope so. In many ways, we are at the beginning of these conversations, but for now I notice more emphasis on what our government owes us, where I feel we should explore the responsibility we each have to larger society. But as you say, hopefully in time this will change and my book will be one voice in the discussion.'

A wave of fear rolls over me as I remember how soon the meeting is and I suddenly feel sick to my stomach. I cannot let her down.

She looks at me sympathetically, reading my expression. 'Are you nervous?'

'How could I not be? You have studied these topics for decades – I've had one summer.'

'Mr Rooke,' she puts her hand on mine and it is surprisingly comforting, 'you are entirely capable. I will be there at the back of the room, and will give you notes for the finer points. You already have the confidence and knowledge to convincingly make the broader arguments.' She sits back, leaning on her hand. 'In truth, it is only the question-and-answer portion where you will have to think on your feet. I have every faith in you.'

I wince at the thought of it – a room full of intellectuals, their fingers jabbing in my face as their voices raise complex questions above my mumbles. Elina's book will fail, it will be my fault and, worst of all, the public will not benefit from her work. And they ought to, for she has something unique to say, adding to the new ideas being deliberated. My humiliation will be nothing compared to this loss for her.

She looks at me, reading my expression. 'No matter how the event goes, I shall always be grateful to you for helping my words and ideas reach this important audience. There is no one I trust more.' For a moment, we bask together in this warm reflection.

Imagining the crowd with their wigs and stern faces passing judgement on me, I realise they are all men in my mind's eye, as they will most likely be at the meeting itself, as these events have always been, and suddenly I understand. 'If we do not appreciate how we all depend on each other, we simply repeat the same patterns and political systems as before. How can we create a new beginning without first recognising who makes up our society now?'

'Precisely!' She beams at me. 'Individual liberties do matter, but our negotiating power will never work if we are fractured and do not make room for everyone to see where they belong. We must be prepared to understand what these freedoms might mean for *every* individual, and then align our shared interests.'

I nod, pleased her ideas are beginning to crystallise. Throughout these lessons, I have felt my mind unfurling and expanding in a way that I've only previously experienced through designing garments, and the empowerment is intoxicating. I still doubt whether I can do her work justice but she leans back again to face the sun, her expression relaxed, and I start to believe that, together, we can make this plan succeed.

—

The next morning, Henry and I are in bed together. I laugh as he tries to worm his cold feet between mine, the constant give-and-take dynamic we have. Since the dinner with his father, we've been distant and it's a relief to return to our routine.

'He has never understood me properly,' Henry is saying. 'My whole life I've tried to please him, yet it's never enough.'

'Why do you keep trying?' I ask.

He looks at the ceiling, thoughtful. 'I suppose somewhere inside, I still believe I can obtain his approval. Eventually, he must see reason – otherwise, why have I struggled this long? What will it have been for?'

I look down and away from him, not wishing to hurt his feelings. If his father does not value him now, he never will. Henry is unwilling to accept it, and I do not wish to argue it with him yet again. Once, there were days when I could tell him that our love justified his existence, that the memories we shared and the future we were building together would be enough. But he could never fully believe it, and now I'm not sure I do either.

I lean over to grab my clothes on the floor, then begin dressing. Henry continues musing. 'When I meet Mr Gerrald in Bath, he will provide additional insights to improve the estate. Father will see that I can be trusted with his legacy.'

Oh yes, the trip to Bath. I forgot he had arranged everything at last. I smile, thinking of our chance to be alone again. 'Will we go for tea and Sally Lunns?'

He laughs. 'Of course, anything you like.'

'When do we depart?'

'Next week! Oh Matthew, it will be such a relief to get away at last.'

Next week? How could he not have told me earlier? 'I didn't realise it was so soon! You have not mentioned anything for over a month.'

'Yes, it took some time to find the appropriate window and arrange everything. But it's all settled now and we shall have a grand time.' He leans in for a quick kiss but, as he does, we hear the tinkle of china outside – Thomas coming in with Henry's breakfast.

Terror seizes me as I hurl myself to the floor and dart under the bed. We are normally careful to watch the time, but I'm distracted today. This is the third instance where I've had to hide under the bed and I hold my breath, listening to Thomas greet Henry and set down the breakfast tray. Henry smooths the strain from his voice in a way that I hope is imperceptible to anyone but me. When Thomas opens the door to leave, I shift uncomfortably in my cramped hiding place. No matter how long I have lived under this roof, even with Henry's protection, the threat of being found out is constant. I have never quite grown accustomed to that sense of peril always lurking just around the corner.

With Thomas gone, I can scurry out from under the bed and brush the dust from my shoulders. Henry and I stare at each other, relieved but also unnerved. It's close shaves like this that remind us it only takes one person, whether they are a servant, a villager or, heaven forbid, Lady Elina, to bring an end to our entire existence as we know it. It's an anxiety-ridden way to live, but we both know there is nothing we can do to change things. 'Do you have everything?' he asks softly, and I nod, glancing around the bedroom to check before stepping outside.

It isn't until I'm back in my own room that I remember our earlier conversation: Henry expects me to accompany him to Bath next week, but Lady Elina needs me in London. I must disappoint one of them, yet will not be able to explain my reasons. What will I do? How can I choose between them?

Chapter Fourteen

Then

Martha watches me, and I stare back at her. The question of Henry hangs between us. The only remaining uncertainty is how I will respond, what each of us will do next.

I consider my options. I could try to explain his presence away, but that feels hopelessly naive. Threatening her is another direction to take, but risky because if she pushes back, it would put me in more peril than her. I could beg her not to say anything, but then I will be admitting the truth and disgracing myself as her superior. There are no good choices.

At last I cast my eyes down, shuffle the broadsheet on the table – I don't know why. Henry's words still sting my memory and I can't think clearly about what to say to Martha. I avoid her eyes as I stammer out, 'That man… whatever you may think, it's not… it hardly matters anyway.'

She makes a quick movement, either towards me or perhaps she's flinching? 'I expect it does matter. I'm not as naive about the world as you might suspect,' she says.

I have never spoken in-depth to anyone about Henry's and my relationship. Very few people are even aware that we know each other, much less our true feelings. As I think about how I can explain it to Martha, I'm stuck in place – my words caught somewhere down at the bottom of my stomach. Each time I think I've gathered my thoughts and begin to open my mouth, my mind clouds over again. I do not know what I want in this situation – I'm caught between my instinct to stay safe and hide from Martha's questions, and the desire to have someone besides Henry know who I am. Can I trust her with the truth?

'Mr Ashby… Henry…' I stop again and sigh, then sit down and lay my arms open upon the table. She watches me, unmoving, as I try to find the right words. 'Have you ever been walking alongside St Paul's, when suddenly the bells peal out? First you're startled, but you recover and gaze up at the cathedral, in awe of the heavenly sound. Not seeing or hearing fully, you simply let their power and wonderful resonance wash over you. That's how he makes me feel.' Once I've uttered the words, a sort of relief slows down my pulse, but still I can't quite meet her eye. I fiddle with the sleeve on my left arm, afraid I won't be able to continue if I stop. 'As the days begin to tighten around me and become impossible to bear, he's my reprieve. When our eyes meet across a room, it's the most exquisite feeling in the world. Everything I take delight in – this city, my work… somehow it all culminates together in one person: him.' I glance at her again – she has not moved. 'I don't expect you to understand, but we share something… unique.'

She does not respond to any of this. I tap my fingers on the broadsheet nervously but carry on.

'Where once I had nothing but my work, I now have lightness and connection. I belonged to the city, perhaps – but now I belong to him. Where life lacked meaning, he has provided affinity. My concerns used to be seams and laces, but now I am fastened to him. Or at least, I thought I was.'

I dare not look at Martha again – her stillness would hurl me over the edge and I've already had the air knocked out of me with the realisation that those feelings Henry once lit up inside me have nowhere to go now. He is gone, taking my happiness with him. Allowing my head to hang down, I lift my hand to pre-emptively cover the tears I feel on their way, when I see the headline on the broadsheet I've been fidgeting with.

RAID ON THE BIRD'S NEST COFFEE HOUSE –
NEW SENTENCING

'No…' I hear myself murmur as I jolt upright, grabbing my jacket from the table in front of me. I practically knock the bell off the door as I twist my arms into their sleeves and run outside.

'Mr Rooke! Mr Rooke!' Martha calls behind me, but I hardly register her voice. I tear through the streets, pushing past carriages and shoppers until I reach Soho. Sweat dampens my neck and my heart pounds but I don't stop, rushing forward through the door of Mother Mack's.

Normally boisterous and smelling of gin, the place is empty. Chairs and stools are scattered sideways across the floor, quickly abandoned in a moment of panic. How many men did the constables grab, and what horrific punishment will they face? I think back to the hanging and nearly collapse with the unbearable pain of imagining a familiar face up on the scaffold. I collect myself, then pick up a seat and gently set it upright, my hand lingering on the warm grain of the wood. It must have been a night like any other, jovial and full of laughter, until the whistles blew. So much joy and merriment, scattered perhaps forever.

I hear the faint tinkle of glass and follow it behind the bar and into the kitchen, where Geoff, Mother Mack's husband, stands over a basin. He moves slowly – painfully? – as he swirls the water inside each glass and places it gingerly on the table next to him. I clear my throat and he turns around with raised eyebrows.

'Oh, hello, Mr Rooke,' he says, turning back around. 'We're closed, as you can see.'

'I heard about the raid,' I say. 'What happened? Is everyone all right?'

'They just came in last week, started grabbing men and making arrests,' he replies. 'Got me and the missus early on. Broke half the glassware while they were at it.'

'I'm glad you've been freed.'

'Wish I wasn't. They let me off because I'm always back here and no one associates me with the Bird's Nest. But my wife... lots of men said they'd seen her here as the proprietress. I can't blame them – it's the truth after all – but now she's...' His voice trembles.

'What?' I ask, remembering the sharp, foreboding angles of the Tyburn gallows while officials tightened the noose around Mr Arnold's neck, the fearful expression on his face as he looked up to the heavens. 'What will happen to her?'

He sniffs. 'She was found guilty of prostituting men and keeping a disorderly house! She'll be on the pillory tomorrow.'

I stand, frozen, unable to even breathe. 'The pillory?' It is a fate nearly as terrible as hanging – the excruciating pain of being held in place and bent over, the shame and abuse, cuts and bruises from items thrown. Sometimes people die, depending on the violence of the crowd.

He nods, dabbing at his eyes. 'If I could just go in her place,' he says. 'It's cruel to make a man watch his wife be tortured with no recourse.'

I've always known the law was my enemy, but it has usually been a threat looming from the distance – a broadsheet headline punctuating an otherwise ordinary day, or forcing my recreation into the shadows where others can be bold. Mother Mack is my first friend who has been the victim of the government's hateful clutches. I promise Geoff I'll go to Smithfield Market tomorrow and support her however I can.

–

The next day, my heartbeat quickens as I move with more urgency, pushing my way through the crush of Londoners. I returned to the shop late and missed Martha, so I still do not know whether she will turn me in. The world is tightening around me, but I cannot think about that right now – the most important thing I can do is stand with my friend. Corners of hats and jacket sleeves hit me in the face but I press on, shoving skirts out of my way and twisting myself through the crowd, eyes straining to see what everyone else has come here to see.

The pillory. Locked in the wooden boards, wrists limp and head hanging, is Mother Mack. I immediately recognise her bonnet and the chestnut hair poking out from underneath it. Her silhouette is dark against a bright blue sky. I hurry forward, trying to glimpse her face. 'Mother Mack,' I cry, but quickly wish I hadn't. She raises her head, looks at me, and smiles briefly before I hear a loud *smack* and see a red tomato running down her face. This seems to encourage others to throw what they have brought: animal dung, putrid fish, rotten eggs. The day is warm and the stench of rotten food permeates my nostrils. Under my jacket I am sweating, though whether it is from the climate or panic, I cannot say. A raw potato thuds against the board behind her head and bounces off her hand. I see her wince and stretch her fingers in a feeble attempt to soothe the pain. 'Stop it! Stop it, that's enough!' I yell, but it makes no difference. A cowpat whirls over the mob and explodes on her face in a cloud of dust and strands of straw. The mess clings to her skin, her hair, and she scrunches up her face to seal her lips against the manure on them. Laughter ripples through the crowd in appreciation of her misery. 'This must end!' I call beseechingly to the Londoners around me. 'What is the matter with you?'

'She's a blowze,' someone roars behind me. 'Whoring out mollies for profit.'

I stand in shock until a throng of men edging forward jostles me back to reality. I try to fight against them, but it's like trying to stop a wave from crashing – I am only one person. A mouldy orange flies through the air, juice dripping down on the crowd, then smashes against the boards with a squelch and covers Mother Mack with its noxious pulp. I try to move towards the front, to block her in some way, but everyone keeps trying to get closer and I am pushed back. The air is thick and smells sour. I desperately look around for Henry, hoping by some miracle that he's found his way here too, but do not see him. Mother Mack is sweating in the heat, her bonnet askew, red splotches on her face and hands where she's been struck. There are heckles and laughs whenever a hit lands particularly hard. Something shiny sails past and knocks her bonnet off – bloodied animal intestines. I scrunch up my face at the smell, even from ten feet away. A few members of the crowd try to shake the pillory pole, and I see her gasping for air.

From my left, a tall man calls, 'Lazy fussock. Shoulda done your own work!'

'Who'd've paid her?' laughs the man behind me, and everyone in the vicinity jeers. I force myself around, pull my arm back, and punch him on the nose. He reaches for me but I stumble backward, knocking into a man and woman who shove me away. The crowd closes in on me, a crushing and suffocating force, but I fight back, pushing and kicking. My breath keeps catching in my chest – am I sobbing? – and my limbs jerk instead of moving with their usual fluidity. I look up towards the pillory for Mother Mack. Through the flashes of bright coats and dresses, I see her head and hands hanging limp. When a turnip hits her, she doesn't move.

'*No!*' I keep wrestling with those around me, pulling items out of hands and throwing them to the ground. I notice blood on my knuckles for a brief moment, then a fleeting image, perhaps a boot, before a heavy force lands in my stomach and I nearly vomit. There's a crystallised period when the only thing I hear is my own gasping breath, filling my lungs before they force the air out again. I can't feel anything, not even my own heartbeat. Then, another sound: a high buzzing, which turns into the piercing whistle of a constable at my side.

'All right, that's enough!'

He wrenches my arm and pulls me from the crowd. I'm still catching my breath and twisting my neck to see Mother Mack. 'Is she all right?' I choke out. 'I think she's fainted.'

'Not your concern,' he says, and I turn to see where he's pushing me – a cage on wheels.

'Wait—' I begin, but there's no time to protest – he shoves me inside and locks the door.

Chapter Fifteen

Then

The cart rolls in front of the gaol, wheels creaking. The sun burns the skin on the back of my hands, torn up with gashes and cuts. My mind races – how much do the constables know? Of everyone in the crowd, why did they grab me? Did someone from the Bird's Nest turn me in as part of a bargain to protect their own neck? No, surely they wouldn't do such a thing – this must be about the punch that I threw. I try to catch my breath, but cannot find it. Suppose the officers accuse me of breaking the peace by starting a fight – what will the consequences of *that* be?

My hands are forced into cuffs, then the cage is opened and I am pulled out, shoved into the imposing brick building. It's dark inside, with low flame lamps flickering on the walls. I try to reassure myself as fear nearly stops my heart from beating. Surely they can only hold me here for a few hours to send me a message – perhaps I will not even have to give them my name? I desperately search my surroundings for anything that could offer more information, but all I see are shadows from myself and my captors. They walk me down a short hallway to a cell filled with soggy hay, dangerous-looking men with furrowed brows, and only one small window for light. I stop walking in shock, before the officials on either side push me forward. With a rattle, they open the door and shove me inside the cell before removing the handcuffs. One of them finally looks me in the eye. 'Magistrate's been called away,' he says, 'so you'll be held here until he's back to examine you.'

'And when might that be?' I ask, panic flooding my body.

He shrugs. 'Several days, maybe a week.' He turns to go, and I press my face to the bars.

'But I have a business to run! Clients and an employee who depend on me – I cannot be held here without end.'

'Should've thought of that before you punched one of your fellow Londoners in the face,' he responds.

'Please!' I beg. 'Send word that I am here to my apprentice. I will give you the address.' I do not know if Martha will answer, what she thinks of me since I told her about Henry, but she is all I have right now. To my relief, the constable agrees to write to her.

—

Several days later, I have heard nothing. I'd initially imagined that I would grow habituated to the smell of stale hay, unwashed men, and old piss but I'm not so fortunate. It continues to sting my nostrils, imposing itself whenever my thoughts begin to wander. Have the constables or prosecutors questioned Martha and learned about me and Henry? I'm not sure they can charge me without a witness, but is there a chance Martha would be willing to testify? Even the threat of a trial for an offence like sodomy would leave my reputation in tatters, no matter the outcome. And if the worst were to happen… it is too dreadful to contemplate.

Around our group cell the other men sit, occasionally standing and walking around its perimeter, dragging their feet in boredom. I join them sometimes, craning on my toes to peer out the window at the city lit up by bright sunshine. They are less dangerous than they first appeared, but it is still a destitute atmosphere, with most of us keeping our own company, heads bent low in shame. The cuts on my knuckles from striking people have begun to heal, but my joints remain sore. I yearn for fresh air and the feeling of stretching my legs as I walk across the city. Being coiled up here with other listless men is agonising and my thoughts dart around my mind, moving in place of my body. I try to manage them by finding small details to focus on – the creases in my sleeve, the way the light changes as each day drags on, the sound of my own breathing. Still, anxiety continues tapping at my shoulder.

I've nearly lost all sense of time passing. Apart from watching the sun rise and set through the sliver of a window, the mean and depressing meals are the only routine that remains. Some of my fellow prisoners have family or friends who visit and bring them fresh clothing and victuals – while they carefully savour sweet apples or pork pies, I slowly stir my spoon in the gruel served to those of us without support from loved ones.

Men come and go from our shared pen a few times a day and, apart from that, time stands still. We take turns pacing back and forth across the long sides of the room, but it does nothing to break up the monotony – every face is unchanging, every heartbeat the same. Occasionally, a guard comes in and takes someone out, but he usually brings them back. At night, we stuff linen sacks to make our own mattresses with some of the damp straw at the back of the room.

I wonder if Martha has stayed on working, or whether she has packed her things and left forever. I try to calm my thoughts by focusing on what I might be doing with my time were I not stuck here, the orders that must go out. The stays for Mrs Lewis have their boning finished, but still need to be lined and completed. There was an order for Lady Ursula that Martha had only begun cutting out when I was forced to come here. While I recently took some measurements for Mrs Gowers, I have not yet drawn up a design for her stays. I feel defeated. Martha may have the skills if she's decided to remain with me, but it is too much for one person to do in addition to delivering the stays on time and acquiring new materials. She does not know the clients well enough to chase new orders – how much future business will we lose? How much longer will the magistrate continue to hold me here, and when can I return to my workshop? I don't know how Martha will handle our rent payment in two weeks, but I desperately hope I will not be trapped here at that point.

Where is Henry, has he heard of my arrest? If he did somehow get the news, would he even write? Perhaps he is off with Miss Hartwell, too preoccupied to notice my absence. Or maybe he is unaware that I am not home, has written to me at the shop, and now wonders why I do not respond. I recall the words we snapped at each other mere days ago. They cannot be the last things we ever say to one another. Even if he does marry his precious Miss Hartwell, I would like our parting sentiments to be generous and kind, more befitting of the feelings we shared. After all, it is unusual in this life to feel such a complete sense of unity with another person, to be effortlessly comfortable yet unnerved by the spark between you. Henry brought a playfulness and fluidity to my days – watching his eyes brighten when I showed him a new part of London or vice versa made my heart feel lighter. Now it is dense, a lifeless organ weighing me down.

There is nothing I can do with these thoughts, these worries. Although accustomed to taking action, while I am stuck here I can only wait until others decide my fate. It is agony.

Footsteps in the hall, heading towards the door. My head jerks up from my palms as keys jangle in the lock. The guard is watching me – has he come to take me to the magistrate? Could it possibly be they're releasing me without charge? Or is he here for someone else entirely? He opens the door and, as he moves, I see Martha behind him. I rush towards her, but the guard puts up a hand to make me stand back.

'Ten minutes,' he says as he lets her through.

She shifts uncomfortably as the gate closes. I see her struggle not to look at the other men, though we both feel their eyes on her. For a few moments, neither of us says anything and I wonder if she is disgusted with me – for the way I look after living and sleeping in the same clothes for so many days, for loving Henry. I cannot know for certain, so try to push those thoughts aside and work up the nerve to speak. 'Thank you for coming.'

She clears her throat – perfunctory. I hold my breath. 'I wanted to update you on things at the shop.' She pulls out a piece of paper for reference. 'I've finished what we were working on for Mrs Lewis and Lady Ursula, and we've had ten new orders come through, including one for Lady Waverley at court.'

I choke up as I exhale. She has not betrayed me – she is working harder than ever before to support my shop. *Our* shop. My skin tingles with gratitude, as if I could begin floating right here in the holding cell. 'That's marvellous news.'

She nods. 'So far, I've been keeping on top of everything, but I don't know how much longer I'll be able to. I'm not as fast as you are with lining and boning.'

I can't help but smile. 'I imagine you're doing better than you realise. It's a lot of work for one person, but you've made great improvements in the last year. Look at you, reading from your paper now.' I gesture with pride.

She blushes a little at this. 'I've brought the measurements for Mrs Gowers and Lady Waverley. Would you be able to draw some designs for me to follow?'

My hand trembles a little as she approaches with a paper and pencil. I crouch down on the earthen floor, brush aside a few pebbles and strands of hay, then begin drawing. It feels good to put my mind to work again, feel the familiar give of the paper under my hand even if the surface isn't ideal for making straight lines.

It feels strange to draw a design for someone I haven't met, although Martha hastens to tell me, 'Lady Waverley desired a pair with shoulder straps, to wear at a winter ball,' which is helpful. Once I've done an initial pass, I ask if she's brought an awl and string. 'Oh yes, I thought you might be needing that,' she replies, pulling the one from my workbench out of her pocket.

I anchor the awl on the paper and loop the string around my pencil so I can create curves on the pattern.

While I work, Martha shuffles her weight back and forth, glancing around the holding cell and towards the tiny window. 'They don't give you many amenities here, do they?' she asks sadly.

I stir uncomfortably on the floor, aware of just how paltry my current surroundings are. The indignity of it stings in front of an audience, but I hold my head up as I hand my designs back to her. 'Have you heard from him?' I ask, unable to resist any longer.

She bristles just for a moment, then folds the papers and tucks them into her pocket. 'He stopped by the shop a couple of days ago. Just that one time. I told him what happened – that you were here – and he left.'

I wait for her to say more, but she doesn't. 'He simply left? Did he seem remorseful or upset in any way?' Perhaps our argument really was the last time we will ever see each other. My heart is more bruised than my hand and I feel desperately alone.

'I can't claim to know his thoughts, sir – he didn't say much.'

'Of course,' I say, disappointed. 'Well, thank you, Martha. For everything.' I gesture at the patterns and paper she brought.

She nods, about to say more, but the guard comes back. 'I'll keep the shop open for as long as I can,' she says.

I nod, the uncertainty in her voice catching me by surprise. Neither of us know how long I'll be kept here, or under what conditions I'll be released. There might be a fine, in which case I would need to borrow money to keep the business afloat. But who would lend to me?

When the door closes again, I crumple against the wall. Henry has clearly abandoned me now that he's found out I've been arrested for defending someone connected to sodomites. The feel of our fingers entwined, of his breath on my neck, the flutter in my chest when our eyes lock – I will never experience these moments again. If only we'd been able to have a proper goodbye, perhaps I would find things easier. As it stands, I must turn my focus to getting out of here and returning to work. But how? What can I do from where I sit? I have become habituated to a certain sense of control over the events of my life, but within these walls I feel helpless. No amount of late-night work or strategic thinking can release me early. I turn my face towards the filthy, damp wall and cry bitter tears, completely alone.

Now

Travelling case open on my bed, I consider a pair of shoe buckles and stockings, then set them aside. I glance around my room, find a clean shift – smell it just to be safe, then fold it and place it in the portmanteau. I pace the room, thinking about what I may be missing.

A knock outside – I open the door to Lady Elina, holding a stack of books. 'I thought we could split these,' she says with a smile.

Suddenly nervous, I nod and reach out to take them from her. She stays in the doorway and watches me pack, holding her breath. I feel her eyes on me, sensing my anxiety, perhaps second-guessing the faith she's placed in me. I try not to think of what will happen if we're found out. There must be a penalty for impersonating someone outside of my station, but worse than that, I will ruin Lady Elina's chances of sharing her ideas with her peers – the great thinkers of our time. Even if she forgave me, I could never forgive myself for letting her down.

If she can sense my stress, she does not mention it. 'We depart in twenty minutes,' she says simply, before turning and walking back upstairs.

I snap shut the clasps on my case and the sound helps me focus. There is still one thing I must do.

—

When I sneak into Henry's room, he is reading by the fire. He smiles when he sees me come in and reaches a hand out, which I take as I sit down next to him. I cannot hide my worried expression, and his smile falls. 'Ah, you have something you wish to discuss,' he says, closing his book.

I look at his fingers interlaced with my own, unsure how to begin. 'My love, I'm sorry... I can't go to Bath with you today.'

His reaction is subtle – he straightens his posture and his hand goes slack in mine, but his face stays the same. I know he is hurt, disappointed, but I hope I can make him understand. He will feel bruised by my deceit, but if I explain things gently, he will come around. 'Why?' he asks in a low voice.

I swallow. 'I have to go to London.'

Now he squints, confused. 'Isn't my wife—?'

'Yes, I'm going with Lady Elina.' He waits for further explanation, but I cannot tell him the truth or there will be consequences for her. 'We have... business in town that cannot be rescheduled.'

He rolls his eyes, annoyed now. 'Some nonsensical dressmaking emergency? Honestly, Matthew, no such thing exists. You know this is the only time away I have available for months... surely your business can wait a few days.'

This stings, but arguing with him won't help matters. 'I'm afraid it cannot. I was looking forward to our trip, but – but this is more important.' I flinch, unsure whether I should have said that last part.

His face changes – his expression darkens and he retreats into himself. 'I see,' he replies, not meeting my eye. 'You and Elina... it's not strictly professional, is it?'

All at once, it rushes over me – how I have betrayed him. I knew cancelling our trip would hurt him but I had not anticipated this, his pain at being passed over. Why was I not open with him from the beginning? My cheeks burn with humiliation – I've been a coward.

His mouth parts and he lets out a small, hollow laugh. 'This is a surprise. I've been such a fool.'

'It isn't that sort of relationship,' I say, but feel helpless to defend myself.

'Clearly your loyalties have changed.'

'We've become friends, that's all.' Is it though? I do not understand it myself.

He nods silently. He might choose to quarrel with me over this – it would be reasonable, expected. But he does not. Whether from pride or contempt for a dispute of this kind, he sits back and quietly accepts my decision. Much as it would break my heart to spar with him, knowing that he is unwilling to fight for our time together hurts too. 'You seem to have made up your mind – I won't try to stand in your way,' he says, his eyes fixed on the faltering flames.

'I'm sorry,' I say, rising to stand, 'I promise I'll make it up to you,' trying to pretend this is just about the Bath trip. He does not look at me again – just picks up his book and pretends to carry on reading. I understand he is upset and frustrated, although he has cancelled several trips with me at the last minute. I debate saying as much to him, getting into a heated argument – but there is no point. I don't have the time, and I've made my decision. It does no good to pretend this morning could go any other way than it has.

Carefully, I leave his bedroom and plunge back downstairs into the servants' quarters. Guilt and shame bind themselves around me, but my mind remains clear. I grab my travelling case, then leave through the kitchen door and walk around to the front of the house where a carriage is waiting. I hand my case to the driver and wait outside until Lady Elina emerges from the front door. As she steps into the carriage, I stare up at the house, looking at its darkened windows. Something shifted between me and Henry that I had not anticipated – until we spoke, I had not realised that I was choosing Lady Elina over him. I must address the matter and apologise to him when we return.

For now, I get into the carriage and sit opposite Lady Elina. The road to London is uneven and jostles us back and forth in silence. We watch the scenery pass outside, each lost in our own thoughts until we share a glance, reading the other's expression. We both feel nervous about how this afternoon will go for different reasons – she, concerned she has put too much responsibility on my shoulders; I, worried about letting her down. And yet I can see in her face that she feels the same gratitude as I feel towards her for opening my eyes to new ideas and believing I have something to offer her as a friend. After a moment, her eyes narrow in her characteristic michievous smile. 'Shall we practise some more?'

I nod, a fresh wave of nerves numbing my arms and fingers.

Focused, she looks at me squarely. 'What will you say if they challenge your position on the role of women in an equal society?'

I take a breath. The nuances of this argument remain difficult for me to remember but I stumble forward, knowing it is essential practice.

'We know that if given the opportunity, women can contribute in equal measure to men.' I pause because it sounds impossible to defend, then sigh in frustration. 'I'm afraid I still do not understand. I know that women are good workers,' I think of Martha taking over my shop – of course I know this better than many, 'but with the majority of wealth already controlled and inherited by men, how can we pretend women will be equal contributors?'

She listens but does not look at me – we have had this conversation before and I sense her strain in going over it again. 'I am imploring the public to use their imagination to seek a more prosperous society. This is important, Mr Rooke. Very few have written about the political and economic role of women before now and we must begin these conversations.'

'I know I lose the finer details of it,' I say, 'but I want more than anything to be a success for you.'

She reaches forward and squeezes my hand in thanks. 'It's easy, really. Think of the difference in your life between your apprenticeship and when you created your own shop. Doesn't everyone deserve that opportunity to find purpose?'

'Of course, no one should be limited to playing a set role dictated by society.' I look down, clasping my hands anxiously. 'I agree with you, I'm just not sure I will be able to articulate the point as well as you do.'

'I suppose if things truly spiral, I can deliver a persuasive argument with a letter or pamphlet in a few days. But I hope it does not come to that – it will be suspicious if my assertions are dramatically improved when writing instead of speaking.'

'I understand,' I reply.

The carriage continues to bump gently over the road and we take a collective breath, each unable to feel relaxed when so much is at stake.

Chapter Sixteen

Now

Still trapped in our carriage, Elina and I travel in quiet anticipation as the grey buildings of Central London spring up around us. I don't know which of us is more anxious, whose situation is worse – mine for holding a friend's future in my hands, or hers for being forced to wait, powerless. She's written up a speech for me and some additional discussion points, which sit folded in my breast pocket pressing gently towards my chest. The horses stop outside a tall stone building and I blanch. Elina sees my expression and clasps my hands. 'You can do this. We've discussed everything they will ask.'

I nod, collecting myself, and we step outside. The sky is close and grey and it has just begun to lightly rain. Out of habit, I adjust my wig in case it got jostled out of place during the ride. I know she's right, that the information is in my head. She has imbued me with the passion and enthusiasm for these ideas that I once admired in her from a distance. But whether I can deliver a convincing performance remains to be seen.

I gesture towards a tiled archway. 'We can meet there when it's over?'

She nods silently, eyes darting around the street nervously. Then she steels herself, grabs my arm with force. 'Good luck, Matthew. I trust you.'

'Thank you.' I turn around to head inside the building, but a thought occurs to me and I spin back towards her. 'Can I ask one question?' Her face looks expectantly at mine. 'Why me?'

She thinks for a moment, then smiles to herself. 'Like you, I prefer the bustle of city life – I want to exchange ideas and meet a variety of interesting people. But there is not much cause for that in a place like Stonehurst Manor. I am treated as a decoration for my husband and to the workers I am the lady of the house who must be blindly obeyed. I am limited to my role. But you – I could see that you would challenge me and speak more frankly, actually exchange ideas. You have been my sole intellectual partner in that house, and I hope the affection is not limited to my side.'

My heart swells and I want to rush forward to hug her, but know it would be inappropriate. Instead, I offer my warmest smile to reflect my new determination. 'It's not just on your side. I will do this for you.' With a quick nod and a parting pat of her speech in my pocket, I turn around and walk up the steps.

The foyer is dark and my eyes take a moment to adjust. I try to muster all my confidence internally as my feet thud gently against the wooden floor. For this to work, I cannot falter even once. I recognise one of the publishers from John Josephson's office and walk over to him. 'Mr Ashby, excellent!' he says, shaking my hand. 'We anticipate a great deal of interest in your work at this afternoon's meeting. Once everyone is settled, Mr Maltby will introduce you.' He gestures across the hallway towards a fellow in a blue satin suit. Behind him, people have begun filing inside and through a door to the main chamber. Briefly, I spot Elina in the crowd but immediately turn away so we do not catch each other's eye.

I take a few breaths to calm my nerves, then pull the speech Elina wrote for me from my pocket and review it.

It's only been a moment when: 'Mr Ashby, they're ready for you,' from Mr Josephson, and I am following Mr Maltby through the door into the crowded chamber. I try to swallow but my throat is too dry, so I clear it instead.

In front of the benches where the public sits is a podium, which Mr Maltby walks up to. 'Ladies and gentlemen, thank you for being here this afternoon to discuss a new work of daring political assertion. You may be familiar with some of his pamphlets on the revolutions in America and France, but this is the first full-length political treatise he has laid out. To share more about his ideas and fuel our afternoon's discussion, may I present Mr E. Ashby!'

There is a polite round of applause and I step up to the podium, nodding at Mr Maltby with a grin before deciding I should take up a more serious expression. Fingers shaking, I smooth the speech on the podium and begin reading.

'Across ancient civilisations, humans have endeavoured to build a working society. We can now strive to build something even greater, a society that recognises the accomplishments and promise of our enlightened era.' I try to make my tone natural so the words are easy to follow – I know if I can present Elina's ideas correctly, the crowd here will find them appealing. 'Many great minds have championed the rights of individuals to pursue freedom and control over their own happiness.' I watch small nods of recognition and agreement, then take a breath as I prepare to introduce the crux of her philosophy. 'As we continue these conversations, I want to draw attention to interdependency, how our lives interlock by necessity.' The rustle of some papers, adjustments to sitting positions, but otherwise the room is quiet. 'We must not forget that negotiating power is strongest when it is collective. We have seen the power of uniting behind shared interests in the Americas, France, and even on our own shores during the silk weavers' protests. If we are to build a society where upward mobility and individual free will are possible, we must use collective bargaining power to achieve these ends.' I pause, looking up. 'Are there any questions thus far?'

In the back of the room, Elina's eyebrows are raised in tension and her eyes are wide, darting around in quick flicks. I purse my lips and take a breath to continue.

'Does this idea of interlocking interests conflict with the individual freedoms we have just begun to earn?' asks a rusty-haired man off to the right.

The blood pounds in my ears, but I remain steady – she prepared me for a question like this. 'Not at all. We must have both, always remembering that one individual will never outmatch the government in power, and using our shared interests to influence the law.'

'But supposing one man did achieve a level of power and wealth to parallel the government, would he also benefit from these shared interests? Who would keep his power in check?'

I falter, gripping the podium as if it can save me. 'In that instance...' I take a deep breath. 'In that instance, the collective power of those with opposing interests would balance the scales. Unless this hypothetical individual acted in the interests of others, which is also possible.'

Murmurs of approval ripple through the crowd. 'This concept of interdependency is rather intriguing,' says a man in the second row. 'Where did you come up with the idea?'

'I...' I hesitate. Curious faces are tipped towards me, eyes blinking expectantly for my answer. I look down at the speech and notes written out for me by Elina. The words, so concise yet representing years of her work, ideas she has puzzled over and thought into creation from a genuine desire to see a more equal world. They are an external expression of her very being.

She belongs on this stage, not me. But will she feel betrayed if I give her identity away now? Can I live with myself if I do not? It is a gamble and potentially dangerous to unmask her, but instinct tells me it is the right thing to do.

'I cannot take credit for these ideas any longer while their true author is in the room.' A murmur of confusion ripples through the crowd. I look towards the back, find Elina's face. 'Lady Elina Ashby, won't you please come up and claim the recognition you so warmly deserve?'

Her eyes lock into mine in shock. I nod in understanding, but gesture for her to come to the front of the room. A flush has crept onto her cheeks, but she stands and begins making her way to the podium. Rows of heads turn to watch her. Everyone is quiet, and for a moment I wonder if I've made a terrible mistake.

'Ladies and gentlemen, this woman wrote the treatise you admire so much. Please direct your questions to her, for she is much more eloquent on the points than I am.'

Shaking slightly, Elina stands next to me at the podium. She takes a deep breath, then speaks with the control and precision so customary to her. 'Thank you, Mr Rooke, for your courage and compassion. Are there any questions on the treatise?' Softly, I step back so she can be the focus of the room.

A man in the middle of the audience calls out, 'So, the fellow wrote nothing? Everything was you?'

'Indeed, sir.'

The man squints with a puzzled expression. A blur of maroon hides him from view as the man next to him rushes to his feet. 'You want to give your own sex more power? Are we to infer that your concern over inequality is driven by selfish interests?'

She chuckles a little, more good-humoured than I would be in her position. 'Shall we ask Patrick Henry such a question? Or Olaudah Equiano? The answer is yes and no – my arguments are driven by reason, by studying the gaps in our current system and a desire to fill them so that we may all function at higher levels. Yet of course, one of the goals of equal individual rights is the freedom for every single one of us to express self-determination.'

Mutters of appreciation from the crowd, but even those who don't nod along seem to take her seriously. As she fields more questions, I find a seat along the edges of the room. I watch her, full of admiration, then join the applause at the end of the event. At one point, our eyes meet and we beam at each other with relief and pride. It feels exquisite.

—

That evening, we meet in a public house on Hanover Street for a celebratory drink. Elina's cheeks glow from the warm air and we keep giggling, in shock at what we've managed to accomplish. We blend in with the crowd, though Elina is probably the only woman in the room who isn't for sale. The atmosphere is jovial and getting louder as the evening wears on.

'You've barely touched your drink!'

'I hardly need it... I've never felt so elated,' she tells me, beaming. 'Mr Rooke, we must make a pledge right now.' She reaches across the table and wraps her hands around mine. I laugh at the exuberant light in her eyes, feeling equally buoyant. 'Let us promise to keep working together in the future.'

'Yes!' I grip her fingers enthusiastically. We are leaning in and raising our voices to hear each other over the rest of the pub's revellers. 'I can help you parse through your ideas, perhaps act as your assistant—'

'You are invaluable as my *friend*, let us not take up silly titles. You have insights of your own and I believe we can work together to inspire new ideas for our shared society.'

'Thank you.' I blush a little, fully aware that my education still has a long way to go. It is strange, I realise, that while Henry and I share commitment and love, I feel valued in a deeper way by Elina. She sees me as someone capable of change and growth – our friendship is built on a shared hope for the future, rather than who we were in the past.

A man walks past with a sense of purpose – we both recognise him immediately. 'Mr Cugoano!' Elina calls to him, and he turns with a questioning expression. 'Elina Ashby and Matthew Rooke, from Mr Phelps' debating society this past summer.'

'Oh yes, of course!' He breaks into a grin and shakes our hands. 'A pleasure to see you again. What brings you to the Stag's Head on such a fine evening?'

'We are celebrating. Mr Rooke has helped me present and garner interest in my forthcoming political treatise. I must thank you for sharing your experience and wisdom from your own work – there are chapters that would not exist had you not opened my eyes to the finer arguments on the political and moral impacts of slavery.'

'I am glad to hear it – I have recently completed an abridged version of my book in the hopes that more of your fellow Britons will read it. But now I must join my friends,' he says with an easy but sad smile. 'It is my last night in London, you see.'

'How long will you be away?' I ask.

'I cannot say – perhaps forever. I am sailing to Saint-Domingue to join their revolution. The people there grow discontented with breaking their backs for another's enrichment and there is a spark ready to burn through the old social order.' It seems there is already a blaze within him – he stands tall and the embroidered threads on his jacket glimmer in the candlelight.

I peer over at Elina and see the warmth of admiration in her eyes. 'You are a brave man.'

He inclines his head in thanks. 'I have the courage of my convictions, ma'am.'

She stares after him as he makes his way back to his table of friends and is lost to us through the din of the crowd. 'Can you imagine doing such a thing, Mr Rooke? Sailing across the ocean to fight in another country's revolution?'

I half laugh. 'No, I'm afraid I cannot.'

'Because of your age?'

'Careful, now.' I widen my eyes at her, teasing. 'I'm not sure political ideals could ever inspire me to something so dramatic. But perhaps I have simply not experienced the society that would push me in such a direction.'

She leans forward on the table over her glass of gin. 'Yes, Mr Cugoano has lived an enslaved existence and knows its horrors first-hand. Perhaps that feeds his desire to help those who are still held in its clutches. Do you think your character is not one that would take on such a dramatic change?'

I frown, casting my mind back. 'I'm not sure about that. I've made significant changes to my life before – learned new trades, lived in strange places – and may do so again.'

'Indeed! What inspired you then, if not political ideals?'

It's so exquisitely simple, I almost don't believe it could be true. 'Love.'

'Ah,' she replies, eyebrows lifted. 'I've heard it makes men move mountains.'

I can't help but laugh at her phrasing. 'You've never heard of a woman doing something ridiculous for love?'

'Well, of course there are some. But in my experience, women tend to be more rational in love than men,' she responds. 'We have to be, in the modern world.'

I laugh at her characteristic drollery, enjoying the conversation. 'Go on, then – would your political ideals ever inspire you to leave England?'

She scoffs a little. 'Where could I possibly go – back to Bengal? Without a husband or money, I would be in a desperate situation almost immediately.'

She's light-hearted but I can see a melancholy shadow cross her features. Perhaps she does feel called to travel and laments her inability to go far without Henry's permission. 'Just as well,' I say. 'Your work is desperately needed here at home.' I tip my glass towards her in acknowledgement, then finish it.

'Indeed,' she replies, back to her efficient manners. She glances at her timepiece. 'Speaking of home, we must make our way to the main road for our carriage soon.'

–

It's late and the manor is dark when Elina and I arrive. As I'm about to step out of the carriage, she puts her hand on my arm. Her eyes are bright and sincere. 'I know it was not easy preparing for today's meeting, but you rose to the challenge and I cannot thank you enough.'

I take her hand and clasp it in mine. 'I must confess, it was all rather enjoyable. I may be a hopeless student, but I am already looking forward to more collaborations in the future.'

She sneaks in through the kitchen door with me, then makes her way upstairs. My heart still feels light – I can't believe how well everything has gone. Perhaps I can help her with research for her upcoming work, or we will begin attending regular meetings with the corresponding society. I hang my coat and untie my hair, then carefully sneak upstairs to Henry's room. The carpet is soft under my feet and I know the way so well by now I can move through the corridors with stealth.

The fire is low and he is asleep when I arrive. It's a chilly night, so I add another log, then slip out of my stockings and breeches to slide into bed with him. His breathing changes and I know he's awake. 'My love?' I whisper in the low light. 'I hope you can forgive me for this morning.' I should say more, but I'm still elated from the meeting so I simply lean forward and kiss him.

I feel his resistance melt away and he turns towards me, his familiar hands cup my ears and his fingers entwine themselves with my hair. 'How did you know I was still here?'

'I saw your carriage as we passed the stables. Why did you not go to Bath and meet Mr Gerrald?'

'I couldn't bear to take the holiday I had intended for the two of us by myself. I would have been too despondent without you.'

It is rare for him to admit so openly that our love matters. More important than attending to his business in Bath, he wanted to be with me. I breathe in the warmth of his body and become hungry for him, reaching my hand down under his shift. As we kiss, our mouths are wet and loud – it is as if we are returning to each other after a long absence.

A familiar gasp behind me – Henry's eyes dart up and he lurches away. Electricity shocks my nerves as my eyes search the room. In the dim light, I scramble to find the doorway but my heart has already dropped through a pit in my stomach. Elina stands there, hand clutching the doorknob, tears silently streaming down her cheeks.

Chapter Seventeen

Then

My arms ache from repeatedly tensing, but I try to stand tall as I'm brought down a corridor and through two imposing double doors. The room is dark – narrow stained-glass windows cast their light upon a man at a long wooden table. His wig is coiffed and perfectly powdered, his black robes slash the air menacingly when he writes with his quill. I sense others on the peripheries of the room but he seems to be the person to set my focus upon – the magistrate. His long nose tips up in my direction as he shoots me an accusatory glare, then slides a piece of paper across his desk.

'What is your name?'

I nod, then realise I'm expected to speak. I clear my throat nervously. 'Matthew Rooke.'

'Age?'

'Twenty-four years.'

'Trade?'

'Staymaker.'

'Residence?'

'Bell Yard, Bishopsgate.'

He nods, reading from the paper in front of him. 'You stand accused of offences against the peace and assaulting several men in a riot.'

'I did no such thing! The crowd was after blood before I arrived.'

'I'm afraid that's not what Mr Barrow has testified,' the magistrate replies. 'He claims you attacked him.'

I glance to my side and see the man I punched, with a prosecutor sitting next to him. I suddenly feel stranded like a wherryman on the Thames when the tide comes in fast, overcome and unable to act.

I'm about to respond but the magistrate continues. 'In addition, there have been accusations that you are connected with the mollyhouse proprietor who was at Smithfield two weeks ago – surname Mack.' He tips his nose up towards me for a brief moment. 'This is highly concerning information that does not incline me to sympathy towards your character.'

I look at the magistrate, but all I can see is Mr Arnold's body twitching in the air. Every fear I have tried to hold in place for so many years is ripped open and I do not know how to defend myself without lying. I feel small and powerless but manage to stammer, 'I can... assure you that my character is very good and I have the utmost respect for order on our city streets.'

'And yet you recently attacked at least two men,' he replies snidely.

'If I did such a thing – and I do not concede the point,' I add, remembering that this man controls my fate, 'perhaps I was provoked.'

The magistrate's face wrinkles as he squints in feigned interest. 'But what could have provoked you, if not sympathy for the woman on the pillory? By all accounts, the crowd was as ordinary as any other.'

The pillory is a barbaric practice and those being punished sometimes die from their wounds at the hands of spectators, but I cannot say this in a court dedicated to upholding the law. Feeling trapped, I look around the room again, searching for a familiar face who might offer me a way out of this. But there is no one here apart from a few clerks and disinterested onlookers. I think back to Mother Mack, her head hanging in defeat, drenched in rotten juices. Did she survive her injuries? Even if she did, our effervescent evenings at the Bird's Nest are over now, mere memories locked in the past. The London I have known for so long seems to fall away from me, leaving only uncertainty ahead. I am completely alone – friends scattered to keep themselves safe, Henry vanished forever, family long deceased.

'Mr Rooke, have you anything else to say in your defence?'

My attention jerks back to the magistrate. 'Since you seem determined to accuse me without justification beyond hearsay, it seems I cannot undertake a defence for myself.'

He nods, writes something down on the paper. 'Very well then, I will recommend bringing the case against you to trial. You will need to hire counsel for your defence, and we will hold you in Newgate until a date is set.'

I let out a gasp of shock. 'But I will lose my livelihood if I am imprisoned indefinitely! It has already strained my business to be held for as long as I have.' My knees buckle – a trial also means a definitive verdict. This could lead to me losing more than the shop – I could lose my life.

His expression does not move. 'Perhaps you ought to have considered your business before you provoked a fight with your fellow citizens in defence of a woman whose trade has corrupted the moral integrity of our city by harbouring degenerates and fostering their ungodly proclivites.'

I feel my face flush with anger, but manage to hold my tongue.

He continues, 'If you had a character reference to speak for you, perhaps I might be convinced of your integrity. But as the situation stands, I have no reason to expect remorse for your actions.'

'I have an apprentice – an upstanding young woman who I'm sure would—'

'A person under your employ, and a woman no less,' he sneers, 'will not be convincing enough.'

He pauses, but there is nothing more for me to say. Even if I could crawl on my stomach and beg a client for such a reference, it would take too much time. Henry might hold the social weight, but he has abandoned me. There is no one here now – I am desolate. Out of options, I lower my head.

I hear the scratching of quill on parchment. 'Off to Newgate, Mr Rooke.'

Firm hands grasp my shoulder and forearm, pulling me backward. My collar tugs against my throat uncomfortably. I turn around, my footsteps echoing as I walk back towards the heavy doors, but before I get very far, a voice rings out through the dim shuffling in the room.

'I will serve as this man's character reference.'

There, in a bright blue suit shimmering with gold embroidery, is Henry. He pushes through the throng of people and towards the magistrate, giving me a look that I immediately know I'll never forget. I can't feel my fingertips or my heartbeat – everything is light now that he's here.

'Mr Rooke is a good friend of mine, a dedicated servant to justice in this city and one of the finest staymakers you'll ever meet. I have known him for years and never seen him strike another person – I'm convinced this is a simple misunderstanding and would urge you to release him.'

At last, the judge's expression changes from hostile to easy, even admiring. He smiles pleasantly. 'Why, Mr Ashby! How delightful to see you again. Regrettably, we do have numerous witnesses against this man.'

I hold my breath, eyes jumping back and forth between Henry and the magistrate. Henry's tone is carefree and familiar. 'Come now, Lord Whitmore! This is clearly a vexatious case brought against my friend by some fellows with a grudge and nothing more.'

The magistrate weighs these words, then smiles again. 'Of course, Mr Ashby – if you can attest to this man's character, then naturally we will release him.'

'I thank you,' Henry replies, about to turn, but the magistrate beckons him closer to the table.

'I shall consider myself to be in your favour, Mr Ashby.'

'Indeed – perhaps something we can settle over cards one evening?' Henry replies blithely.

What feels like a deep breath later, I walk out to the yard and find Henry waiting off to the side. As I approach him, every fibre of my being burns to kiss him, clutch his body to mine, but I strain against the urge. 'Martha said you left when she told you what had happened,' I say in wonder.

He chuckles lightly – together, we walk through the gates and down Ludgate Hill. 'I always knew I would help. First I went to the prosecutors building a case against you to try and talk them out of it, but they were determined. So I told them I'd come here and make the magistrate throw the whole thing out.'

I'm overcome with gratitude and love, but all I can do is thank him repeatedly. As we pass a tavern, I remember the pillory. 'Do you know what happened to Mother Mack? Is she out of prison?'

He looks down, doleful. I stop in my tracks. 'I haven't heard anything – the Bird's Nest is still closed. Apparently her injuries at the pillory were quite severe.'

Even though I expected as much, a heavy sorrow wells up inside me. The cruelty of this city might have irreparably injured my friend, perhaps even killed her. 'Can you believe we'll never spend another evening there?' I ask, a slight fog in my throat.

'No,' he shakes his head. 'It's an excruciating pain to think she may not have survived her sentence.'

Slowly, we keep walking down the street. Our sombre attitudes contrast sharply with the sunshine spilling onto bright dresses and jackets – most people are carefree and laughing as if blind to the horrors this city might inflict on them at any moment.

After a few paces, my thoughts turn to the shop, how much work has stacked up, how Martha has been coping without any respite. I say as much to Henry.

'You needn't worry – I've given Martha a small loan to hire additional help.'

I can't believe all he's done for me. The terrible things we last said to each other are forgotten in a silent communication between us that comes effortlessly and with perfect understanding.

We make our way towards St Paul's, its colossal dome towering over the city streets. The air is hot and still, so we bask in the shade cast towards Cheapside and watch pedestrians and carriages going about their daily business. My entire world has shifted and yet London carries on.

As if reading my thoughts, Henry turns to me. 'I cannot be apart from you again.'

'No, never.'

'The city isn't safe for us any more.'

'Yes, I see that now.' I feel pliable, warm and safe as long as he is nearby. This arrest was a narrow escape and if houses like Mother Mack's are coming under stricter scrutiny, there will only be more like it in the future.

With a lack of restraint unlike him, Henry clasps my hand next to the wall of the cathedral. It would be impossible for a passer-by to see, yet his confidence still makes my heart skip. 'You must move to Stonehurst Manor with me,' he says.

Can I really leave London, the only home I have ever known? The city where I have struggled to build my staymaking trade and where I have only recently begun to see the fruits of my labour? The answer comes up from nowhere, clear in my mind: if I stay, I could pay with my life. It will be an effort – I'll need to make arrangements with the shop and Martha, decide what to take with me and what to leave behind. But there is a security in being together right now – perhaps in a year or two, London will feel safer again and we can return. 'All right. I must see to my shop, of course – shall I keep it open? Perhaps only during the season.' The thought of not working is unsettling, and perhaps some income during the social time of year would be enough to sustain me. Yet these nerves are nothing compared to being without Henry.

His eyes darken. 'I thought...' He stumbles, clears his throat. 'I thought you might be my wife's dressmaker.'

The street tilts out of focus. Were it not for his hand on mine, he would slide away. 'You've... you're married?'

His eyes, sweet and anguished, don't quite meet mine. 'I'm afraid so.'

I must focus on his touch, his firm grip is steady. 'Constance Hartwell?'

'No – someone my parents found who's just returned from Bengal. She's a lady – they insisted on the opportunity to step closer to the peerage.'

'Oh. I see.'

He leans forward, his breath warm against my cheek. 'Please, Matthew, I can't lose you again. We'll be safe in Surrey, I'm in charge of the servants and everyone who comes and goes. We'll be in each other's company each day, and every night.'

My stomach is still in knots, whether from the meagre meals provided in Newgate or from this shock, I cannot determine. 'How have you convinced her that a live-in dressmaker is necessary?'

'I tried to pass it off as a display of the family fortune,' he replies. 'Besides, she's accustomed to a large household staff after her time in the colonies. It's cheap to hire servants there.'

I nod, but still feel nauseous. 'I will be your servant?'

'Certainly not! You'll have your own quarters and can remain independent. I won't let anyone task you with any responsibilities beyond dressmaking.'

I sigh, remembering another problem. 'But I don't know the first thing about dressmaking. Only stays.'

'Of course you do – you're clever enough to figure it out, and I'll help you. Please, Matthew – I know I'm asking you to sacrifice your ambition, all your work to this point, but I will do whatever I can to keep us together and safe.'

Though the challenges at the outset will be immense, there is something appealing about learning a new set of skills. Across the street, a bailiff waves his arms at a woman walking past. I feel myself yielding. 'And I can return for frequent visits?'

He smiles, tears of relief shine in his eyes. 'As often as you like! My love, believe me, this will work. We shall remain side by side forever more.'

Now

'Elina—' Henry begins, but she cuts him off.

'How could you do this to me? After everything we've shared?' Is she speaking to him, or to me? I cannot meet her eyes so have no way of knowing. Henry does not answer her, which makes me realise he had nothing to say when he began talking before. 'This is unforgivable,' she continues. 'I… I must go…'

'Let me explain,' I begin, but Henry has found his voice.

'You're right, it is unforgivable. But let's not wake up the household with bitter words tonight. We should all return to our own beds and discuss the matter afresh tomorrow. Allow me.' He jumps up and begins to usher her through the door, but she slashes her arm out, her fingers splayed wide.

'Do not touch me,' she says emphatically.

'Elina, please.' His voice is gentle, almost intimate, and this seems to soften her. The two of them stagger back to her rooms.

I remain where I am, paralysed. My mind whirls – not only have Henry and I been caught and exposed to whatever punishment Lady Elina cares to inflict upon us, but the full impact of my betrayal collides into me. She confided in me, and I have broken that trust. If we once passed a thread back and forth to one another, growing closer and tighter, now that cord has been ripped away and I am the one who pulled it. Without her, I feel myself begin to drift aimlessly. I replay the events in my mind, the way Henry jumped, how it felt when I heard her cry out. She was at the door – but why? Why had she come to Henry's room tonight? Is it possible that she was elated after the events of the day and wanted to celebrate with him?

Henry creeps back inside, closes the door behind him. 'You still sleep with her?' I ask him.

He rubs his eyes, sighs. 'Yes, of course – she's my wife and we have to produce an heir. It would be suspicious not to have... conjugal relations on occasion. You heard what my father said.'

I can't feel myself breathing. 'You said that you stopped after the first few years – you're always so distant with her, I hardly knew you spent any time alone in each other's company.'

He reaches towards me – his hand is on mine but I do not feel it. 'I had to do it for my family... surely you understand that?'

The bedclothes wash in and out of my vision. I have no reply – after all these years I thought I had his full devotion, but it seems I was mistaken.

He looks over at the embers smouldering in their hearth. 'Elina and I do not have very much in common, and being with her is not like it is with you. But we do share a connection, a duty to carry on our lineage for the future—'

'Please stop, I cannot bear to hear more.'

We sit on the bed in silence, a gap widening between us.

'Leave it with me,' he says quietly. 'I'll speak with her and smooth things over.'

'No,' I tell him, standing with a sudden passion. '*I* will speak with her.' Whatever connection he thinks he has with her, I know mine is more genuine.

I leave his rooms and walk to the opposite wing of the house. A faint light glows around the edges of her door. Without knocking, I softly press it open and peer towards her desk, where I know she will be. She stands, scribbling something down, then sets the quill aside and rests her hand on the back of her neck with a heavy sigh. I clear my throat to signal my presence and she turns towards me.

She stares at the floor between us and does not look me in the eye. 'How could you?'

'It isn't what you think.'

'What I think, Mr Rooke, is that you have betrayed my trust and forsaken our friendship by seducing my husband. Any explanation you may have will simply be finer details of this infidelity.'

How can I make right where I have caused such suffering? All I can do is tell her the truth – something in me trusts that she will understand. In my heart, I feel that our friendship is not broken just yet.

'If I'm honest, I do not remember who seduced whom — it was so long ago. Twenty years, in fact.'

At this, her eyes widen and she sits down.

Instinctively, I pull another chair over and join her, leaning forward. I do my best to explain some comprehensive version of the life Henry and I have shared together, from the thrill and romance of our youth to the comfort and routine built over time. The memories meld together in places but I try to be specific where I can, knowing that I must paint as honest a picture as possible.

'Do you recall your annual springtime trips to London, how he often disappeared after the evening meal?'

'Yes, although I hardly noticed at the time.'

'We would meet for drinks at a discreet coffee house friendly to… our sort of men.' The King's Head, although it was never as warm and genial as Mother Mack's.

'I see.' She looks away for a moment, exhausted. Behind her eyes, I see the struggle between her overwhelming pain and keen intellect already calculating and sifting through her memories. 'I knew you were friends, but I never imagined — how could I be so foolish? Never questioning his departures or noticing when the two of you went off together.'

'I am the guilty one, not you. And as for noticing, only those in a certain network do. The way we identify each other is very subtle — a certain stare, a twitch of the arm.'

Her brow furrows in comprehension. 'I suppose you have both been lying to me from the very beginning, then. When Henry suggested a private dressmaker I assumed he was trying to show off his wealth, but came to understand you had a sort of friendship with each other. How could I not have recognised it might be something more?'

'You certainly saved both of our lives by not questioning it,' I reply. 'And perhaps you found it convenient not to look too closely?' I say this gently, but know by now that she is not offended by my impertinence.

She acknowledges this with a familiar tilt of her head. 'I have always been very focused on my work. There have been times I have baulked at Henry's lack of affection, but knowing how traditional he is, I chose the convenient rationale that he was not given to expressing emotion excessively.'

I look down at my knees, deciding not to rub salt into the wound I have already caused by mentioning Henry's affection when we are together. 'Elina, I am truly sorry for the pain I have caused. You've opened me up this past year, not just my ways of thinking, but in my heart as well. I now feel a stronger kinship with my fellow men and hate to think I've repaid this favour with cruelty.'

She casts her eyes aside, deep in thought. 'It has not been cruelty purely... I will not report you and Henry,' she says suddenly, focusing back on me. 'I do not wish to cause any further suffering between the three of us. Your deaths would be an unfair punishment for the grief you have inflicted upon me.' She stands and reaches across her desk, stacking papers and books together in neat piles. 'Yet I cannot remain here – I still have some money in my trust and will use that to move to Paris, where I have a group of friends and can continue to write and shape society in a more democratic direction. Perhaps in time, a divorce and annuity would be appropriate.'

'He's reasonable – I'm sure he would agree to that.' I watch her tying her books together with leather bands, realising she is already packing. 'When will you leave?'

'I will make enquiries in the morning.'

So soon, and then we may never see each other again. 'Won't it be terribly unsafe in Paris?'

'Without wishing to underestimate the situation there, I do not think it is quite so violent as some reports would lead us to believe. The poet Helen Maria Williams just moved there a few months ago.' She straightens and sighs, thinking. 'And if it is unsafe, then I shall adapt and learn to live carefully. But I am not at high risk – my only enemies are close-mindedness and tyranny.'

'As you say. Well,' I stand, reaching out my hand, 'I admire your bravery nevertheless. It is not easy to move so far from home.'

'I'm used to it,' she replies. 'You know I spent my formative years overseas, amongst violence and famine.'

After bidding her a good night, I walk downstairs to my room, feeling heavy but hollowed out. It's all I can do to slip myself into bed, easing my body against the mattress. I try to relax but my mind is still working. Will Elina keep her word? Is there any way the three of us can forgive each other and remain under one roof? Are these relationships worth fighting for, or should I cut and run given the deceit rampant between us?

At last, my thoughts begin to lighten their tread around my mind and I drift off to sleep. There is a rumbling, perhaps movement from somewhere far away, but I ignore it. The noise gets louder and when I hear voices, I sit up. Is that someone yelling in the distance?

A door slams – I bolt out of bed and rush down the corridor without even putting on a dressing gown. I rush to the front windows and crane my head towards the lawn. A carriage sits on the path, driver ready to depart. My heartbeat quickens and my throat closes up as I cast my eyes around, finally spotting movement as two male figures – one appears to be Henry – pull Elina from the house and thrust her towards the carriage door. She tries to fight them off, arms reaching outward and clawing, but she is outnumbered and they push her inside.

I open my mouth to yell, but no sound comes out. The carriage drives away – Henry and the footman stand watching it bounce off into the darkness. I remain paralysed for a moment until my knees suddenly buckle and I fall to the floor underneath the window. All I can do is stare into the darkness in front of me, wondering what Henry has done.

Chapter Eighteen

Now

When I wake, my limbs are stiff. Each breath feels like it's my first one. I roll over to fall back asleep, but then I remember what has happened.

Elina, gone. My gaze falls to the windowsill, upon my long-borrowed copy of her French discourse. I'm hollow, numb. But I must roll out of bed and attempt to begin the day.

It feels wrong to wear bright, celebratory colours so I dress simply in black breeches and a dark green jacket. I open my door and begin down the hall, nearly bumping into Henry.

'Ah, Mr Rooke,' he says. 'I was coming to find you… would you like to join me for breakfast?'

Still in a daze, I want to interrogate him immediately, demand to know what he's done to her. Opening my mouth, I notice Mrs Ferrers standing behind him and realise it will have to wait. 'Do you have enough food prepared?' I ask her.

''Course, Mr Rooke,' she replies with a little too much neutrality. My familiar terror of being found out by anyone and everyone returns to taint each interaction. With Elina gone, how could any of the staff refrain from speculating now?

I follow Henry up to the smaller dining room, the one overlooking the south garden. Eggs, toast, and jam are set out on the table and we help ourselves when Mrs Ferrers leaves.

'It should be a crisp day,' he says, 'perhaps we might take a walk in the afternoon.'

I put my knife down with some force. 'I don't want to spend more time with you than is absolutely necessary. What have you done?'

His expression inscrutable, he is controlled and aloof when he speaks. 'I did what was necessary to protect us both – I declared her mentally unfit and sent her to Bethlem Royal Hospital.'

To Bedlam, notorious for rotting the minds of its occupants! I stare at him, aghast. 'What? How could you?'

He jumps to defend himself, reaching for any justification. 'She is perfectly safe, kept in the finest conditions available.' He reads my expression and adds, 'My love, what else could I do? She'd report us and have us killed.'

'She wouldn't!'

'You don't know that. She has a powerful, calculating mind. Even the rumour of any impropriety is too dangerous for us.'

His words stagger me – I stare at him in disbelief. 'Have you always been so selfish?'

He pierces me with his eyes. 'Haven't we both?'

I look down at my full plate in shame. Can it be indulgent to give in to one's innate urges, no matter the harm that may come to others? Is placing my love and loyalty to Henry above all else a selfish act, or is it something I cannot control? Being in love is learning how to walk the line between self-interest and the addictive desire to entwine yourself with another person. When we give in to our desires, is that submission self-indulgent or is it living truthfully?

Henry looks hurt, still bruised from my rejection yesterday morning. For me, the time between then and now stretches out behind us, too long ago to focus on properly. While I may have felt regretful for choosing her over him at one point, now my rage against him overwhelms me and it is all I can do to stay in the same room together.

He speaks softly. 'All I have done, all I have risked, has been out of love for you. You owe it to me to try and see this from my perspective.'

I push my food around the plate, too guilty to eat anything. I do not understand him, but nor can I cleave myself away from him so easily. We are still part of each other's composition, even through the anger and betrayal. 'And what is your proposition to justify my existence here?' I ask. 'What will be my role if not Elina's dressmaker?'

'You see, that is the best part.' He reaches across the table and clasps my hand, but I cannot return his vigour. 'You are an accomplished artisan – my established friend – and shall be my guest.'

'That is not a sustainable solution.'

He returns his attention to his breakfast. 'Perhaps not, but it will hold us for the coming months – maybe even the year.'

No one will believe Henry having a guest come to stay for an entire year, especially someone who had previously been working for the estate. 'You haven't thought this through at all – you've imprisoned Elina and destroyed her life on a whim.' I can still hardly believe it.

'Enough,' he says emphatically. 'It is done now and we must move forward.' He swallows a mouthful of eggs. 'Since you will now be here as my friend, I will have your things moved upstairs to one of the guest rooms.'

Is he trying to buy my acquiescence with softer sheets and a larger fireplace? My allegiance is not so easily earned. 'Only if you agree to let her go.'

He looks away, lifts his wig and runs his hand through his hair. He fixates on the pepper grinder, lost in thought. Finally, he sighs and replies, 'Perhaps one day.'

Outside, heavy mist blurs the outlines of the trees. I look down, the future unclear and out of focus.

Henry's grip on my hand tightens. 'My love, try not to be downcast. With Elina gone, we can live as if this were our shared home. Equals at last.'

I can see no way forward – it is impossible to remain and yet I have nowhere to go. I abandoned my options and connections long ago when I committed to Henry and now, with Elina gone, he is all I have. There is nothing left to do but hope he is right and that the heaviness in my chest will lift with time. I pick up my buttered toast and take a bite, but it is dry and tasteless in my mouth.

Days pass without my noticing. I sit at the rosewood table in the guest room, looking out the window at the pond and rolling lawns until I work up the energy to take a walk. The leaves have begun to turn on the trees, preparing to fall for the winter. When they do, the lawns seem to sprawl endlessly and the manor feels completely isolated. I suppose we will be – Henry prefers to attend parties than to throw them, and with Elina gone, he has every excuse to disconnect.

What will I do now? Even if my presence in the home as a guest is not directly questioned at first, how will I fill my time without anyone to design for? How will I earn money? Henry pretends he can take care of me, but as each day ticks past, I grow less certain that's true. His value of propriety may soon eclipse our love and, even if it doesn't, I'm losing faith that he knows the best path forward.

An invisible force compels me down the corridor, to Elina's rooms. I don't expect to find anything meaningful there, I just want to feel closer to her again. The expensive carpets silence my steps as I walk over to her desk, papers askew from her packing and the subsequent struggle with Henry and the footman. She must have been frantic, clutching for the pages she'd spent months labouring over. My heart pangs as I turn towards her bookshelves. I pick up an edition of John Locke, lift it towards my face, and take a cautious whiff. But all I smell is stale ink and paper. Nearby is an armoire, its door askew. A flash of turquoise – the dress I made for Lord Newington's ball last summer. Without warning, hot tears begin falling down my cheeks.

I return to the guest room, where a letter from London waits on the table. Immediately, I recognise Martha's handwriting and my senses heighten – I'd written to ask whether she has heard reports of anyone sneaking out of Bedlam. As a born and bred Londoner, I understand some of the infrastructure is weak and a small part of me is optimistic that Elina might be able to free herself. Eagerly, I open the letter.

> *Dear Mr Rooke,*
>
> *Thank you for beginning the proceedings to sell the staymaking shop to me – I know it marks a new chapter for you and you must have complicated feelings. I signed some forms just last week and don't believe there is much left to do.*
>
> *We were so terribly sorry to hear about Her Ladyship's confinement to Bedlam. I have kept my ears and eyes open but am not aware of any reports of someone breaking out. As you know, the north-west corner has been crumbling, but maybe she is not being held on that side of the building. Keep hopeful! She sounds very clever, and perhaps in time her husband will see reason.*
>
> *Your loving friend,*
> *Martha*

With the dramatic recent events, I had forgotten about selling my staymaking business to Martha. Yet another door closing. And no nearer to helping Elina.

After dinner the next day, Henry shows me into the drawing room. 'Let's have a game of draughts,' he says. 'I want to help you see what our future life together might look like.'

Sullen but aware that I must give him a chance, I sit down and watch him arrange the pieces on the chequered board.

'That's a nice suit,' he says, looking at my waistcoat. 'New buttons?'

'Last year,' I murmur, running my finger along one of them. They are gold-plated and had been a treat to break up the monotony of life at Stonehurst, before Elina dissolved the clouds overhead.

He picks up a piece and moves it forward. 'Did you have a pleasant day? I had a lovely time spotting birds on the terrace earlier.'

'Is that so?' I ask, trying to veil the impatience in my voice.

'Yes, there were colourful robins, jays, and magpies. I put out some seeds to attract them. How diverting!'

I skip my piece forward, capturing two of his. 'No doubt, the grounds here offer some wonderful opportunities to spot nature,' I reply. 'But perhaps you might spend some of your time deciding whether it would be worthwhile to free Elina from the prison you have put her in.'

'Matthew,' he sighs, 'don't spoil the evening with that kind of talk.'

'How can we hope to return to any sort of normalcy when her incarceration haunts us?'

'It doesn't have to! The hospital assures me she is being kept in comfort. You must try to put those concerns behind you.'

But it's no use. Guilt eats away at me as my thoughts turn back to Elina repeatedly. I must find out how she is and what conditions she is being kept in.

—

Iron screeches against steel – a key clanging into place and turning. 'Women's ward is through there,' a pale man with thinning hair says, gesturing down the hall. Small candles flicker on the walls but it's so dark, I squint to make sure I'm not tripping on anything.

My shoes clop against the stone floor, echoing, but otherwise the corridor is completely quiet. Where are the patients? Then, through the stony silence, I begin to hear it: moaning. A chorus of lamentations rings through the air. I stop for a moment, listening to the mournful cries. My eyes begin to adjust to the darkness and I see with horror that there are pale fingers reaching through bars near the floor along the stone tunnel. They slowly reach out, then pull back again. My instinct is to recoil, but I overcome it and bend down, peering into the darkness that houses them. Pairs of eyes and knots of hair are all I can see. The wails continue and my nerves tighten, wanting to flee. But I must push on – Elina is somewhere in this nightmarish place.

Towards the end of the corridor, I spot what might be a thin ray of sunlight on the floor. I turn right and stifle a gasp. She is lying on a straw mattress, mere inches from the ground. Her face is streaked with dirt and tears, still wearing the dress I made for her. What a difference in just a week – the last time she wore this dress in London, it was in triumph. Now, it is encrusted with stains and smears of dirt. I inch closer, but she stares at the wall as if blind and numb. 'Elina,' I whisper, stretching my arm through the bars as far as it will go. Her eyes snap into mine and she stumbles to her feet, coming over to face me from behind the bars.

'Mr Rooke,' she breathes, 'why are you here?'

For a moment, I'm taken aback both by her uncharacteristic frailty and her unmistakable hostility. But I deserve it – I have betrayed her unforgivably.

'I'm so sorry about my part in putting you here.' I reach out again to take her hand, but she stays back from the bars between us. 'I have asked Henry to let you out – he is stubborn, but I will keep trying. He does not know what the conditions are truly like – surely that will sway him.'

'He is worried about himself,' she says, looking away. 'It is clear that he places his and your safety above what is decent and kind.' Another woman from a nearby bed of straw gets up and wanders past, a glassy expression on her face. I glance around the cell – there must be about eight or so women kept here together.

'I cannot believe he will keep you here once he knows the extent of horror that you face. It is far worse than I had imagined.'

I can feel her softening, her body begins to crane towards me like it used to when we were colluding together in her rooms. 'I can hardly believe how cruel and shocking it is. My own imagination falls short, and every day grows worse. Women cry out for help and go ignored. We are underfed, confined to these cells and yet rest is impossible.' She breaks down. 'My mind has always been my greatest treasure and pride, but I fear if I remain here I shall go mad.'

I have seen her confident, angry, even insecure, but never so fragile. It is heartbreaking and distressing, but all I can do is nod along. 'How could anyone stay here and keep their sanity?'

Suddenly fierce, she lifts her chin. 'It is designed in opposition to rational thought. Even our keepers display no capacity for reason. They disregard everything we say, disputing our own memories and driving us to madness all the faster. On top of which,' she holds out her forearm and I realise it is bandaged, 'they have begun a bleeding treatment despite my cries that it was unnecessary.'

I grip the bars anxiously, trying to get as close to her as I can. 'Please tell me I am not your only visitor, that you have not been on your own here all this time.'

Her eyes are dull, their usual spark dimmed completely. She shakes her head in response. 'I have been utterly abandoned in this pit of despair.' With a violent jerk, a woman lying behind Elina is sick on the ground. I watch, amazed at the lack of response from anyone nearby. Clearly in distress, Elina closes her eyes and purses her lips. 'You are still free – you should leave,' she says at last.

This is a terrible place for anyone to be, but it is a particular nightmare for someone with such a brilliant mind to be locked away and unable to write or converse with intellectual equals. Anger towards Henry sears my throat. How could he sacrifice her very essence, throw her in here without a second thought or without considering another option? She would have been true to her word, moved to France and never returned. But he could only see his own needs.

'I will get you out,' I promise her.

She shakes her head solemnly. 'I wish it were possible, but only a male member of my family can have me discharged. If Henry will not be swayed, then there is nothing that can be done.'

I hang my head in shame and embarrassment. How can I return to Stonehurst and leave her here? There must be something within my power. A flicker of hope as a thought occurs to me: 'What about your friends from the debating society? Perhaps their connections could ensure your release, and since I've met them—'

'Please, Mr Rooke,' she says a bit sharply. 'I cannot depend on false hope – it will only hasten insanity's arrival.'

I am not willing to let her suffer here. 'I'll go to them, they've met me before and they understand the value of your intellect. I will convince them to help – I won't leave until they agree.'

She nurses her bandaged arm, then slowly paces to the other side of the cell, pops onto her tiptoes and cranes her neck to look out the window. 'I will not allow myself even a glimmer of hope, but I cannot stop you.'

It's painful to hear her talk like this, in a state of total despair. I try to plead with her. 'You must remain hopeful – your intellect will not abandon you, nor will your friends.'

She scoffs, but does not smile. 'I understand perfectly my position as a woman in this society – the moment you think you have reached solid ground and can catch your breath, you are pushed back down further than before. Fighting for change is futile.'

This place, these conditions have shattered her very core. If left to remain, she will be destroyed completely. 'You don't mean that,' I try to remind her, but she does not look at me.

Leaving her like this feels impossible, but I am galvanised to try anything in order to free her. 'I'll think of something,' I assure her, trying to convince myself as well. 'Do not lose heart.'

'Goodbye, Mr Rooke,' she says, lying back down on her straw bed and turning away to face the wall.

-

Back at Stonehurst Manor, I walk the grounds and wrestle with my thoughts. The earth is soft from recent rains and misty clouds hover above the lawns. I oscillate between fury at Henry and knowing that he was unaware of how she would be treated when he sent her away. Guilt consumes me but I try not to wallow – Elina needs me to take action rather than indulging in morose feelings. What can I do to help her?

I walk around the large fountain, avoiding my reflection in the tumultuous waters. I think of how different everything felt just a week or two ago – I saw a future with Elina opening up before me, working alongside her and promoting her ideas to a more enlightened world. How foolish I was.

I return to the house and head upstairs to Elina's rooms. With all her reference books and political pamphlets, surely there is something here I can use to get her released – perhaps a loophole or new law only passed in the last year. I pull books from shelves and rifle through pamphlets, skimming everything I can get my hands on. Every law I can find seems to defer women's rights to those of her husband, enshrining that she be treated only as he suggests she should. After two days of frantic researching, I still have nothing that I can use to help her.

As every hour ticks past, I grow more convinced that I must intervene on her behalf – she cannot be allowed to remain in Bedlam. I will speak with Henry again, make him see reason and release her. He is not a monster – surely he will listen. Yet it is equally possible that he will be ruled by fear, pushing back again and demanding that we focus on our future. If he does, I have resolved to abandon him. It's an intimidating thought – I don't know where I would go or how to begin anew, and it may still not convince him to release her, but threatening to leave is the best leverage I have.

With new determination, I walk across the house to Henry's office. A quick rap on the doorway and I open it without waiting for a response.

Henry is at his desk, face down.

'We need to talk,' I tell him firmly.

He looks up, ashen. 'Oh, Matthew...' He sees my expression. 'You already know?'

I falter, trying to understand his meaning. 'Know what?'

He holds up a creased letter with a few lines hastily scribbled in the middle. 'Father has died.'

Chapter Nineteen

Now

The days drag along, washing over me. Footmen ebb and flow through the house, carrying boxes up to Henry's office – papers relating to managing his father's business. Henry works non-stop, making final arrangements for the funeral and maintaining correspondence with distant family and friends. In the days following his father's death, I have tried to give him space but there are necessary conversations hanging between us like empty air.

I have to free Elina and I cannot do it without him, but each time I try to ask about her or say anything of significance, I feel his energy wane and cannot bring myself to demand what I know he has no capacity to receive. He never did win his father's approval – even in death, the man overwhelms him. At meals, he moves heavily and his sentences trail off.

I attempt to comfort him. 'I'm sure he did love you, in his complicated way.'

But he shakes his head. 'I'm so angry – all the things I never told him, falling into line and for what? I almost hate him, but there is enough pain here,' he gestures towards his chest, 'that I think I may hate myself. He certainly taught me how.'

I try not to drown in guilt and keep out of the way so he can work. Dressed in a black suit, I sit on my bed and bury my nose in a book of poetry by Anna Laetitia Barbauld – a recent discovery from Elina's shelves. I've begun reading some of her books in a lopsided effort to continue the education she began – now that I remember what it feels like to be connected to the broader world, I do not wish to stop. It is also a way to feel close to her again. I read through her pamphlets and notes, running my finger along the pages her pen once touched, trying to put myself in her mindset. But she is cleverer than me, and it is not the same experience without her by my side.

I didn't expect to attend the funeral, but Henry asked me to be there for silent moral support. I sit at the back of the church, trying not to stare at him for too long lest someone notice and become suspicious. Henry delivers the eulogy with gravitas, and the whole thing is over without too much pomp. After all, his father was an old man – clever and wealthy, but also dour and irritable. He did not have many friends. While crowds of family and business partners line up to pay their condolences to Henry, I hang back by the side of the church, waiting for some kind of signal from him. When none arrives, I turn and walk up the road back to the house alone.

That night, Henry crawls into bed next to me and grabs at me with a kind of desperation. As we begin kissing, I pull away and lock eyes with him. A deep pang hollows out my chest. 'It has been two weeks since you locked up Elina – you *must* release her.'

He looks surprised and a bit confused, as if he hardly knows who I am talking about. 'How can you ask such a thing of me on the same day I buried my father?'

'And I might ask how you imagine I can sleep with you as if our life has continued unchanged? It is solely within your control to free her, and yet each day you choose to let her suffer in that prison.'

'You've seen what my days are like – shut up in my office with the estate's lawyers and managers. I am exhausted and can hardly think clearly.'

This is true. I've seen the stress deepen on his face daily as he tries to meet his new obligations. His father always held control over the family business, and now his son is unprepared and overwhelmed. 'So do something easy and let her go! If you knew the conditions she has been left in—'

'Her doctors assure me she is being cared for.'

His willful ignorance is infuriating, and I feel the colour rise in my face. 'They are lying to you! I have seen for myself the dark rooms, the unsanitary environment. It's inhumane, you must believe me.'

At this, he jumps out of bed and stares at me with a confused, bitter expression. 'You went to see her? What is wrong with you? And why did the hospital let you in? They had no right.'

For the first time in my life, I want to strike him. How can he say these things? 'You would deny her the small comfort of visitors when she has already sunk into a state of despair? That is too cruel, even for you.'

'Even for me?' he repeats, aghast. 'I am trying to protect us both and manage my father's affairs to keep this whole household alive! You have no idea what my days have been like, and still you demand this indulgence from me.'

'It is not an indulgence to show mercy to someone who has done no wrong. Come, Henry.' I try to change course and speak more gently. 'There is no shame in admitting you were wrong and correcting your mistake.'

But his face is fixed and I can see that between his grief and his new responsibilities, something has hardened within him. 'I have not made a mistake. In time, you will see my reason. Think of all the others you saw in the hospital – do you trouble yourself about their futures? So it must be with Elina, you must dismiss her from your mind.'

A new wave of ire crashes over me. 'If you refuse to see reason, go back to your own room.'

At last we are silent and I watch as he puts on his jacket, slips on his shoes, and walks out the door. I twist the bedclothes in frustration. I will not, cannot let Elina be forgotten – if Henry will not entertain the idea of her release right now, I will find a way to get her out myself.

—

I step out of the carriage and into the busy London streets where pedestrians mill about in the late morning air, breath escaping from their mouths in little puffs. I can smell coals burning, interrupted occasionally by the whiff of yesterday's manure.

There isn't much time today if I'm to make all my necessary stops. From the main road, I plunge into Piccadilly and towards St James's Square.

I walk up to an impressive, familiar townhouse and knock on the door. When a footman answers, I ask if Mr Phelps is at home and am shown into the drawing room. It's empty, so I take a turn and observe the opulence – gold leaf decorating the walls and marble for the fireplace brought in from the Italian mountains.

'Ah, Mr Rooke,' Mr Phelps says in greeting, and I turn around. 'How delightful to see you again.'

He gestures to a set of ornate chairs and we both take a seat. I wonder if he's going to offer me tea, but he simply smiles and watches me patiently until I realise he's waiting for me to explain why I'm in his home.

'Mr Phelps,' I begin, 'I've come here to ask for your help. You may have heard that our mutual friend Lady Elina Ashby has been unlawfully and cruelly confined to Bedlam.' I'm buoyed as I watch his eyebrows furrow in concern. 'I'd like to ask for your help in getting her out.'

'This is most unfortunate news,' he begins, eyeing the parquet floors. 'How did such a terrible event come to pass?'

I pause, considering the best way to answer. He does not know that I have been living with Elina and Henry for twenty years – as far as he is aware, I'm merely a concerned friend. 'I believe there was a disagreement with her husband – tempers were raised and he made the extreme decision to lock her away. Now, he refuses to see reason and let her out.'

'Ah, so it is a private dispute between husband and wife,' Mr Phelps replies, interlacing his fingers together and nodding with false wisdom. 'While I agree that it is a tragedy, I'm not sure what either of us can do, Mr Rooke.'

I work to control my expression so he does not see my shock at his indifferent manner. 'Sir, we cannot let a mind such as hers rot in Bedlam. She will lose all sense of herself. You are a powerful man – do you not know someone who might be able to help? Perhaps a physician with the hospital who could sign her release forms?'

But he is shaking his head before I even finish the question. 'As I'm sure you know, Bedlam only allows a woman's existing male relatives to sign her out. You have already spoken to her husband?'

Henry, so constrained by his new responsibilities and distracted by his grief. Will he continue marching forward and forget about her completely? I worry that he might – after all, he does not know her like I do and does not understand how accomplished and gifted she is.

Mr Phelps continues to speak, leaning back and crossing his legs nonchalantly. 'As saddened as I am to hear about Lady Elina's current circumstances, in my experience it is best to keep these matters between husband and wife. They tend to work themselves out in the end.'

'How can you be so callous?' I ask, unable to stop myself this time. 'You saw at the corresponding society how well her ideas were received by radicals and important thinkers! She is brilliant, she is your friend, and she needs help.'

'She is my *acquaintance*,' he says over his nose, 'and you, Mr Rooke, are not even that. I'm afraid there is nothing I can do.'

Without another glance, I stand and make for the door. 'Then I will find someone else who can.'

I storm outside and into St James's Square. How can he be so snide, so polite, while standing idly by and doing nothing? Someone who knows Elina – who has borne witness to her genius and spent time socialising with her? Someone who considers himself progressive unless it requires any real effort? Walking towards a line of waiting drivers and horses, I realise my anger at Mr Phelps really belongs to Henry and, by extension, myself. If I had been more honest with Elina and Henry, would that have changed the course of events? Even if I manage to get Elina out, will she ever forgive me?

'Paternoster Row,' I tell the first driver I see, dashing into his hackney. We turn out onto the road. I stare at the window, half in thought, half noticing London's strange familiarity once more. As we travel east, I notice paved pathways where there once was dirt, new stone and ironwork where there used to be wood. How happy I once was simply walking down these roads – ambitious, full of potential, willing and able to tackle any challenge I might meet. As we slow down, I watch a man struggling to hoist bags of sugar onto a waggon. The streets that once invigorated me now feel foreign and hostile, reflecting back a city that is more memory than reality.

When we stop, I jump out and throw a shilling at the driver. I hurry across the road and push open the door to John Josephson's. It is darker today than it was last summer, but then again, the sky outside is overcast and doesn't let as much sun in. I remember the path down the corridor and turn left, walking with increasing confidence until I reach the office door and knock before turning the knob and peering inside.

Mr Josephson is behind his desk and smiles when he sees me. 'Ah, Mr Ash— excuse me, Mr Rooke! Delightful to see you again.'

For a moment, I regret crediting Elina for her own work at the corresponding society – if I hadn't, this man would think of me as Mr Ashby and could verify my identity for the hospital as a male relative.

But there is no sense dwelling on those actions now, when they could have only been what they were in that moment. 'Mr Josephson, I'm sorry to stop by unexpectedly. But as you may know—'

'Yes, I can imagine what this is regarding,' he interrupts, his expression dropping to one of fatigued concern. 'We have tried to help her, to no avail.'

Perhaps Elina's pessimism was justified after all. 'Is there nothing you can do? I thought perhaps you might write a letter certifying her sanity—'

'Yes, I attempted something to that effect,' he replies. He pauses, about to elaborate, but simply sighs and shakes his head. 'My efforts fell on deaf ears.'

I pace across the room in frustration. 'I refuse to believe that there is nothing any of her friends can do to help her out of such a desperate situation.'

'I'm afraid it is one of many unfair systems that are alive and well in Britain today,' Mr Josephson agrees. 'Short of breaking in and sneaking her out, which of course would be illegal, our options are severely limited. For our part, we are saving profits from her book, which is already selling quite well, to give to her in cash. I won't let her husband get his despicable hands on her money.'

'Quite right,' I say, avoiding his eye. Henry still does not know about Elina's professional writing, nor how well respected her ideas are. That I have kept this secret from him is a small vindication, but guilt still torments me. I cannot help imagining Elina's face, crestfallen and beyond hope, in that dark cage. I stand and extend my hand to Mr Josephson. 'Thank you for trying. I will continue thinking until I find a way to get her out.'

'I hope you do,' he says, shaking my hand. 'No one deserves to spend even one night in Bedlam, much less someone with the perception and intelligence of Lady Elina.'

I walk outside, hardly noticing my surroundings. Everything seems washed out and grey, but I must return to Stonehurst before dinner or Henry will notice I've been away. I do not wish to attract his ire prematurely. I feel my way through the narrow streets and down to Ludgate Hill, where I catch a mail coach back to Surrey.

The Three

I am back to walking the grounds and reading Elina's books in a poor attempt to keep my shame and remorse under control. The next morning I sit through a tense breakfast with Henry, then he retreats to his office while I perambulate and consider what to do next. Perhaps I could break her out of Bedlam myself? I could probably find my way back to the group cell she is being kept in, but how would I get inside? I must find a way to get through to Henry, to make him understand that releasing Elina is essential.

My mind aches to work and I sketch a few ideas for stays and jackets based on the latest fashion plates, but even this act, once easy and familiar, feels hollow. After lunch, I wander around the quiet house almost in a trance, finding myself back in Elina's rooms searching for the connection we once shared. When the post arrives, I hurry downstairs to intercept her letters and protect her privacy from Henry, but nothing has arrived thus far.

After flipping through Adam Smith's *Theory of Moral Sentiments*, I drift down to the kitchen. Abigail is there, peeling chestnuts. She's only been here a few months, replacing Clara after she married, and we don't know each other very well yet.

'Hello,' I begin, standing across from her. 'Would you like some help?'

She nods, pushing a bowl of shells and skins towards the centre of the table. I sit down and begin cracking the chestnut shells open, so I can painstakingly peel off the thin brown skin from the nut, then drop the finished results into another bowl.

'Are these for tonight?' I ask in an attempt at conversation.

'Yes,' she replies. 'Well – I think they're for dinner downstairs. Now that it's just yourself and Mr Ashby eating at the main table, most of the food stays right here in the kitchen.'

'That makes sense.'

The chestnuts are warm from being steamed but still firm in my hands. Abigail reaches into the bowl and picks out one I just threw in, removing a sliver of skin that I'd missed.

'Are you enjoying working here?'

Her eyebrows raise like she's trying to push away some unspoken thought. 'The work's good enough,' she replies. 'Same as most places.

But it's an odd – I mean, a different sort of house, isn't it? No mistress and everything.'

My eye strains as I try not to wince. I focus my attention on picking off a piece of stubborn peel. 'Yes, I suppose Lady Elina left shortly after you arrived.'

'Wasn't much entertaining before then either, from what I've heard.' She looks up, suddenly aware she's not gossiping with a fellow servant. 'Beg pardon.'

'No, you're right, the Ashbys have always preferred to seek out entertainment rather than bring it to their doors.' I throw my peeled chestnut into the bowl and grab another from under the towel.

'I suppose it makes our jobs easier. Well, not yours…'

My hand tenses, snapping the shell into several pieces. I concentrate on dropping them into the discard bowl, avoiding Abigail's watchful eyes.

'Are you still working as Her Ladyship's dressmaker?' she asks slowly. 'Or did Mr Ashby withdraw your employment when you moved into the guest room upstairs?'

My heart begins racing, but I try to stay calm. It's understandable that there might be jealousy and confusion about my change in status, but she's still too audacious to bring it up. If this is what she's willing to say to my face, the gossip must be even worse. 'I am here as Mr Ashby's guest. We have known each other for many years and are friends. He has… made an effort to help me, financially, over the years.' The words stick in my throat.

'Oh, I see,' she replies. 'Then I suppose you'll be leaving at some point? Will he find another house for you to work in – one with a mistress?'

Her tone is difficult to read – does she believe me, or is she trying to catch me out? My response will be the same either way: 'Yes, I suppose I will be leaving soon.'

I must make Henry aware that these questions are circulating amongst his staff. When Abigail pulls the bowl of peeled chestnuts towards her and carries it across the kitchen, I push back from the table and turn down the hall, passing my old room for the first time in two weeks. The pale white walls look drab, void of the decorations adorning the main part of the house. Yet the way the light comes in through the window is familiar and I feel held between these walls I lived in for so many years. Soon, they will belong to someone else – I'm a little surprised Mrs Ferrers has not assigned the space to another servant yet. Perhaps there have been quibbles over who 'deserves' a space to themselves. I scoff to myself – none of us deserve anything beyond the right to pursue the life we want.

Retracing the path I've spent the last two decades sneaking along in the middle of the night, the grandfather clock and chandelier now illuminated by the cold winter sun, I make my way upstairs to Henry's office. He's hastily scribbling something down when I open the door. Only his eyes flick up to meet mine for a second. 'I can't speak right now,' he says.

'It's important.'

He rubs his jaw, frustrated. 'All right – but let me just finish this so my valet can post it.' He quickly folds the letter, seals it, and rushes past me across the threshold.

Feeling a bit foolish, I glance around the room. His desk has become a disorganised mess of papers, no doubt files from his father's estate that he is working his way through. I glance out of the oriel windows behind his desk, overlooking the grounds. In the pond, a pair of swans swim. There's a haze up over the trees in the distance, likely from a hearth burning in a nearby property. Outside and in the house, the air is still and quiet. I feel a kind of energy inside myself, a potential simply waiting for something to shift. I must take action, but which sort? Could I use the tools in my hussif to pick the locks at Bedlam? I wonder how many guards they have…

I turn around to face Henry as he returns, his eyes watching me expectantly. 'We must make a change,' I tell him. 'Your staff have begun asking questions about my place here.'

He inhales sharply, brows furrowed together. 'Right, we need to figure out who is the culprit and remove them—'

'It isn't one person, it's everyone. What we are doing is simply not sustainable.'

Clearly overwhelmed, he sits in a chair against the wall. I want to help him see a way through this, to believe that all is not lost yet.

'We could have what we had before, if you'd just let Elina go. Bringing her back would justify my existence here, and now that she knows about us—'

'Matthew, I cannot. It's too great a risk.'

I try again. 'Your father is no longer a threat and she has such a brilliant mind, she might devise a way for all of us to coexist harmoniously.'

He stands and paces across the room – I can see he is not hearing me as I would wish. 'I know perfectly well what will happen if I let her out. She will publicise our weakness and I will lose you.'

I feel a familiar wave of tenderness towards him when he says this, but a voice in the back of my mind also wonders whether his own self-preservation is his primary concern.

I'm still thinking of how else to frame my argument when he returns to his desk. 'Please, do not ask me about her again. I have tried to see it your way, but found it impossible. I will consider what to do about the servants. Now, please leave me to work.' He reaches for a stack of papers and begins reading.

I turn away, heading back to the guest room. I must make things right, both with Elina and Henry. We all deserve a new beginning.

-

It's dark, but the streets in Bishopsgate still bustle with workers. I walk along London Wall, keeping my face down and trying to blend in. As I pass Bedlam, I notice the street seems quieter, as though people make an effort to avoid this particular section. The air is crisp and cold – I breathe into my cravat and shove my hands further into my pockets.

The moon is bright, but I don't see any guards or constables patrolling. I skirt up the lawn and around the side of the hospital, looking for the areas of decay that Martha mentioned, but find nothing. I realise I will have to climb over the fence and search for loose windows.

I take quick, furtive glances over my shoulders once I reach the backside of the building. Looking up, the top of the fence feels endlessly far but I decide there is no room for second-guessing. I grip the iron bars on the fence with all my strength, then pull myself over in a quick motion, falling heavily to the ground on the other side. The earth is frozen and hard – I gasp for air, refilling my lungs. As soon as I can, I flip over and lie on my stomach, watching for guards in the windows or doorways. Everything is quiet.

I get up, run to the nearest door, and try turning the knob. It rattles, but does not budge. Growing desperate and increasingly cold, I look up at the stone building and scan the windows. They're all dark – it seems I must take my chances. I knew it was possible I'd have to break a window, so I wrap my cravat around my hand and punch through the nearest one on the ground floor. The shattering glass seems to shriek in the quiet of the night – I scurry to the side for a minute in case someone comes to inspect. But again, nothing. I manage to get the window open and jump down into a room filled with a large metal chair, medical instruments, and pieces of furniture covered in cotton clothes.

I creep towards the door, carefully pulling it open. There is a staircase nearby and I cautiously follow its steps up. As I reach the top and inch around the corner, I catch a faint sound trailing from down the corridor: the cries and wails of those trapped here. Hardly daring to breathe, I inch along, following the sound to get closer to the ward. As I approach another corner, I hear the shuffle of heavy shoes and a faint light begins to appear. My eyes nearly spring from my head – it must be a guard. I find a doorway and leap towards it, willing myself to disappear into the shadows. The guard keeps trudging down the far corridor, away from me. When I no longer hear his footsteps, I breathe out. I must be careful – to be caught would mean imprisonment, and Henry would certainly not save me again if my crime was freeing his wife from the institution he put her in.

The surroundings are dark, but what little I can see all looks the same – what had I expected, breaking in with only a vague plan and one previous visit? I follow the heartbreaking cries softly echoing down the corridors. Delicately, I run my hand along the wall just ahead of me as a way to compensate for what my eyes cannot see. The bricks are rough and old – small pieces crumble if I brush my hand too hard against them. I tread slowly, not daring to make a sound. After another careful turn, my fingers touch something new: metal. I stop and hold my breath with excitement, realising I must have reached the cages.

Where I had previously leaned against the wall, I now step back to hide in the shadows. Moonlight might pour through the narrow windows above, but it is a cloudy, cold winter night and quite dark. Looking down, I can make out the shapes of patients sleeping atop piles of straw on the floor. Some are not asleep and seem to shiver, whimpering. My heart tugs for them, but I stay in the shadows and keep walking, looking for Elina.

At the end of the corridor, the surroundings begin to look familiar and I squint a little harder until I spot the blue glimmer of her dress, contrasted with the threadbare blanket draped over her. As before, she is in a cage with several others, all huddled in crumpled mounds on the ground. My muscles tighten and a jolt runs through me. Slowly, I creep forward until I am up against the bars. 'Elina,' I whisper, but my voice is too soft, the sound barely escaping through my throat. I eye the others in her cage for any motion, but they are still.

Perhaps I will change strategy – open the lock, then wake her. I have heard that padlocks are easy to pick with skeleton keys and various devices, so I remove my hussif from my pocket, open it, and pull out the awl I have used for years. I have never picked a lock before, but am confident this will do the trick.

Once the awl is inserted, I shake it back and forth, trying to prise the lock apart. It makes a clicking noise, then begins to rattle as I grow increasingly desperate. One of the women lying on the ground stirs and I freeze, but it's too late. She lifts her head, spots me, and gets up from her modest bed. I wait for her to cry out, say anything, but she does not. Perhaps she understands that her freedom and my success are intertwined. I nod my head towards her, then begin fiddling with the lock again.

'No,' the woman moans, watching the lock. Is she criticising my methods, or does she fear what will happen when I break in?

'Shh – it's all right,' I tell her hastily. 'I mean you no harm. I am here for Elina, over there.'

'No,' she says again, and others in the cage begin to stir. Panic rises in me and my heart, already pounding, beats harder. Through my pulse, I try to listen for the sound of footsteps from the guards.

'Matthew?' Elina whispers from my other side, carefully standing and brushing herself off. 'What are you doing?' She joins the crowd of women standing opposite me, eyes down on the stubborn lock in my hand.

'I told you I wouldn't let you stay here,' I reply, my voice tight with agitation.

'No!' the first woman cries, more forcefully this time. Elina wraps her arm around her shoulders and hushes her, but she breaks away and begins wailing loudly.

'Dammit!' I cry, shaking the lock in frustration. There's no use being quiet now – the guards must be on their way. I pull the awl out and kick the lock, hoping brute force will break it. Doubts infiltrate my mind – what if the guards come before I can break it? Will I run and hide until they are gone, or will I be caught and arrested? Why did I not devise a plan to confront them? I am unarmed and middle-aged, not as fast as I used to be. Why didn't I acquire a skeleton key? How could I have come here without a foolproof plan? I glance to my right, thinking I hear the inevitable footsteps.

'Here – try this!' Elina passes a brick through the bars to me. I catch it in a clumsy, desperate motion, turning it in my hands and quickly assessing its weight. I stare at the lock, then hurl the brick at it with the force of my entire body. The impact rings through my wrists and forearms, and my shoulders knock painfully against the bars. Gasping with the effort, I look down and see with relief that the lock has broken open. But there's no time to catch my breath. Down the hall echo rapid footsteps – the guards at last.

'Hurry!' I cry, sliding the door open as the women flood out like water over a broken dam.

Instinctively, Elina and I clasp hands. 'This way,' she says, pulling me behind her. We run away from the guards and down the corridor, skidding around the corner. All pretence of stealth is abandoned as we make our way, followed by some of her fellow inmates.

'There's a surgical room,' I pant as we run down a long hallway lined with foreboding doors. 'I broke the window there.'

We bolt down the stairs so quickly, we nearly fall. 'Stop!' shouts a voice behind us. The guards are gaining ground. I look for the other women who were running with us, but they have darted into open rooms and down new corridors. It is only me and Elina left.

She is ahead of me and hurls the door open – I pull it shut behind me and barricade it with a nearby chair. I spin around to find Elina struggling through the window – her skirts are too big to make it an easy manoeuvre. I pause for the slightest moment as a tinge of modesty overtakes me, then put all thoughts to the side and push her. One ripping noise, and she is through. I scurry after her and we sprint across the manicured lawns designed to appeal to wealthy benefactors who are willfully ignorant of the torturous conditions at the hospital.

When we reach the fence, Elina falters. 'Step into my hands!' I kneel down on the freezing earth with my palms linked together.

With a determined expression, she grips the iron bars and gingerly treads into the cradle I've created. My knee sinks into the frozen grass, and she lets out a loud grunt as she struggles to pull herself up. She's nearly there – I stand and her feet flail before I help her find my shoulders. With this effort, she is over.

'Hurry, Matthew!' She points and I turn around to see a guard scrambling out of the window we've just crawled through. My heart jumps into my throat and I grab the fence, hurling myself over. Elina braces to soften my fall, and we dash into the safety of the narrow city streets.

Here, I'm better prepared. 'Head for the river!' I cry as we slow down, but keep running. When we reach the quayside, I scan the scene for the correct ship and then nudge her to the right. Our path is slowed by stacked crates, bales of hay, and a flock of sheep being herded into the city. Chests heaving, we pick our way through the crowd until the air cools and we're next to the water. 'Here we are – first ship to France.'

She stares at the mast looming above, topped with a small lantern glowing against the dark sky. She turns back to me. 'How can I repay the kindness you have shown me tonight? It would be impossible even if I weren't leaving the country.'

I shake my head. 'Inaction was intolerable – I could not have done otherwise.'

A sailor drops the gangway and people begin to board. I hand her a pouch with ten guineas inside – my life savings.

She clasps my wrist. 'I can't help regretting all the time we wasted by not befriending each other sooner.'

I nod. 'But perhaps the timing was appropriate for each of us. We were both primed to grow closer last year – hungering for our lives to mean something more. We've given each other the gift of transformation.'

'That's true.' She watches the ship for another moment then fixes her gaze on me, her eyes piercing through mine. 'Won't you join me? In a strange way, I am more myself when we are together.'

I feel the same and ache to go with her, to leave the claustrophobic world of Stonehurst Manor behind. But I cannot. 'My place is by

Henry's side.' Now that I know she will be all right, I hope to take the lessons I have learned back to him so we might begin anew.

She nods, casting her eyes away and wiping a tear from her cheek. 'I hope you will write,' she says, looking back at me with a smile.

It is the sweetest, most generous expression I have seen – my heart swells and my throat constricts. I beam and embrace her. 'I hope you will do the same, for your words will sway minds and build new civilisations.'

She returns my hug, shuddering with a sob. 'Thank you.'

Chapter Twenty

Now

Exhausted from the late night, I spend the day after Elina's liberation oscillating between dread and self-doubt. I do not sleep, passing the early hours by walking down the sprawling lawns away from the house, debating whether or not to tell Henry what I've done. If I say nothing, that gives her more time to escape but it means he will be angrier when he inevitably does find out. I want to take responsibility so that we can settle and move forward at last, but am also worried. Will the hospital write to him immediately, or will they hesitate admitting to a security breach? I dislike carrying the anticipation of this necessary conversation, but manage to stay away from him most of the afternoon and then retire early, too tired for my anxiety to coax me into what I know will be a difficult discussion.

The next day, breakfast is a bleary-eyed affair and I hardly say anything as I swallow my tea and listen to Henry muse aloud about estate affairs.

'The Jamaican sugar plantations might be worth a visit in the future.'

I nod along, exhausted and nervous. If I tell him now, while he is fresh and rested, will he be able to forgive me? How much time do I have before the hospital writes to him? I do not want the news to come from anyone other than me – I should tell him today, right now. 'Henry?'

'...Then again, perhaps I ought to give up the trade side of the business altogether. It's such a lot of unnecessary work. What do you think?'

I haven't been paying close attention and nearly drop my fork as I try to recall his last point. There is so much I want to ask him. What of *our* future? How long can we be cloistered here together before the suspicious whispers grow louder? What kind of life can we hope to build together? But all I say is, 'It's your estate and you know how best to run it,' which seems to please him.

'Did you have something you wanted to ask me?'

I swallow, my blood freezing with a sudden dread that the moment is here and he will be furious. I must find the best way to order my words. 'Do you have time to speak later today?'

He has finished eating, wiping his mouth and taking a last drink of tea. His expression is hardly on me, he is half turned towards the door to go back upstairs. 'Of course – stop by my office after lunch.' I nod as he pushes back from the table, squeezing my shoulder in a goodbye.

Alone at the table, I pick up the newspaper and read about the larger world. Out there, time still moves forward, unlike at the manor. The French have a new legislative assembly and there is growing frustration with the lack of food supplies. Some British correspondents fear that war is on the horizon, others are less certain. I wonder whether Elina will be safe if war comes, and what it will mean for Henry and me.

After walking the grounds, reading from Elina's library, and nibbling on a light dinner in the kitchen, I glide across the first floor to Henry's office. I pause, considering the ornately carved wood in front of me. I hope I've found the right way to tell him what has happened – what I have done. I crack the door open and poke my head inside. The room is brightly lit against the approaching winter evening and Henry hunches over a stack of papers at his desk. He glances up and notices me.

'Ah, come here – what do you make of this?' he asks. '"The African Company of England, having received by your order a copy of one clause of the grievances represented to be his master from Antigua, they thereupon humbly answer..."'

'I couldn't say – perhaps someone is in trouble?'

'I don't know how my father kept up with so much correspondence,' he says, an edge to his voice. 'I never heard him mention this plantation, but apparently he sunk five thousand pounds into it.'

I'm sympathetic to his struggle – his father should have been a better guide as he grew older. But as I cast my mind overseas, my thoughts immediately turn to Elina and her escape. She must have reached French shores by now.

Henry takes off his wig and scratches his head. His hair has begun to thin and recede just like mine. Reading the papers, he sighs, 'I am beginning to suspect I will need to travel to Antigua myself.'

I sit down in surprise. 'Will you go as often as your father did?'

He shrugs, sits down too. 'Perhaps. I do not know how things are done there and it might take me multiple trips to understand.' He watches me over the desk. There's something guarded about his expression, like he's hiding something. Or perhaps it is just my own guilty conscience. 'Matthew, I've been thinking… would you consider joining the family business? It would allow me to keep you on the payroll, and we could travel to the West Indies together without drawing any attention to ourselves.'

Although his reasoning makes sense, it is a proposition that catches me by surprise. I consider his words – perhaps it would solve some of the problems we face being together now. But is transatlantic trade the direction I want my life to take? 'I'm flattered, but I'm not sure I know enough about the industry to be an asset to you.'

'You've run your own business in London, albeit on a much smaller scale… still, you're clever and could learn.'

That might be true, but this is not a subject I want to learn more about. I set my jaw, my heart sinking a little over what I must say next. 'I don't think I can be involved in such an evil practice as slavery. It is immoral.' After hearing Mr Cugoano's story and reading additional letters in Elina's library by Ignatius Sancho, I do not wish to partake in such a gruesome business.

Henry is still standing on the other side of his desk and he leans forward, alert and agitated. 'For clarification, you can bear to live with the lifestyle purchased by means of the slave trade, you can sew fabric made from cotton grown by enslaved people, but your moral compass draws a line… where, exactly? Somewhere in the middle of the Atlantic?'

I had not considered the implications of buying cotton from the Americas. Perhaps silk from the East is also associated with this corrupt institution. 'Maybe you are right and I cannot live with this lifestyle if it is funded on the back of free labour.'

He stands and walks over to me, catches my hand in his. 'I am trying to do what's best for us. What other choice do we have – would you prefer I hire you as a servant here?'

'I don't know! I need time to think,' I respond, feeling trapped. Are there really so few options available to us? I must find a way to redirect the conversation back to Elina and Bedlam so I can say my piece and from there we might look towards the future.

'Perhaps you will find you have a knack for it in time.' He walks back around his desk, grabs another paper. 'Here, look at this one.'

'I'm really not qualified—'

'Aren't you though?' His anger flashes hot, upon me in an instant. 'I thought you were quite knowledgeable, posing as a political philosopher for my wife?'

So he knows everything – but how? Who could have told him? I stand to prevent myself from being shouted down at. 'How long have you known?'

He lets out a strained laugh. 'This is my estate! I know about everything that goes on here.' It must have been one of the servants, a bargaining chip when Henry threatened to fire them for speculating about our relationship.

I open my mouth to defend myself, but can think of no excuse. 'Why didn't you say anything sooner?'

'I wanted to pretend it didn't matter, but clearly it does.' He pulls a letter from his breast pocket and slaps it onto the desk, sliding it closer so I can read it. 'How did my wife escape from Bedlam in the middle of the night?'

I stammer a response but he interrupts, bitter hurt spilling from his lips.

'Don't bother answering – I know it was you.' While my thoughts whirl he turns away, walking towards a cabinet on the other side of the room. 'How could you betray me after all these years?' he asks, his voice now tinted with sorrow.

I let my breath out in a shallow exhale. Already I feel the lie lifting from my tongue – that it did not feel like a betrayal at the time. It would be so easy to feign ignorance of my actions, to paint over them and pretend we can go back to how we once were. Instead, I opt for the truth. 'I wanted to help her. I'm sorry.'

We stare at each other across the room, both suddenly aware of how wide the chasm between us has become. How could this have happened without either of us noticing? I want to speak to him openly, but I cannot. He is almost a stranger to me in this moment – I cannot ask him anything. He's right, I have betrayed him, but he has hurt me too, so distant for years that I no longer know who he is. All I can see is a projection of who he used to be. I feel almost breathless, lost in thought. Where do we go from here? Is our love salvageable, or is it already gone? What remains between us?

As usual, Henry is the first to act. He walks back towards his desk and leans on it as if to steady himself. 'Let's get through tonight – there's that French associate of Father's coming to supper.' He wants me there in part for support, but also to give the table a more festive air than the dreary atmosphere of only two dining, as has become obvious during our meals together.

We have so much more to say to one another, but how can we if we've lost the intimacy that was once between us? I cannot even meet his eye, staring at an out-of-focus paper on his desk. If we say nothing today, how will we broach the conversation again? How will we get past this moment? Perhaps we won't.

'All right,' I say.

A few hours later, I tread carefully down the carpeted hall leading to the dining room. This is the first formal dinner Henry has hosted in months, well before he sent Elina away. I'm vaguely aware of how to behave, but am out of practice and distracted. Our words to each other spin around my mind – have we passed a point of reconciliation? He has been such a fixture in my life, his gravity guiding all my actions back towards him. Without him, where will my sense of direction come from? Who will I be?

The table looks grand as ever, with candles lit and silver serving trays set out. To think, all this finery for one guest – I almost chuckle at the thought, but am too sombre to laugh. This associate must be very important to Henry, or perhaps 'useful' is the more accurate term.

I glance behind me at the open door, unsure of what to do with myself while I wait. I check the buttons on my jacket are in order, no loose threads to diminish my appearance. I suppose I could pour myself a glass of wine – yes, that seems the appropriate thing to do. Sitting down might overstep the mark, indicating that I am too comfortable in this home. I suppose, in a way, there are two guests tonight if I am included in the group. Hardly realistic to the world we inhabit, but it's probably what Henry has told this gentleman and the narrative he's tried to sell to the household staff. I remember standing outside Mrs Ferrers' office, hearing his voice ring down the corridor: 'In the time since my beloved wife has been hospitalised, Mr Rooke has become a constant source of support and fraternal goodwill. As such, I would like to have a room prepared for him in the guest wing of the house.'

When I first moved to Stonehurst, I'd felt such a rush wondering if we'd get away with it, but that feeling of anticipation and shared strife against the odds has dulled. After all, we are not the ones struggling to get by, we are protected in this world that Henry controls and reality is only what he says it is. I wonder where Elina is now, whether she is settled—

'...All the way from Tunis!' chortles Henry as he and his guest arrive. I spin around, taking the man in. Surprisingly tall, bright gold buttons on his maroon jacket, a hand tucked into his vest as the other reaches out to take mine. His smile is warm and inviting, completely unsuspecting of my real class.

'Bonsoir, you must be Monsieur Rooke?'

A luscious French accent, clearly he has not been in England for long. 'Yes, it's a pleasure to meet you, Mr...?'

'Balise,' Henry chimes in, filling his glass. 'Please, sit down.' He gestures at the table.

'After you,' I say to Mr Balise. I suspect he will take my usual seat and I'm to sit at the other side of the table, but want to have my suspicions confirmed. I sneak a glance at Henry, but he is cold and aloof when his guest isn't looking.

Mr Balise sits to Henry's right and I sidle around the table to sit opposite. Daisy brings in a tureen of soup and Henry begins serving.

'How long have you been a guest here at Stonehurst Manor, Monsieur Rooke?'

Panic rises, my neck muscles tighten – but I dare not look at Henry. I try to sound relaxed when I vaguely reply, 'I suppose it has been a number of years, now.'

'You are fortunate to have such a dedicated friend.'

Now, I do turn towards Henry with a smile. 'Indeed I am. I hope I have proven myself useful to the household over the years.' That seems to be sufficient to keep me out of trouble.

Henry's eyes slide away from mine and he turns back towards his guest. 'Mr Rooke possesses a sharp business acumen – he is going to help me handle some aspects of the family enterprise now that my father has passed.'

'Is that so? You must both be pleased – to work alongside a friend makes each day pass more pleasantly.'

I keep my face pointed down at my bowl, swirling the soup without taking a spoonful. Did he place extra emphasis on the word 'friend' or was that in my mind? My back feels tight towards the middle, the tension of the evening burying itself there. Does Henry mean to force me to join in his father's business, or is he only saying this for the benefit of Mr Balise? I just need to get through this supper, then Henry and I can broach the discussion later.

'Yes,' Henry responds, 'we are both looking forward to it.'

'I am sorry your wife cannot join us tonight,' Mr Balise says innocently. Instantly, the soup loses its flavour and I carefully set my spoon down. But Henry looks calm.

'So am I – regrettably, she has not been well and is seeking treatment in London.'

'How unfortunate.'

I sense Henry wants to change the subject, but I interject, 'I'm sure she would have loved to speak with you about your homeland. She is very interested in French politics.'

At this, Mr Balise becomes animated and his eyes brighten. 'It is a constantly changing situation, very exciting at the moment.'

At this point, Daisy returns with a joint of roast lamb on a platter of vegetables. She sets it down in front of Henry, who begins carving while I keep my focus on Mr Balise. 'It must be quite frightening on the streets of Paris.'

'Some days, but not most of the time. Depending on who you are! But I am pleased with the changes currently being proposed – in the new penal code, we are removing tyrannical Catholic punishments and decriminalising private sexual acts between men.'

Henry, passing the plate of lamb back to Daisy, freezes for a moment, and I notice my breathing stops.

'It will usher in a new progressive world and set France's place as a leader in Europe!'

I force myself to recover as quickly as I can. 'Let us hope Britain follows your example.'

He begins serving himself from the plate Daisy now holds before him. 'For your sake, I hope you do. Being on the front lines of such revolutionary change is exciting – you can bear witness to history being made even just by walking down the street.'

Henry clears his throat. 'As fascinating as this is, I do want to make sure we discuss sugar cane while you're here. You have travelled to the West Indies before?'

'Yes. It was a beautiful, terrible place,' Mr Balise says with a shudder.

'Well, this shouldn't bring back any unpleasant memories. I'm just hoping you might parse some of the language for me.'

'Of course, Mr Ashby. You are my host and I am happy to oblige.'

I sit back and let them talk, mulling over the changes France is making. What might this egalitarian society look like, where one's personal life does not put him at risk of imprisonment? How much lighter would his existence be? With extended rights for women and her sharp mind, Elina should flourish there.

After Mr Balise has gone to bed, I approach Henry's room. The door is cracked so I silently push it open. He is sitting in an armchair by the fireplace, reading. I shiver a little despite not feeling a draught. I stay back and he does not look at me, but there is a change in the room's atmosphere and I know he can sense my presence.

'I must go to London,' I tell him.

Henry nods in understanding. He does not move, but there is restrained anguish in his voice when he asks, 'And will you return?'

Despite the tension between us, we are past lying to each other now. 'I don't know,' I answer.

—

It seems like every time I visit the East End, the air is a little bit darker. Looking up, hundreds of chimneys erupt with black smoke, though they are difficult to see from the narrow alleys I wind through, shoulder to shoulder with manufactory workers and traders. Through windows, I can see the new machinery – large looms weaving cotton from the colonies into beautiful fabric for this season's dresses and coats.

Turning down Bell Yard, I open the glass door of my shop – the last time I will ever call it mine. I peer between the orphans seated along the workbenches until I hear Martha calling me from the back of the room, by the staircase. I weave over to her and give her a hug. 'I've brought the final papers,' I tell her.

'Excellent – let's talk in here.' She opens the door to the back room, with its simple furnishings of a bed for Bess and Georgie, a washbasin, and a chair. Bess plays in the corner with some letter blocks. I reach into my inner coat pocket and pull out the deed of ownership for the business, its wax stamp bumping against my fingertips. Martha's smile shines as I hand them to her. 'Thank you – this means so much.'

'Of course, I was happy to.' I look down, knowing that isn't entirely true.

She studies my face, her eyes kind, then says, 'I know it may be hard to formally step away from the shop, but it's not going anywhere – I'll be here until my hands are too weak to sew.'

I smile fondly, thinking back to the young girl sitting on my stoop who had never made a pair of stays before and couldn't write. I know in my heart we have helped each other over the last two decades – I just wish I knew what the coming years will hold for me. 'You are part of a new generation of women staymakers,' I tell Martha, 'and I am happy you have more experience than the competition so you can continue to thrive. My weariness is not on your behalf, but my own – with Lady Elina gone, my future is uncertain. I must work, but doing what?'

She crosses to the washbasin where dry laundry is piled up, begins folding the shifts and chemises. 'Come now, you've learned so many new skills since you left London – dressmaking from the inside out, trimmings and notions. Not to mention all those political ideas this past year! You're adaptable and will find a way to use your skills. You'll always have a place in the clothing trade.'

'I don't know,' I reply. 'Between enslaved labour and these new weaving machines, fabric prices continue to fall. Perhaps soon, people will expect their clothing to be so cheap that those of us who work with textiles will no longer be able to earn a living.'

'No,' soothes Martha, 'the fabric's cheaper, true, but it just means more people can afford custom-made products like our stays and there's more business to be had. Why do you think I've got a whole room full of girls out there?'

I shift my weight, ashamed at my sense of resignation. I used to have passion and zeal – energised by challenges or uncertainty, I stood tall and fought. Now I feel adrift with no sense of which direction to take next. There is nothing to keep me occupied at Henry's house, yet if my skills are no longer useful to society, I will not be able to find purpose outside of Stonehurst either.

Martha is down on the floor, helping Bess dress her doll. She squeezes the figure's arms through narrow sleeves, then flips it over and buttons up the back while Bess clings to her arm impatiently. I'm sure she designed and sewed the doll's dress herself. She feels my gaze and gives me an exasperated smile. 'I sometimes wonder where your resilience comes from,' I tell her.

'I've never thought about it myself,' she replies, standing and brushing off her skirts. 'I suppose not treating it like a choice has helped.' Maybe she's right. With too much time by myself as of late, perhaps I've fallen into the trap of overthinking and overcomplicating my problems. 'But you know, I'm proud I wound up in this trade. Clothes are great equalisers,' she muses.

I try, but cannot hide my bemusement. 'What do you mean? Clothing dictates class faster than anything – its expense is visible for all to see, whether from fabric selection or literal jewels hanging from it.'

'I know,' Martha urges, 'but no matter who you are or what your station, you've got to wear *something*. In that way, we're all connected by clothing.'

'That's true,' I reply, thoughtful.

Chapter Twenty-One

Then

I stand outside the front door, uncertain whether I should knock or go around the side through the servants' quarters. The manor is magnificent – never before have I seen a house so grand and wide. They must have twenty bedrooms! Walking up, I was astounded by the number of windows reflecting the sun back at me with blinding efficiency. And the surrounding grounds, so trim and organised. I thought I could see a lake behind the home, but it was difficult to tell with all the trees on either side of the path. I'm sweaty and my back aches after carrying my bags from the town. Henry offered to send a carriage, but I didn't think I would need it – after all, I walk so much in London.

Tired as I am, I feel an overwhelming urge to turn around and run before I'm spotted. This is all too sudden – how will I live with Henry and his new wife? How will I pass for a respectable dressmaker when all I have done before now is create stays? But remaining in London feels too dangerous and, besides, I trust Henry. I raise a hand to the knocker, which is shaped like a stag's head, but pause. Everything goes dark for a moment – the sun passing behind some clouds. I'd probably get rained on if I headed back to town anyway, and who knows when the next coach arrives? Of course I'm going inside. Finally, I gather my nerves and knock loudly.

An older footman in full livery answers, looks at me without a question in his eyes. 'Good afternoon, sir, you must be Mr Rooke.'

'Indeed I am. I believe Mr Ashby is expecting me?'

'Of course, right this way. May I take your things to your room for you?'

I hope I won't be spending much time alone there. 'Yes, thank you.'

He leads me down a grand passageway, through an elaborate drawing room. I slow down instinctively to admire the opulent decor, but realise

I will be left behind if I do, so I quicken my pace to keep up. We pass through a room with sculptures, a pianoforte, and towering shelves of books. Finally, we arrive at a third room, a lounge of some sort.

'Sir, Mr Rooke has arrived.'

I peer past the footman at Henry, who closes the book he's been reading and stands from a plush sofa. He doesn't look at me immediately.

'Excellent, thank you, Ramsay.'

The footman nods and continues down the hallway with my things.

Harry watches him go, then beams at me. 'Finally! Why have you been so long?'

'I should have taken you up on the offer of a carriage.'

'Such a silly man.' He grabs my hand and pulls me towards him.

'Wait – should we?'

He kisses me before I can say anything else, and my nerves begin to rest. 'It's all right. Of course we'll be discreet, but the servants leave me alone when I've got the house to myself.'

'Where is... she?' I feel my chest and neck tighten with the question, unable to speak about her directly with him.

'In Chipping Norton visiting her aunt.' He anticipates my next question. 'She'll return tomorrow evening.'

'Won't it seem suspicious, you staying behind to see me settled?'

'Not at all – I feigned an illness so I wouldn't have to travel.'

'Do you think that was wise?' I look around, incredulous in these new surroundings.

'Matthew, you are still on your guard! You needn't fear – the manor is much safer than London and I am master here so I can keep us both secure. You will be my talented guest and we'll remain above suspicion.'

I nod, beginning to soften against his confident words. Of course he's right – London is far more dangerous.

He glances at the door, then takes my hand. 'There isn't anyone else I'd rather be with than you, right here. Shall I show you around? Or would you like a drink first?'

If we only have tonight, then we must make the most of it. 'Let's do both – give me a tour, but bring the drinks along too.'

Harry laughs. 'I've missed you. This house was so depressing by myself... we'll get up to some fun, won't we?' He crosses the room and opens a drinking cabinet, pours two glasses of amber-coloured wine. He brings them over. 'Cheers, my love.'

'Cheers.' It's a buttery, sweet flavour that compels a quick second sip.

'Right, I'll give you the tour. There's not really much to keep track of – it's more work for the staff than any of us. Ridiculous, isn't it? Anyway, this is the dining room.' We stand in the doorway of a long room with a sturdy oak table and stag heads interspersed between portraits on the walls. 'That staircase leads down to the servants' quarters... I think you'll like this next room. It's always everyone's favourite.'

We turn a corner and my breath catches a little at the beauty – a gorgeous, long room with a wall of gilded windows overlooking the back garden and lake. The wall opposite the windows is lined with mirrors, reflecting the gold and the sunlight and the sparkles coming off the water. 'It's stunning,' I say.

'Yes... a clever design by the architect, though of course each generation always makes their improvements. My father opened up this wall so it was only windows. It's bloody cold in the winter, but at least it's nice to look at right now.'

I peek out the windows, down towards the extensive lawn. 'I can't believe you have a lake all to yourself.'

'Ha, that's just a pond, really. We can go swimming if the weather stays nice.'

'You know, I never learned how to swim.'

He leans towards me, a bit mischievous. 'Really? Something I can teach you, then.'

I can't help but laugh. 'You know, you're much bolder here than you ever were in London.'

He pours more wine into my glass. 'Do you think so?'

'Yes, you're so confident and self-assured. I suppose we're in your territory, now.'

'Don't think of it that way – I'm sure it seems like an intimidating house, but once you spend a few days here you'll get used to it.'

I scoff, looking around again. Will these rooms ever feel like home?

'Besides, London isn't exactly *your* city. It's ours.'

Ours. Yet I've spent my whole life in London, made a life and future for myself in that city long before Henry and I ever met. And when we began seeing each other more intimately, it was I who acted as guide, showing him the side of the capital he'd never seen before. 'I only mean that you're taking the lead. You were always open in London, but usually to suggestions I made. Here, I feel like you're the one steering things.'

He considers this. 'I see what you mean… Yes, I suppose so. What can I say? I'm a good host! If my upbringing taught me nothing else, it's that.' He glances at his watch. 'Come on, shall we have a bath before supper?'

'Together?'

'Why not? I'll just have the valet draw two baths, and then we'll leave yours alone. They won't notice and, even if they did, they'd never say anything.'

'I'll do whatever you bid while I'm here. After all, you're the lord of the manor.'

'Come along, then!' He jostles me playfully and I laugh, chasing him up the stairs.

—

The passion and carefree atmosphere kindled between us dissipates as we lie in bed together the next morning. This is the day I will meet his wife, the person to whom he has publicly avowed himself because it is impossible to do so with me. We lean towards each other in bed, kissing tenderly before rolling to our opposite sides. I sigh, then peel myself away from the soft sheets and get dressed so I can return to the guest room. After breakfast, Henry shows me the grounds of the estate but his generous, convivial nature has dulled and tension pulls at the edges of his posture. I feel it too – the uncertainty over whether his plan will work, the terror of being found out. How will I watch them together without reaching out for him? Surely my inner agony will spill across my face and we will be caught immediately.

At last, evening arrives. I stare from an upstairs window, watching the horses pull her carriage around the path to the front of the house. A footman rushes forward, opens the carriage door, and bright emerald skirts flow from it before I make out lightly powdered hair coiffed to a fashionable height. She turns her face up, skimming the house, and I pull back as if, by seeing me through the window, she might feel the fire emanating from me. I would burn her if given the chance. I retreat to my room for the rest of the night, staring at the ceiling. We are all three under the same roof now – I will the entire house to crumble into a thousand pieces and crush me.

The next day, Henry brings me to her rooms for a proper introduction, but we both know it is more professional than social. Before knocking on her door, he squeezes my hand and gives me a sweet smile for reassurance, which I feebly return.

'My dear,' he says as we step inside, 'I'd like you to meet my friend and the talented dressmaker fresh from London, Mr Matthew Rooke.' I hope my face is powdered enough that she cannot see how red my cheeks are.

She is sitting by the fire with a book – I hear it snap shut with a quick flash of her hand as she stands and walks over to us. 'It's lovely to make your acquaintance, Mr Rooke.'

I try to take her in, but am overcome with emotion. I must try to think of her as any other client. 'The pleasure is all mine, Your Ladyship,' I reply. 'If there is anything I can do—'

'Actually, there is,' she responds briskly. 'I have a pair of quilted petticoats that are lacking a dress to accompany them.' She gestures to her maid, who hurries over to the clothes press and removes the petticoats. They are a luscious, soft silk in a warm ochre colour. I am only too happy to turn my attention away from her to examine them but remain aware of Henry next to me, observing our conversation in silent support, hoping we will get along and that she does not detect what he and I share.

'Do you have a fabric already in mind?' I ask.

She nods, a jewel necklace glimmering on her throat. 'I brought some embroidered cotton back with me from Bengal that should be suitable. Perhaps a robe cut in the English style?'

Although her tone suggests a question, we all know it is a demand. Over the last month, I have begun researching the methods for designing and measuring robes though have only attempted a few model-sized mockups in economical linen. Part of me is relieved that she wants one of the simpler designs, but I also scoff a little at her lack of taste. Surely something more ornate like the French or Polish style is more befitting a lady. I recall the cotton gowns I have seen women wear in recent years – so many seem to wrinkle in the front. Perhaps I can add some boning to the front panels, where they clasp together, so it would not be obvious. Baleen at the back might also smooth the fabric and she should not feel any impact with her stays on underneath providing the main support. Should I mention this to her now? But perhaps there is a reason I have not seen this done in designs and will make myself look as inexperienced as I truly am. Instead I simply reply, 'Of course, if that is what Your Ladyship wishes.'

She smiles demurely, but her skin is fresh and bright. She seems more innocent than I had imagined her last night, or perhaps she is naive. 'Wonderful. I will have the fabric sent downstairs for you. I look forward to working together, Mr Rooke.'

I take a slight bow, understanding I have been dismissed. The word 'downstairs' runs circles in my mind – a new place I must become accustomed to. I turn to go, expecting Henry to follow, but she is asking him a question about that evening's meal, a small indent of concern on her forehead, and as I watch his hands reach out to reassure her, I force myself to turn away.

Now

I walk into the drawing room where Henry sits, watching the fire. I sense a familiar wave of tenderness towards him, but it strikes differently now, almost taking on the feeling of pity. He turns to me, sees the portmanteau in my hand, and a wilted expression appears on his face. We both know it's time for me to leave, but that does not make it any easier to say goodbye.

I approach him, looking up at the surrounding walls. The portraits and decorations that have become so familiar as to be boring suddenly seem important to remember, knowing this is the last time I will ever see them. So many details I will have to surrender but, as difficult as letting go will be, I am ready to make my own choices again. Living in the shadows for so many years, I was depleted, but now I am confident and optimistic that I can thrive in a future I will create for myself.

Henry and I face each other with no regrets between us. We are both tired but there is something vigorous in the air – the understanding that these are our final moments together. I open my mouth, but Henry's face crumples and he embraces me. 'I can't,' he says.

We pull apart, our fingers lingering in a gentle interlock out of habit. Warm tears flood my eyes. 'I don't think two people could have loved each other more completely than we have these last two decades.'

'Yes,' he smiles.

All is still and quiet – the coals smoulder silently, the clocks too distant to hear. My eyes trace the lines in his forehead, the pink tone of his lips, the wet streaks on his cheek. We turn and walk into the hall, towards the front door. In a quick move, Henry pulls the door open and the cool winter air hits me in the face with a shock.

'Where will you go?' he asks. I look across the green lawns, over the woods, and towards the horizon.

–

The sky is white with clouds and a fine rain drizzles the dirt road underneath as the coach bounces forward. I tilt my head back and nap as often as I can – it's been a long journey from the coast down through the countryside, but I believe we're nearly there. I'm a bit nervous about how the next few days will go, but have no doubts that I'm doing the right thing. The next time I open my eyes, we are passing through a grand wall made of clean ochre-coloured stone. An official stops the carriage and checks the papers of everyone on board. We each hold our breath as we pass our information to him, but after the control he waves us through. There is a small field, and then the city begins to spring up around us – markets and monuments, towering churches and half-timbered houses.

We pull up in front of the Hôtel de Ville and at last I can stretch my legs. I look around the square, smelling bread baking in the freshly rinsed air, and try not to be intimidated by how unfamiliar everything is. I look towards the river, which stretches away towards clusters of bare trees on its other shore. Another coach pulls up behind the one I've left, and I scurry out of the way. The aroma of coffee cuts through the air and I can hear bowls clattering gently in their saucers as patrons of a nearby café debate passionately, emphasising their assertions with pointed fingers. I spin back around uncertainly, peering through the sea of faces, until at last Elina's emerges forth. 'Mr Rooke!' she calls out jovially. 'You've made it!' We embrace, then she loops her arm through mine and begins to steer me. 'Welcome to Paris. Come this way, the shop is not far from here.'

I pick up my portmanteau and follow her up the street. The sun has already begun to push its way through the clouds and, as we walk, I feel its warmth on my cheek.

'Prenez ce dépliant!' someone calls out, thrusting a pamphlet at me. I stare at him in confusion and look towards Elina for an explanation.

'The streets here are lively, but there's nothing to worry about – you can ignore them if you wish.'

My shortcomings and the amount of work ahead rush over me and I nearly drop my case. 'I can't very well share political ideas when I don't even speak the language.'

'You don't speak it *yet*. But you will learn! It's not so different from English.' She hasn't lost her characteristic confidence and perception – I can already see that she is thriving here. Hopefully I will too.

We turn down a narrow street, where half the shop windows are plastered with broadsheets. 'Why have they done that?' I ask.

'It's to keep the authorities from seeing inside. Look there...' She points above, where signs jut out towards the street. 'Those depict the lawful products being sold, or at least what the shopkeepers pretend they are selling.' I follow her finger upward. A pair of scissors suggests a barber, while a painting of a cow indicates a cheesemonger. We pass a shoemaker's and then stop as she pulls a key from her pocket. I stand back, surveying the small shop – its windows are clean and it seems well kept, difficult for anyone to object to.

Elina opens the door and we step inside. She gauges my reaction as I set my bag down and look around.

'There's an office in the back where I can write, and I thought you could use this front space for your new business.' She smiles knowingly.

There is a little counter facing the window, and I try to imagine myself working here. I recently had the idea of using what I've learned of dressmaking to suit the needs of working-class women by buying old clothes and recutting them into new, fashionable shapes. It will be more affordable than working with new fabric every time. I can imagine myself haggling with customers, cutting and stitching new panels, all while Elina carefully works at her desk in the back.

She rocks back and forth on her feet, watching me consider the space and waiting for my response.

'I think this will do very nicely,' I smile. Already I'm feeling more optimistic simply from being with her again and seeing how the pieces of our new life will fit together. My imagination tingles with the anticipation of restoring old gowns to new glory and my fingers itch to work again.

She rests a supportive hand on my shoulder, eyes twinkling. 'I look forward to wearing your designs. And you must create some tricolore cockades for ladies' hats, though we'll have to sell them under the counter.'

I laugh. 'Focus on your work and let me worry about the fashion!'

She checks her watch and her eyebrows jump up in surprise. 'Oh! We must go and get ready for your welcome reception.'

That evening, we gather with Elina's friends in a large, candlelit room with glasses of wine. The lights of the city sparkle through the windows at us and Elina glows, giddy with the pleasure of lively company and free debate. She has shown me how to speak with rigour and form strong opinions that I can actually defend – an unthinkable notion even two years ago. I comfortably chat with her friends about interdependency and why we all deserve an equal political voice. They kindly ask about my new shop and I explain my plans to make affordable clothing from pre-existing garments, which they agree is preferable to catering to the wealthy. It will be a different manner of creation – using pre-worn fabrics in simple, tailored designs cut close to the body to make the most of the material – but I already feel capable in this new environment.

'I do think that society has an important role to play in individual happiness,' I hear Elina say from another cluster of guests, 'for when we become too enamoured with our own lives and lose awareness of our responsibility to the larger world, we cannot unite in our demands for improvement.'

I turn to meet her eye amidst the tight crowd and we grin at one another. It feels as though an entire world exists between us, invisible to everyone else even as they are bathed in its radiance. We have torn apart the stories of who we were expected to become, and now the future is uncertain but resolute. No matter what happens, we will retain the strength and courage we have given each other to choose our own path. I glance down and notice her glass is empty – with a small gesture and questioning expression, I offer to refill it.

I cross the room to a table, where several bottles have been left open for everyone to enjoy. A large mirror at the back doubles the selection and replicates the party to pleasing effect. I set our glasses down and take in my own reflection. I step closer, letting the din of the party fall away. I run my fingers along my coat sleeves – a sapphire wool I acquired a few years ago that everyone here has complimented. My fingertips feel every ridge of the fabric, its subtle peaks and valleys. I look down at each thread, interwoven with the ones around it, bound tightly together to create something whole.

A Letter from Kelsey

Dear Reader,

Thank you so much for reading *The Three*! I hope you felt transported to eighteenth-century England and enjoyed your journey. If you did, please review the book online – this is a great way to support me and helps others find the book as well.

This novel is no longer mine; it is *ours* – the combined result of what you invented in your imagination as you read, and what I wrote to guide you. I firmly believe that readers are a powerful part of the writing process and I don't take your trust lightly. With that in mind, here is some background on how this story came about:

Many years ago, I attended an exhibit at the V&A in London about the history of underwear. There, I discovered what stays were (not corsets!) and was amazed to learn that they were traditionally made by men. This got me wondering what sort of relationship a working-class staymaker might have had with his upper-class clients. I dashed off an email to myself with an idea for a staymaker who keeps his clients' secrets yet has his own to guard as well.

Over the years I worked on the idea, put it away, struggled to untangle its many threads, fell in and out of love with it. I went to the British Library and read eighteenth-century reports of prison conditions. I visited historic homes to get a sense of what spaces these characters might have inhabited. I scrutinised paintings in museum collections all over the world to determine how people looked and moved. I read every available guide from the incredible Old Bailey Online for an idea of what London was like in the past. I fell just a little in love with Rictor Norton and his impeccable research into gay life in eighteenth-century England. I stumbled upon the incredible community of historical costume makers on YouTube while trying to understand what the actual process of making stays and dresses would have been at the time (so much work!). I learned about the Haitian Revolution, an essential moment to consider when we think about the Enlightenment. I cast my mind back to the philosophy classes of my university days and brushed up on arguments about individual liberty, though I crafted Elina's ideas to be a bit more modern to meet some of the discussions we are having today.

In part, I wrote this novel to celebrate friendship and the loose social ties that knit us all together. I love connecting with fellow readers and can be found around the internet, as well as the streets of Paris:

Website: https://kelseyobrienauthor.com
Instagram: @kelseyobrienauthor
Substack: https://kelseyobrienauthor.substack.com
Bluesky: @kelseyobrienauthor.bsky.social

Happy reading,
    Kelsey

Acknowledgements

This is entirely a work of fiction, but I want to pay my respects to the historical figures alluded to throughout the novel:

- Gabriel Lawrence (? – 1726), Thomas Collins (1686 – 1743), and Richard Arnold (1700? – 1753), were all men killed by the British government in the eighteenth century for the 'crime' of sodomy. Today, homosexuality is still criminalised in over sixty countries around the world.

- Mother Mack is inspired by Margaret Clap, who faced violence on the pillory in 1726 and likely died in prison from her injuries sustained there.

- Ottobah Cugoano was the first Black writer in Britain to argue for the abolition of slavery in his 1787 book, *Thoughts and Sentiments on the Evil and Wicked Traffic of the Slavery and Commerce of the Human Species*. His personal story as related to the corresponding society is heavily borrowed from this work, though he disappears from records after 1791.

- Lady Elina's publisher is an homage to Joseph Johnson of Paternoster Row, who published such ideological progressives as Mary Wollstonecraft and William Godwin.

I'd like to thank my editor, Jennie Ayres, for her unwavering enthusiasm for this novel and championing it with such dedication. The questions she asked and notes she offered have undoubtedly improved the story for readers. In plucking this novel from Hera's general submissions email and advocating for its publication, she has made my longest-held childhood dream come true and I'm eternally grateful.

I must also thank the rest of the team at Hera for bringing this book together: exquisite cover design by Head Design, brilliant copyediting from Ross Dickinson, eagle-eyed proofreading from Vicki Vrint, as well as the in-house team including Nicole, Nick, Micaela, Kim, Keshini, Kate, Iain, Hannah, and Dan.

While researching this story, I stumbled upon the incredibly rich historical costuming and dress historian communities online, many of whom make clothes by replicating past techniques. It's incredible to me that people have done such extensive research and documented their sewing journeys online – their experience was invaluable and spared me from spending three months handmaking a pair of stays myself! Thank you to Gracie Patten in particular for offering kindness and encouragement at a key moment.

Support takes many forms and can come from anywhere if we engage with one another. On a trip to Thailand many years ago, I chatted with a few young women who were very enthusiastic about this story idea and gave me some influential feedback in the space of a thirty-minute car ride. If you are someone who listens to writers, whether friends or strangers, talk about their work, it is a true kindness and form of encouragement. Thank you.

I'm so grateful to my friend Satu for her reassurance and insights during the acquisition and publication processes. For their formative feedback on the early chapters of this story, I must thank the rest of our MA writing group: Nancy, Helen, Gina, and Afy.

I was lucky enough to be connected to wonderful beta readers through the History Quill and want to thank Sue, Kate, Gary, Esther, Emma, Christine, and Alison. Knowing that this story was out in the world, existing separately from me in the minds of seven complete strangers, was a jolt of euphoria that kept me going after my first draft was 'finished'.

Writers need not only inspiration, but new energy to tackle their second drafts. For this, I'm incredibly appreciative of the support I received from Imogen Hermes Gowar's *Writing the Past* group: Ruth, Rachel, Melanie, Katie, Karen, Johanna, Jessica, Jennie, Hope, Claire, Caz, and Bindy.

To my friends in the Paris Writing Collective: thank you for your enthusiasm and support at the naissance of our meeting. I can't wait to see your work published in the coming years, too.

I'd like to thank my friend Rob for helping me research by finding some of the most useful books I didn't know I needed and gifting me lovely artefacts from London's past.

I am indebted to my parents for developing me as a reader through tireless bedtime stories and countless trips to the local library. Thank you also to my siblings, Lily and Hunter, for playing and imagining with me.

While hand-stitched clothing is a largely historical practice today, our clothes are still made by hand with the assistance of sewing machines. In an intimate yet invisible connection, everything we wear across all levels of fashion has been touched by garment workers making paltry wages for their skilled work. Thank you to these essential workers and those who fight for their improved wages and working conditions.